THE LIES WE TELL

IRON OUTLAWS MC
BOOK 3

S. COLE

Published By: Kadelo Group Ltd.
Edited by: Manu Shadow Velasco
Cover design by: Letitia Hasser at RBA Design
Photographer: Wander Aguiar

E-book ISBN: 978-1-7392843-1-2
Paperback ISBN: 978-1-7392843-2-9

For the ones still figuring out where they belong.
It's okay, Lovely! You've got time.

NOTE TO READERS

The Lies We Tell runs in parallel to *The Games We Play* for part of the book. There are a handful of scenes that appear in both books told from Saint and Spark's POVs. Both books are designed to stand alone, but for enhanced enjoyment, you may wish to read both.

Dubious consent (in the second epilogue that introduces the hero and heroine of book four)

PROLOGUE: SAINT
OCTOBER 25

"Fuck. Fuck. Fuck," I mutter as I dash around my undercover apartment, shoving anything that might keep me alive for the next four hours into a backpack.

I yank open the cabinet beneath the bathroom sink and grab my medical kit, one with more than simple over-the-counter remedies. Antibiotics. Synthetic monofilament sutures. The kind of painkillers that can cause addiction.

When I stand, I see my brown hair and beard trimmings in the sink and wonder who the real me is; I run my fingers across my cheek, beardless for the first time in years. Spark, the Iron Outlaws' sergeant at arms, had teased me about how I looked like Jesus. Now I actually look like who I am. Who I'm supposed to be.

Fuck.

I don't even know who that is anymore.

Am I clean-cut Special Agent Ryker Miller, undercover for the Bureau of Alcohol, Tobacco, Firearms and Explosives? Former army bomb disposal expert? Because that guy surely wouldn't have recklessly detonated his career as I've done. Or am I Saint, preacher and strip club manager for the Iron Outlaws Motorcycle Club? Or, in Ryker's language, an Outlaw Motorcycle Gang.

For two years, I've danced between the two.

And today I picked a side.

My brothers'.

But doing so has made me the ATF's enemy number one, collapsed a huge interdepartmental investigation, and will likely cost me my life. At some point, I'm certain my Iron Outlaws tattoo, the one I was forced to receive, will be burned off my body.

Bates will do it. He loves the sound of pain.

I suppose it's cheaper than laser removal.

This is the price of the path I've chosen.

One day I'll look back and realize I did this for two women. For Iris, so she can love my friend back to life. And for Briar, so we can love each other, and I think we're starting to.

Until I'm out of danger, I need to keep my distance from Briar. She's been through enough. And I can't let her get hurt for me.

I run back into the bedroom. "Think," I mutter. My electronics are packed. My wallet with all my fake identification was tossed in a dumpster halfway between here and the shoot-out at the warehouse. My legitimate identification is in my real house in Portland, Maine. In the past few weeks, I procured another set of documents that neither the ATF nor the Iron Outlaws know about. I also stole two weapons from the club.

If I'm fucked, I might as well be properly fucked.

I maybe have another ten minutes.

I chose to help Spark save Iris because of the kind of man he is. I've seen the sacrifices a man like that makes.

And for once in my life, I wanted to do the right thing. Because he's a good friend, a shit fisherman, and a hypervigilant veteran with PTSD.

He deserves the love Iris gives him unconditionally.

And seeing her hurt will kill him.

It would also kill me. Iris was born into a life she didn't want. Daughter and niece of Irish crime family kingpins. I know how it feels to live a childhood in the shadow of that kind of legacy.

I've made calls I shouldn't have.

I've made calls I should.

I stuff my fleece, waterproof clothes, and hiking boots into the suitcase. I'll buy more, but the basics are good. Maybe I'll head to my sister Rae's house in Michigan. But in case I don't, I've already thrown my tent and sleeping bag into my truck. Not the truck the club knew about, but the one I kept parked on a patch of dirt a mile from the clubhouse. I left my bike there. They'll figure it out eventually, but by then, I'll have made it to Maine and swapped it with my own ride. Switching things up—directions, license plates, lodgings—will make it harder to trace me.

My phone rings, and I know I'm in deep shit. Because instead of it being Weicker, my boss, it's Special Agent in Charge Harry Davis. They know enough that they can call my undercover phone now.

Instead of answering, I hang up and then make a call I don't want to.

"Saint, what happened, man? Where the fuck are you?" Uther "King" Hills, president of the Iron Outlaws, says when he answers. I admire him as a man and a leader. He makes the toughest calls with the greatest ease. Two months ago, I'd watched him put a bullet in his girlfriend's head after he found out she was a traitor to the club.

I also saw the look of pure anguish on his face as he did it.

Which tells me he's still redeemable. It's why he's my friend.

All these men are.

"Listen to me and listen good, King. You've got about an hour. I know you're at the hospital for Spark and Iris, but you need to get the weapons out of the warehouse. You've all got to clean down your homes. Cash. Weapons. Fake IDs. All of it. You need to get Track out of town. Send him and Tessa to Philly, just for now. He was the only one dumb enough to talk on tape."

"On tape. What the fuck, Saint? What did you do?" He's yelling by the end. I know he's going to be tugging on the ends of his dark hair.

"I did what I had to for the women. For Iris. For Br—" I nearly say Briar's name, but King doesn't know about her. And I want her to be a part of my real life, not my pretend one. If they know her name, they'll have a link to me. If they find her, they'll use her to get me.

"You're undercover?" King snarls as I slip my cut off my shoulders. I lay it on the bed, feeling naked without it already. I run my fingers over my road name patch.

Saint.

For two years now, I've been him and he's been me. I feel like I'm leaving my best friend behind.

"Doesn't matter who I am. Just promise me. They'll come for the club. I blew everything up today so you guys won't go down for what happened in the warehouse, when we rescued Iris. So they'll try to close in on what they've got."

"And what have they got?" King asks hoarsely.

"Everything, King. They've got everything."

1

SAINT

FOUR WEEKS EARLIER

"Davis wants to know when you're going to be able to wrap this up."

I roll my eyes at my boss, Derek Weicker, grateful he's on the other end of the phone and can't see my contempt. "If Davis had ever actually done undercover work, he'd know that it's a long timeline to go undercover with an outlaw gang. You don't join on Monday and then get the keys to all the intel by the weekend."

"When you become special agent in charge, you get a frontal lobotomy on the ATF that removes details like that. Regardless, I answer to him. You answer to me. That's how it works."

"Are you calling because you wanted to debate our organizational structure, or do you have a point beyond requesting an estimate you know I can't give?"

I catch sight of myself in my cover apartment's mirror. My hair is so long, it deserves its own shampoo ad. And my beard itches like a motherfucker. The blue eyes that look back at me confirm they both help me get plenty of pussy, but beyond that, I can't wait to trim this beard back to the scruff I prefer.

I began growing it two years ago when I started hanging with our ATF informant, so the club could get used to seeing my face. It's when I officially became a hang-around. Then there was the brutal level of hazing as a prospect. Davis doesn't know half the shit I had to deal with. The worst was probably getting pissed on by the president of the Los Angeles Iron Outlaws chapter, a brutal guy who's now serving twenty years thanks to information I passed to the FBI.

The president of the New Jersey chapter, Uther "King" Hills, nominated me for my patch. Said he valued my loyalty and counsel. And I got my name from Cue Ball, the now-deceased father of our vice president, Clutch. Said I was the patron saint of fucked-up brothers.

"You're sounding more and more like one of them," Weicker notes.

"It's method acting. I'm tired of this shit too."

Except . . . I'm not.

I used to have a strong moral compass. Joining the ATF after serving with the 720th Ordnance Company felt like a no-brainer. Time spent clearing bombs in Kosovo and Afghanistan made me an explosives expert, and high-pressure undercover work felt like a breeze. Plus, I've got friends missing limbs because of land mines and shit. Thought I could take down the explosives market.

Instead, I simply felt like an underappreciated cog in a broken machine.

Time spent with the Iron Outlaws has helped me find myself.

I've found the sense of unity I lost when I left the army and never found with the ATF. When you're sweating beneath all the gear and everyone else is back behind a perimeter, bomb disposal and mine clearing can feel isolating. Even so, you know everyone has your back. With the club, it's the same sense of belonging that happens when you know each and every man would die for you. And you'd die for them.

Something deep inside me stirs around these men, something I didn't feel when I went undercover with a group of incels in Portland, Oregon, inciting violence against women. Or when my assignment was joining a Nazi group in Eufaula, Alabama. It was easy to take down those fuckers. It was easier to see the pain they were both inflicting, the harm they caused.

With the Outlaws, it's been utterly different. I feel like I can breathe.

But with Davis and Weicker breathing down my neck for results, I feel suffocated.

Now I'm cutting corners, not reporting everything that involves my friends. I'm letting trails go cool. I'm bending rules.

My guilt stops me from sleeping at night.

Sometimes.

"A month ago, you mentioned a large gun delivery. Has it been made yet?" Weicker asks.

It was. Last week. I was there. I rub a hand across my bicep, tracing the healing gunshot wound gently. "No. I'll let you know when it does."

I can't explain even to myself why I lied.

I'm becoming Saint more than I am Ryker.

"Well, give me something I can tell him. Anything?"

"Niro has some weapons he's hoping to sell, I believe they were from an earlier gun run. If we can get the cash from Davis, I can buy them, and they can become evidence."

"Even if Niro sells you the guns, we're looking at third-degree and fourth-degree crimes. Niro's never been in prison. He has no record. Worst case, it's five years. It's a temporary removal of a gang member."

The phrase *gang member* makes me itch.

Niro, our penny-pinching treasurer, can be an asshole. But he's also funny and a talented tattoo artist. Helped Track, one of the old-timers, build a pergola for his daughter's wedding. Pisses King off with his one-liners. Got a scar down his face that he never talks about, but tells me he's been through some shit.

"Understood," I say, glancing at my watch. "I gotta be going."

"Bring me something I can use." And with that, Weicker hangs up the phone.

I'm fucking screwed.

I dial my favorite person, hoping she can brighten my day.

"Hey Rae-Rae," I say when she answers. I have a million names for her. Rare-bear, Raester, Rae-parade, Hoo-Rae.

"Hey, Ike. I was just thinking about you." My sister only has the one name for me. Ike. When she first started speaking, she couldn't say *Ryker*, so she'd call me *Ike*. It stuck. Anyone else calls me *Ike*, they get a fist in the face.

"Yeah? Why's that?"

"The kids across the street tried to build a skateboard ramp with a couple of pallets and some ply. Remember when you tried that?"

I laugh as I look down at the long white scar on my forearm. "I remember spending a miserable summer in a cast. You teased me and called me *half-baked* when they took it off because I had one tan arm and one white one."

She laughs, and her laughter makes me smile. Took her

a long time to laugh again, after what happened to us. "You had to wear long shirts until your tan faded in winter."

"Not sure my arms have ever quite matched since."

There's a moment of quiet. It's not uncomfortable. Things never are between us. "You keeping safe, Ike?" she asks.

"Safe as I can ever be," I answer honestly. She knows I'm undercover but doesn't know where I am or what I'm undercover as.

"Yeah, well. Keep it that way, yeah?"

"I will."

"Did you call for a reason in particular?"

I shake my head, even though she can't see me. "Nah. Just checking in. It's been a couple of days."

"Good enough. I love you."

"Love you too, sis."

I hang up, power the phone off, then slip it beneath the floorboard next to the bed. Phones are tricky. They could be taken off you at a moment's notice to check who you're calling and why you're calling them. This prepaid burner is my secure way to contact Rae.

I pull my cut, the leather vest that declares my allegiance to the club, over my shoulders. It's protection, like the gear I used to pull on for the long walk to an explosive device. The Iron Outlaws patch makes me feel more powerful than my ATF badge. They're both symbols I believe in, even though one contradicts the other.

There's still enough ATF in me to realize I'm trying to protect communities from violent criminals and criminal organizations while being a member of the Iron Outlaws MC.

It doesn't make sense.

I lock the door as I leave and climb onto my bike.

To match cover, my Fat Boy is old, but man, is she a sweet ride. I'm sure a psychologist could explain why riding down the highway with your legs on either side of a powerful vibrating machine is the closest thing to heaven that a guy can get, outside of sex.

I embrace it, letting the freedom of it soothe me. Sun on my face, cares left behind for a few precious moments.

"Preacher man," Halo, the club's perpetually tanned road captain says as I pull up at the clubhouse. He spends his life outdoors, hates being penned inside. The former navy SEAL is watching a prospect clean his bike. "You want yours done?" He tips his chin in the direction of my bike.

"Sounds good."

Halo looks at the guy on his knees polishing chrome with a rag. "Better hop to it, prospect."

I don't miss being one of the grunts, but I'm no closer to truly being one of the members either.

Three hours later, as I lie on my bed in the clubhouse, I'm still thinking about how the hell can I get what I want from the rest of my life.

"You seem distracted," Jessica, one of the club girls, says as she strips.

She's right. I am, even as my dick hardens.

"Club business, babe," I say—code for *none of your fucking business*.

The words roll off my tongue with ease.

In truth, I wonder how much longer I can last under-cover. It's not because I'm at risk of being found out. My cover is rock solid. With his father's permission, I'm using the name Phillip York, a dear friend and army chaplain assigned to my battalion who died at forty-two from an undiagnosed heart condition, two years after he got out of the service. Most of the outlaws will do just a quick military check on members, and a search for Chaplain Phillip York will prove that he served.

The spiritual side is covered—my brutal preacher father had a passion for whipping his unrepentant children who couldn't repeat Bible verses. I enlisted as soon as I could to earn cash and get Mom and Rae a place of their own, so they weren't financially dependent on Dad.

Rae left, taking her scars and nothing else with her.

Mom stayed.

Last time I saw Mom, she had a bruise on the side of her face, which she said came from walking into a door. She's walked into at least a hundred of them over the years.

With an army chaplain as cover, I can pick and choose what I do that skirts the law.

My ability to create a believable background is unquestionable. I know what I can legally do versus what constitutes entrapment. Problem is, I'm following those rules less and less. Worse, I'm enjoying it.

"Well," Jessica says, her voice cutting through my thoughts. "Technically, I'm club business." She pushes her tits together, knowing how much I like to fuck them. "How about you take care of me?"

This part of the role is easy to get into and, honestly, a distraction from the whirling thoughts in my head. I'm naked. My dick is hard.

She's here willingly, and club girls know what they're getting into.

"Then get on up here," I say, patting the bed.

She slips her panties down her legs and straddles me, her thick thighs wide across mine as she rubs her pussy up and down my dick.

When her lips reach mine, it's hot. We kiss, but we both

know what this is. A fun release. Neither of us sees wedding bells.

"How about I fuck your tits, then lick you out, then fuck your ass?" I say, knowing she likes it when I'm blunt.

Jessica smiles. "You think you can recover that quickly?"

"Depends on how long I tease you with my mouth."

"I like the sound of that." She reaches for the oil I keep on the bedside table and stands before drizzling it all over her chest. By the time she's rubbing it in, I'm on my feet and taking over. They're fake, firmer than I normally like, but big enough that they totally wrap around my dick. And yeah, I'm a visual guy, so the thought of watching myself come all over her is a turn-on.

I might be an ATF agent, but that doesn't mean I'm not a dirty fucker when it comes to the bedroom. In fact, the best part of this whole gig has been confirming the kind of woman I'm gonna look for when this gig is over. One who is sexually open and into trying new things.

"On your knees," I grunt. "It's been a rough week, and the only action my dick has seen is my hand." I've been on the road with Spark for a couple of long days of hard riding.

She hops onto the bed and pushes her breast together. "Then let me help you with that."

I stand in front of her and take my dick in my hand, stroking it twice with the oil. It feels good, but I know Jessica will feel better.

I ease my cock between her breasts and tip my head back as I suck in air, then groan. Everything in me clenches in anticipation as she lowers her head and sucks the tip.

And then I move, coiling my ass before sliding back between her tits. In my mind, I focus on how it feels, not who I'm with. It's better this way. Pure sex, no emotion.

In minutes, I come all over her.

I'm still gasping for air as someone hammers on my door.

"Need you to make a ride," King shouts. "You're meeting Spark at his place."

"Shit," I mutter, as I place my hand on Jessica's shoulder.

Jessica pouts. "Guess I'm gonna need to find someone else to take care of that oral, huh?"

I look down at her and smile. "Guess so."

I pull some clothes on while she cleans up, and we leave my room together. There's no hug goodbye, nothing so intimate.

"What do you need?" I ask King when I get to the bar. His dark hair falls forward over his face, and he shoves it back.

He slaps an envelope of cash to my chest. "Need you to drop this off at the docks. Haven needs paying."

Jasper Haven is our contact at Port Elizabeth, the largest docking terminal on the East Coast. For the cash in this envelope, he smooths weapons deliveries for us, enables our access onto the docks to pick them up, and gives us a heads-up about the activities of the Mafia members who think they run the New Jersey docks.

"Same place?"

"Same place. Midnight. You hit that tonight?" he says, tipping his chin toward Jessica.

I shake my head. "You interrupted a decent tit job. She's all yours."

King grins, then chugs the last of his beer. "So generous. And keep an eye on your boy."

"Spark?" The brother I'm probably closest to.

"Yeah. Caught him poking around outside Iris O'Connor's house. When he didn't know I could see him, he told me he was down by the shore. No pussy is worth bringing our club into dispute with the Irish, or lying to your president for."

Iris O'Connor was shot because of the club, and Spark got her out of trouble. I never believed in the whole love-at-first-sight thing, but man, there was some wild tension between the two of them.

I drive to Spark's house, where he's waiting on his bike. It takes us fifty minutes to get to the docks. The parkway is clear. The moon, bright. And our bikes are in the mood for speed. At times like this, I forget what I'm meant to be doing. There's a harmony between man and machine that's almost meditative.

I didn't call Weicker, my handler, to let him know I was on a run. I'll write a report when I get home tonight. I've done this run before for my club.

And there I fucking go again.

My club.

Like I really belong.

2

BRIAR

I watch him. The man I've been told will become my husband. He tugs his jacket over his arms and fastens it around his stomach.

I tug my knees up beneath my chin, wrap my arms around them, and try to breathe through the shivers and shudders.

The room is small, all concrete, like the foundation of a house never finished. There is a toilet in the corner and a bed across the room. It's a king, soft bedding, and I'm grateful that I haven't had to use it with this man who hit me so hard I'm still seeing double.

He touched my skin—nothing sexual. But from his words and his tone, I know it will be expected of me wherever I end up, because I'm here to breed. I can't imagine being so scared and hateful of a changing world that my solution would be to create as many white children as possible. And worse, that the mother of those children would be stolen and raped and abused.

He talked about my new home so calmly. Like this was normal.

God, please don't let it be another concrete prison like this. I won't survive it.

The first chance I get, I'm going to run.

Even now, acid rises in my stomach, and I know I'll be sick again if I don't swallow and breathe and try to calm down.

The thin black slip I'm wearing is no help against the cold.

My eyes burn. Tears and not sleeping for an undetermined period of time are the cause. There are no windows in the room, so I have no idea how much time has passed since I was taken on Wednesday evening. Two days, maybe.

I haven't been fed or given water since I arrived.

He slips on a jacket that I recognize is expensive from the label. "I'm very happy with you, Rose," he says, like I didn't just fight him for two hours.

I spat in his face and got slapped hard for my efforts.

I say nothing because I have nothing left in me right now.

"You'll like our home," he says as if this is normal.

Consensual.

When it's anything but.

The red light beneath the camera in the corner blinks approximately every two seconds. The floor is blissfully cool and agonizingly hard against my beaten body.

I can't look at him. His thick eyebrows, high forehead, and the wide nose of a drinker make me feel ill.

But he crouches in front of me and grips my chin. The scent of powerful cologne assaults me. It's the kind you find in those all-American-type clothing stores that gets pumped in through vents and gives you a headache within minutes. "You can have the kind of life you choose," he says. "You can have nice things, your own space. Or you can have this"—he gestures around him, then smooths a palm down my long blonde hair.

Whether I am in a concrete room or a decorated room will make little difference to the fact I am here against my will.

I say nothing.

"We'll make arrangements for transport, and we'll be reunited soon," he says as he stands. His shoes clip across the cold floor.

As he walks to the door, my captor opens it. "Here's the number for the two police officers, in case you have any transport problems," my new keeper says.

I jump and suck in air as the door slams behind him.

The panic of the police being involved overwhelms me as locks click back in place. Tears threaten to fall.

This cannot be my life.

This is not how it ends.

Not when it has barely started.

No one will report me missing for days. My relationship with my parents is patchy. I'm a freelance graphic designer who works from home. I recently moved to New York and don't have friends here yet.

I've walked this room a hundred times and not found anything useful. Nothing I could use to pick the binding on my wrists. Nothing I can use as a weapon. The thought that it's all futile flickers through me, but I refuse to believe that yet.

There is a rattle outside the door. In a Pavlovian reaction, my heart rate escalates, fight-or-flight kicking into overdrive. I'm not ready to fight again. Not yet. Not when the wounds haven't healed. Not when my wrists are still bleeding from the handcuffs fastened tightly around them.

One of the men who kidnapped me opens the door.

"Time to go," the man says gruffly. He has overly greased dark hair and is wearing fatigues and black boots.

"I'm leaving?"

He nods.

"What time is it?"

"Let's go." He pulls a gun from a holster beneath his arm and waves it in the direction of the door. I realize the handle of that gun has been slammed into the side of my skull once already. I was unconscious for a while after I was brought here.

I try to compartmentalize my thoughts. Surviving the next hour is all I can think about. Focusing on what happened in this room is not going to get me out of it.

"Where am I going?"

I should know better than to ask questions. The answers rarely come.

Instead, he points the gun at my head.

My joints crack as I scramble awkwardly to my bare feet, and my head spins as I follow him into the hallway. He blindfolds me, but not before I notice that it's dark outside and the moon is high. Surprisingly, the metal cuffs are removed and replaced with rope that burns against my sores.

"Easy there, Joe," someone says as I'm scooped up into the man's arms. Now I know his name, not that it helps.

I hated the concrete room, but at least I knew where I was. We're no more than an hour outside New York, where I was taken. If they move me again, I'll lose all concept of where I am.

Shit, they might even put me on a private jet to somewhere.

I start to shake uncontrollably again. It's been

happening more often. Violent shudders that wrack my body.

Cool night air tickles my nose. They must have carried me outside. I'm shoved into what feels like the back seat of a car. Someone tugs a seat belt across me and straps me in, a strange act since they have done no other thing to keep me safe.

"Sit still if you don't want to be shot and dumped in the Hudson," Joe says.

The car jiggles as people climb in. Two doors slam. The car starts, and I sway with the motion as we move down an uneven road.

The blindfold moves enough so I can see a thin sliver of what is going on beyond it. Joe in the driver's seat, and another man I don't know sits in the front passenger seat. He sits facing Joe, his arm over the back of the seat, a gun pointed in my direction.

The car's windows must be tinted. They'd be foolish to move me like this if they weren't.

I try to move the blindfold higher by rubbing the back of my ear against my shoulder in an attempt to move the tie. It works in a fashion and enables me to look down and see my hands.

Grating country music suddenly blasts through the vehicle.

"You still jonesing for the Knicks this year?" the passenger asks.

Joe's laughter fills the car, as if he doesn't have a woman tied up in the back seat. "You better believe it."

"I don't buy it. They can't attract the top players."

I test the give in the rope. There's the smallest amount of release. I can work with that.

"You're kidding me, right? New York is the epicenter. The Garden is the best arena to play in," Joe says.

I can only pray they remain distracted by their conversation. The music helps cover my actions.

The knot across my wrists slips a little. Or maybe I'm imagining it after a prolonged period in unforgiving metal cuffs.

Biting back a hiss as the rough hessian scrapes across my wounds, I slowly tease my hands back and forth, determined to not bring attention to my actions. Each time I tug, I feel as though I make a little more room.

There's more laughter. "Dude, you haven't had a franchise player since Patrick Ewing."

"Maybe it's our turn this year. The streak can't stay cold forever."

I pull a little harder. Warm air blows from a heater by my knees. I'm not going to waste my opportunities for escape. This vehicle could have a trunk, and the last thing I want is to be placed in it.

I narrow my hand, pressing my thumb and pinkie together against my palm, and attempt to tug it through the loop.

"Yeah, but there are too many teams on fire, and the draft was deep this summer," Joe says.

His indifference brings tears to my eyes. How can they be so nonchalant about kidnapping me?

I have to use it to my advantage.

I've been biding my time until there is a real opportunity to escape, but perhaps my lack of resistance has lured them into a false sense of security that I'm not going to try anything.

With one last burst of exertion, I manage to slip the loop

off one wrist. I feel the car slow and stop; I'm guessing we're approaching the stoplights.

Now is my chance. Fear looms large, but I can't wait. Not any longer.

I yank the blindfold off my face and try to open the door. It's locked, but I don't have time to unlock it.

"What the fuck?" the man in the passenger seat yells as he tries to grab my arm, wrenching it backward. Pain burns through my wrist as he squeezes where it already hurts.

My elbow collides with his shoulder, and this time I manage to unlock the door and reach the handle. My breath comes in short gasps, my heart racing at such a frantic pace I worry it will burst.

A scream escapes me as the truck swerves.

We all get thrown around. As the stranger aims his gun in my direction, I slam into his arm, causing the gun to clatter into the dark footwell.

Pain floods through me as he grabs my hair in his fist.

It's dark.

The road isn't busy. We careen.

I mistimed everything.

And now I'm going to die.

3

SAINT

Once we're parked at the lot for the drop, I get off my bike and cross my arms. "What were you doing tonight?"

Spark shakes his head, blond hair whipping in the wind before he secures it with an elastic. "Nothing much. You?"

I don't believe him, but I'm guessing it was related to pussy. The corners of his mouth turn up in a slight smile he manages to stop. But I'm not the man to be holding others accountable for lying right now.

Not when I'm up to my eyeballs in lies and half-truths.

"Was doing Jessica when King hammered on the door and asked me to do this," I say.

Spark laughs. "For a holy man, you don't know the meaning of the word *abstinence*."

I wish I could tell Spark the truth. I hate the fact he thinks I am something I'm not. But I search my memory banks anyway to find a response that Spark expects.

Though Dad's sermons were all about fire and brimstone, I have a wider range of knowledge from reading the Bible every day for the past two years. Decent stories if you ignore everything that's wrong with organized religion. Sometimes, I lose track of which Bible the verses come from, but it's not like these men know the difference between their King James and their New American Bible. "A loving doe, a graceful deer. May her breasts satisfy you always. Proverbs five nineteen. It's as if God personally instructed me to worship those double Es of hers."

Spark chokes out a laugh as a black sedan pulls into the lot. "This him?" He places his palm on his gun.

I do the same, purely for protection. It's not his usual ride. "Probably."

As I'm carrying the envelope, I walk to the sedan, and the window lowers. "New car?" I ask when I see Jasper's nervous face.

He reaches for the envelope I'm holding. "This has helped pay off some debts."

I like the kid. Vex, our resident tech genius, checked him out. Young, hungry. But a mountain of debt and two kids before he turned twenty. I don't begrudge him the cash. In fact, I've not reported that I know his name. Because when the web closes, I don't want this kid caught up in it all.

Some in the ATF might think that makes me corrupt.

I'm past the point of giving a fuck.

"Don't flash the cash around," I warn. "It'll make it easier to find you if anyone comes looking, yeah?"

He looks confused by my concern. "Yeah?"

"Sort your debt out first. Or you'll be stuck doing shit like this for the rest of your life, kid."

Jasper nods, but I know he doesn't really hear me.

The car peels out of the parking lot. I watch the dust swirl as I walk back to Spark. "Well, that was easy." I smooth my hand through my beard. I don't love it. It itches. But it does the job of helping me blend in with bikers well. And it will make it harder for the Iron Outlaws to identify me in public later, as they have never seen me without one.

Spark grins at me.

"What's funny?" I ask.

"Just thinking you look a lot like Jesus, the one on those cheap candles with the weird-looking heart."

I shake my head as I climb on my bike. "That's the sacred heart of Jesus you're shitting on."

"I'm not shitting on it . . . but you've got to admit, they could have gone with a better design."

"O Sacred Heart of Jesus, for whom it is impossible not to have compassion on the afflicted, have pity on us miserable sinners."

"Miserable sinners? It's either us or a seventies rock band."

I flip my middle finger in his direction, and he laughs. I can't help but grin. He's right. If Jesus were a white man with blue eyes as opposed to an actual man from the Middle East, I probably would agree that I do look like Jesus.

I reach to start my bike when a large black truck careens into the parking lot. It's swerving erratically. When it slides to a halt about thirty meters away, the rear passenger door opens, and a young woman leaps out and runs towards us. She's barefoot, wearing a black dress or negligee. The cut is revealing. It's short, the color harsh against her pale skin.

My first thought is that she's hot, but then I realize as she gets closer that she's running for her life.

She runs straight toward us; the stones and gravel must be carving up her feet.

"Help me. Please. Help." Her voice is tortured, her face covered in fresh scratches and bruises. She's young. Maybe mid to late twenties.

"Fuck me," Spark mutters and climbs off his bike. I do the same, mentally urging her to keep running to us.

When the driver gets out of the truck, I see he's a slimy-looking fucker. A military wannabe. A weekend warrior.

"Get back in the truck, girl," the man yells to her.

"No," she shouts, then looks up at Spark. "Please help me."

"How many in the truck?" Spark asks me.

I squint. "One in the passenger seat." The man makes a move to open the door.

"Were you alone in the back of the truck?" Spark asks her.

She nods, rubbing at her wrists. Oh, sweet Jesus. The wounds have all the markings from trying to get free of rope or cuffs. "They tied my wrists."

Spark steps towards the guy, and I tuck the girl behind me. "We've got you," I whisper.

"Get the fuck out of here," Spark yells. "I don't rate your chances."

The first bullet whizzes by my ear. The next hits the fence behind us. Spark and I start firing rounds. Neither of us wants a body to clean up—that would be hard for me to explain to the ATF—so we aim to wreck the truck. The tires, the radiator, the windshield.

The shooter dives for cover.

"You got her?" Spark shouts.

I take her hand and help her onto the back of my bike. She's shaking. Numb. Silent. But those brown eyes of hers, so filled with fear, tug at me. "Yeah. Know a place I can take her. I'll meet you at the clubhouse."

I exit the lot, racing ahead of Spark. After ten minutes of her shaking behind me, I pull over and climb off the bike. Slowly, I remove my cut and tug my hoodie over my head.

No sudden movements; I don't want to scare her more than she already is. "Here," I say, handing it to her. "It's not much, but it'll keep you warm enough until I can get you to a police station."

"No," she says, fear causing her voice to waver. "Please. I just need somewhere safe to sleep tonight. I can't face the police yet."

"But . . . evidence," I say, reaching for her chin and tipping her face so I can see her injuries properly. She jerks back from me as if I stung her. Classic abuse signs. I nod in the direction we came from. "You know that guy? Husband? Boyfriend?"

She shakes her head. So not a battered wife or girlfriend.

Her body is wracked with tremors, so I ease my hoodie over her head myself. "I can take you to the ER. Or to Switch, the medic in our club. You want me to call someone to come get you?"

Again, she shakes her head. "Please. I need some clothes. And some cash maybe."

"Nothing open this late at night," I say. "Cash I can do. I got some at my place. But you sure I can't take you to the cops?" I get paid by the club, but it gets handed straight to the ATF. At least, it did when I patched in and finally got paid. Recently, I've been taking a little off the top. The bureau has been getting pissy about my expenses. Complaining that the sting is dragging on. They don't realize the predicament I'm in. I shouldn't end up out of pocket because the expenses policy doesn't currently cover everything I have to buy.

Tears fill her eyes. And I'm a sucker for tears. Want to fix what's broken. Like I used to for Mom and Rae. Because for all dad was a preacher, a saver of souls in the pulpit, he was the taker of them in our home. A violent and malevolent presence.

"I need a minute," she says.

I want to tell her I'm an undercover agent, that she's safe with me. Instead, I fight it down. "Look, my place is clean, safe, and about an hour away. I can take you there, help you get some clothes in the morning, then help you figure out what you want to do. Okay?"

She blows out a long slow breath. "Okay."

I offer her my hand. "My name's"—I flip through the options, my undercover names merging with my real ones—"Saint."

"My name is . . ." She looks around for a moment. "Briar."

It's a pretty name, but to me, it's clear we both lied.

4

BRIAR

You got a trusting heart, baby girl.

That's what my pop used to say to me every time my heart was stomped on by some asshole boy who didn't deserve my time, let alone my love. He'd make me a hot chocolate if it was raining or take me for a walk around his rose garden while he smoked a slim cigar. The scent of one appears out of nowhere every now and again, and I like to think it's him making his presence known. The warm tone of his voice would soothe my hurts, and while it couldn't fix my heart, knowing somebody loved me while it was fixing itself was enough.

Yet I somehow kept on giving my heart away, giving it over and over until I realized that true love doesn't exist.

True romantic love is a falsehood.

It's a fantasy.

I've built a life for myself that I love. Sure, it's a lonely one. But I'm an in-demand graphic designer. And I earned enough money that I decided to try and make it in New York. My apartment was small, my freelance work flowing. And I recently signed a contract with a major ad agency right in Manhattan. I felt good about how my life was shaping up. But maybe that was all a fantasy too.

Four weeks. That's how long I lasted in New York before the very thing my dad had worried out about happened.

It's not safe, Rose. You're the kind of girl who runs down dark alleys at night. They'll eat you alive.

My dad has belittled and doubted my capabilities my entire life.

Looking at myself in the mirror of Saint's sparse bathroom, I still can't bear to think about how he might have been right.

Because all it took was one date. That was it. He'd said his name was Kris. We'd talked for a few days before. In person, we'd flirted. He'd been a gentleman. And now it makes sense why he was such a good listener. He'd asked about my family back home and how I was settling in the city. I'd been honest. Too honest.

So, when I saw him two days later in a van near my apartment, I trusted him. I stepped forward, moved closer, believed him as he fumbled over the seat to get something out of the back of the van. A gift, he'd said, for me. Even when he asked for my help to reach it, I still trusted him. Until strange hands were on me, and I was dragged through the side door.

My thick blonde hair is a sweaty mess. Scars and scratches run along the side of my face, and judging by the pus oozing out of one of them, they are infected. I feel my forehead. I'm hot. Yeah, sure sign of an infection. My body is covered in bruises, and the welts on my wrists sting like vinegar is being poured on them.

My brown eyes are devoid of emotion. Flat, as I stare into them.

Steam fills the bathroom, the water hot and plentiful, but I can't move.

I fought with all I had.

Until there was nothing left.

I hate that I let them take me, beat me, and grind me down.

The man who thought he owned me had a high widow's peak and an aquiline nose. He looked at me as if I was everything but treated me like I was nothing.

And I hate him with every fiber of my being.

My teeth start to chatter again, and I shake uncontrollably.

"Move, Rose," I tell myself, using my real name and not the nickname Pop gave me all those years ago.

My sweet Briar. You have the beauty of a wild rose but need to use your thorns to stop your petals from getting stomped on.

The name stuck.

I step into the shower and wince, trying to visualize all the infection and pain washing down the drain with the swirls of my blood, but . . .

I sob.

I slam my palms against the cool tile, wanting anger to replace the agony. Either is better than thinking about what has happened to me.

But the thoughts and pain become too loud of a buzz in my head. I can't keep it in. The box I've forced every feeling and emotion into shatters open, and the sound I make can't be described.

It's too guttural to be a scream.

Too piercing to be a moan.

It's wild.

I sob as I reach for the soap on the shelf and begin rubbing it into wounds that reopen and bleed.

The pain takes everything else away. It's all I can focus on. I turn the heat up on the shower. Scalding their touch from my body. Sterilizing my wounds. Cauterizing emotions I can't name.

The bathroom door smashes open, falling off its hinge. And I see Saint through the steam.

His face looks like thunder as he slides the shower door open, stepping around me. "Jesus, no, babe. Not like this," he says softly, turning the heat down.

He's still dressed in boots and jeans and a leather vest that identifies him as an Iron Outlaw. Tall with broad shoulders, he could easily overpower me.

I'd be at his mercy.

I shy away from him, pressing my back against the corner of the shower. With all that I am, I try to cover my naked body, but it's no use. My knees give in, and I sink to the floor.

Why won't my brain think? Why won't my legs work? Did I escape one monster to end up in the bathroom of another? I was so reckless coming to the home of a stranger.

God, and now I'm berating myself on top of everything else.

I put my hands out in front of me to keep him away.

He switches the shower from the overhead to the hand-held unit, running it onto the back of his hand before he looks at me. Then he crouches about two feet away from me. "Me telling you you're safe doesn't mean shit, I know. But you are." His voice is calm and quiet. "Let me rinse you off so we can get you dry and treat these wounds, yeah?"

There is nothing left in my tank, so I nod.

"Close your eyes," he whispers.

He tilts my chin back and gently rinses my hair and my face. He takes my fingertips in his hand and elongates my arm so he can rinse it thoroughly, being careful around the cuts on my wrist.

When he tugs me to my feet, I let him, forgetting I'm naked. Tears fill my eyes as I receive a tender touch I never thought I'd feel again, but I don't open them. I can't look at this man. He's a stranger. A reminder of what happened to me.

I simply need to get through this night.

The shower stops, and I open my eyes.

Saint isn't looking at me in any way that's sexual; it's more like he's assessing me as he wraps a towel over my shoulders. Then he tries to wrap one around my hair though it immediately starts to slide off as he gets a third and wraps it around my waist. Then he pats me dry.

Tenderly.

"Thank you." It's all I can think to say.

"You'll get through this," he says. "You washed a whole bunch of evidence away, though. I wish you'd gone to the police before showering."

"I have my reasons."

"You wanna share 'em?"

I think about what I have to lose and gain here. "On the night they took me, they joked about being able to kidnap me. I threatened to escape and tell the police. But they laughed. Said they have cops on their payroll to make things disappear. That they'd been watching me. They knew I had no real friends. That I lived alone. It wasn't random. They targeted me. A date through a dating app two days earlier. I answered every question he asked honestly."

"Shit, Briar," Saint says as he dries my feet and then sits me down on the side of the bath. "I'm going to put some antiseptic on you. I'm sure it's going to sting, but it's the best I can do."

Exhausted, I nod. "Just do it."

I watch him as he works. He's an attractive man. Kind, blue eyes and sharp cheekbones. His beard is out of control. A wiry mess. His hands are rough.

He's also a danger to me. I know about these clubs, what they do. The weapons, the drugs, the misogyny.

But for tonight, I'm willing to let him be my safety.

He saved me after all. "The guy who wanted me as his new wife was at the building I was held in earlier today. Before he left, he said he'd arrange transport for us to be reunited. But I managed to get my wrists free. My main thought was to crash the truck. To cause chaos and escape. I'm grateful I found a parking lot with two men on bikes."

Saint smiles, but it's a soft one of understanding. "Glad I could be of service." He puts his head back down and focuses on treating my wounds.

"Who was your friend?" I ask.

Saint stops what he was doing and looks up at me. "That was Spark."

"What day is it?"

"It's Friday evening. Well, early hours of Saturday morning now."

A silence falls between us again, but it's not uncomfortable. The tight band around my chest, the one that has been there for forty-eight hours, releases a little.

I doubt anybody looked for me. Two days without contact is not unusual between me and my parents. Dad's still sulking that I moved here against his wishes. But at twenty-eight, with a good degree from a good school and a strong work ethic, I can do as I please.

Even my clients won't be too concerned. I'm usually pretty responsive, but they won't worry if I don't reply for a day or two. And now it's the weekend. "I don't know where my phone and my purse are."

Saint applies the last Band-Aid and gathers all the debris before dumping it in the garbage. "One step at a time. Basic needs first. We've treated your injuries. We'll find you some clean clothes to wear for now. I'll give you some painkillers and antibiotics after we've got some food in your stomach."

"They know where I live. They have my keys. I bet all my things are gone. They know how to find me again. They could be waiting for me."

"Not going to happen, Briar. We can figure all that out in the morning." He leads me out of the bathroom and into the bedroom. The bed has been made, a pair of jogging pants and a hoodie on it. "I figured you'd want something that covers you and keeps you warm but doesn't rub against those cuts."

I look at the soft cotton. He's right. "Thank you."

"There's a lock on the bedroom door. Use it so you feel safe. I've grabbed some things already, so I won't need to come in again tonight. I'm going to go make you something to eat."

I look at the width of his biceps. "If you wanted to break the door down, you'd be more than capable, given how you smashed the bathroom door open."

Saint smiles at this. "I'll take the compliment, Briar. But I want you to feel safe. Slide the dresser in front of the door if it makes you feel better."

Safe.

Such a suddenly foreign concept.

He leaves me standing in the sparsely furnished room, my mind reeling. I don't know who I am right now or what

I'm going to do. But my gut instinct tells me Saint will help me figure it all out.

5

SAINT

Something tickles my nose, and I bat it away.

Then there's a flash of light as I turn my head.

I open one eye, and everything comes flooding back as the sunlight hits me.

Briar.

I rub a hand over my face and stretch out on the sofa the best I can. My back creaks, and my legs groan as I stretch them out after being bent like a pretzel all night. The cover house was meant to be simple: Small. Basic. No need for two bedrooms.

There had been no backup plan for finding a devasted young woman.

I'd done the best I could to help make her feel comfortable, but Briar had gone quiet on me as we'd eaten. And I rage silently as I relive treating her wounds. I've triaged in a war zone. But everyone knew why we were there, knew that injuries were a risk we took willingly. Looking at the large welts on her wrists and the score marks on her cheeks, I knew she'd been caught unawares by what had been done to her.

The way she'd shivered so badly on the back of the bike reassured me of that horrific fact.

I'd not had the balls to ask her whether she'd been raped. The thought makes me sick.

At three in the morning, I debated letting Weicker know what had happened. But something stopped me. Briar needs to be in control of her own journey of dealing with this. The last thing she needs is a guy she doesn't even know making calls for her.

Plus, I strongly doubt Weicker would have given a shit if it hadn't led to useful information for our investigation.

None of it feels any better in the cold light of day. Except for the fact she's safe.

It's absolutely stupid to have her here. I should take her somewhere: a shelter, to her family, friends maybe.

There are cardinal rules in undercover work. Never reveal your role or any details about the deployment without express permission. I can't tell Briar who I really am, even though knowing might help her.

And don't unnecessarily increase your risk. Keeping a woman around does that. She could see something, say something, overhear a call with Weicker and others. The club can't know she's here because it becomes a whole other world of figuring out how to extricate her too when this is all over—which could be in two years or two days.

Carefully, I ease my aching body until I sit upright on the sofa. As soon as I hit forty, it always takes a minute to get the bones and muscles moving. I'm starved. My phone says it's ten in the morning, and there's a message from Spark checking in on me and the girl.

I fire off a quick text telling him it's all taken care of, even as I glance at my bedroom door and know it hasn't been.

After a quick shower, I wander into the kitchen in the pair of shorts I changed into last night.

While Briar showered the previous evening, I grabbed my emergency phone from beneath the floorboards, and I dial a number on it now.

"Jensen," I say before he has a chance to speak.

"Ryker. What gives? Heard you were deep." We served together in Afghanistan. Left around the same time. He went FBI; I went ATF. Two branches of the government alphabet soup. Our paths crossed on the incel case.

"I am. Gotta be quick. Operating sex trafficking groups in New York—can you get me any info?"

"That's a broad range. You got specifics?"

I tell him about Briar without giving any personal details that would identify her.

"She definitely said there were cops involved?" he asks.

The kitchen counter is cool beneath my palm. "Yes."

"She needs to come in. Make a statement. If you can't get her to trust someone, you need to take the statement there while all the details are still fresh."

If only it were that simple. "I'm undercover. Can't be acting like an agent while I'm here."

"Shit," Jensen says. "Maybe encourage her to write it all down, every detail. Tell her it'll be cathartic and will help her process her memories correctly. Then get me a copy. But I can't run down a crime with no witnesses if she won't come forward."

"Understand. Just get me the info on anything that looks similar."

"On it. Look after yourself."

"Will do."

While I have the phone out, I fire a quick text to Rae. *You heard from Mom recently? I forgot to ask.*

It only takes a minute before she replies. *Dad got some big-ass donation for the church from some old dude in his congregation, so . . .*

My dad's church is filled with hypocrites who hallelujah the fuck out of services on Sunday, then vote against civil rights and gay marriage on Tuesday.

I know what that means. It means Dad will be happy for a while, which means Mom won't be his punching bag.

Got it. I'm gonna be unavailable for parts of this week.

She replies straight away. *Understood. Take care of yourself, Ike.*

Thinking of Mom and Dad makes me think of Briar. When my dad got drunk and went into one of his rampages, Mom would get up the next morning and make pancakes for me and Rae. No matter how whipped, beaten, and bruised we were. It was comforting, those precious hours when he'd sleep off his hangover and we'd all reassure each other we were okay when we were anything but.

I turn on the oven to warm, then whip out the pan and ingredients. There's a rhythm to making pancakes. Pouring the right amount, flipping at the right time, allowing them to cook to perfection with a hint of color on each side. I make them three at a time, moving them into a casserole dish in the oven once they're done to keep them warm while I cook some more.

It's kitchen mindfulness in a world of chaos.

I've always wanted to give people an anchor in their tumultuous lives. As a kid, I was always outside, camping in the yard, then farther afield as I grew older. Anything to get away from Dad. Beneath the trees and stars, I felt closer to the God Dad held over us like a sword of Damocles than I did anyplace else on earth. The summer before college, I hitchhiked Route 66 to prove my faith in the basic goodness of human beings. Dad called it rebellion and abuse of people's charity.

Yet the man has been saving up congregational cash like he's going to be picked to fund the next ark.

While the pancakes cook, I set the small table. Cutlery, plates, butter, and syrup. Would be better with blueberries, but all I've got are bananas. It'll have to do.

My club phone rings; it's King. "Yo, what's up?" I say, glancing toward my bedroom door.

"Spark said you guys ran into some trouble last night. You good?"

Lying in this job has been second nature for years. My whole identity is a lie. My father would have a cow if he knew what my real job entails. He'd have some beef with how it's at odds with what the Bible teaches. All the *thou shalt not lie* rhetoric. Which is ironic, for as much as I have started to get comfortable lying to my bosses, I find myself less comfortable lying to these men, these outlaws who have become my brothers.

"It's all good. Got her shelter." It's not a direct lie. And she *is* sheltering. *Here*, in my home. It's the dumbest decision I could have made. For a moment I wonder why I lied, beyond it becoming my MO these days. Then I realize the less everyone knows about her, the safer she is.

"Okay. Good. You think it's anything we need to worry about? The last thing we need is sex traffickers flowing through here. Especially if they bring law enforcement with them."

"Pretty sure the people being trafficked have it worse than we do," I say and then curse silently. I don't usually disagree with King. I go with the flow.

"Yeah. Well, I'll let someone else worry about them. Just don't want anyone sniffing around here looking for 'em. Don't need any more eyes on us than we already have."

I run a hand through my hair. "Fair. But I think we should definitely monitor the situation to be sure."

"I'll let Vex know."

"I got some errands I need to deal with today. Call me if you need me, otherwise I'll see you at the club tomorrow."

"Deal. Catch you later."

When he hangs up, my other phone rings. "What's up, Weicker?"

"The request you made for the cash to buy those guns from . . ."

"Niro," I add helpfully. He's selling a handful of his weapons. Offered them to me. Well, he offered them to Spark first, but Spark suggested I might want 'em. Truth is, if I buy them, they become evidence. His fingerprints. Bullet tracing to every death at the hands of the club.

"Yeah, well, didn't get approved."

"You wanna turn your back on evidence?" I whisper, my eyes focused on the handle to the bedroom.

I step through the door into the rear yard. The previous tenants left a load of shit. Old car bumpers, a broken swing set. The lot had never been tended. And while that plays on my last nerve, it fits the character I've built.

"Nickel-and-diming from the top," Weicker says in agreement.

I need to remember that out of everyone at the ATF, he's the only one I feel truly has my back.

"They're getting impatient," he continues. "Right now, we would rely on your testimony for much of what you've seen. We have one audio worth any salt. They want you in a full wire for the next weapon drop at the docks. And they are going to intercept it."

Intercept it? Jesus Christ.

And that's my first sign of the day that I should tap out. Because I don't get the usual buzz of excitement at the idea of a sting. My head isn't whirring with ideas about how to make it error-proof. Or how we could catch as many club members at one time as possible.

Instead, my head goes to evasion. How do I ensure Spark, as sergeant at arms, knows he needs to be prepared? How does Halo, as road captain, ensure the exit route is open and protected?

A screeching siren pierces the air, and I run back into the house and see smoke rising from the pancakes still in the pan. "Fuck, I gotta call you back," I say, slamming the phone down on the counter.

Tugging the pan off the heat, I reach for the dishcloth and wave it beneath the smoke detector six times before it turns itself off. My heart is still racing as I open the window and waft the back door open and closed a couple of times to let some air flow through.

"That's one heck of an alarm clock," Briar says, her voice thick with sleep. As she inhales deeply, she stretches her hands over her head, reaching for the top of the door frame. She hangs there, stretching her spine for a minute before letting go, a puff of air escaping those plump lips of hers.

"Sorry, got distracted by a call and forgot I was cooking them."

She doesn't move from the door frame. "If you could help me get some clothes, I can pay you back when I get my bank cards. I'm good for the money."

I take a step toward her, but then realize I should give her space. "I can take you to the store to pick up some things now, or you can eat some pancakes first, my mom's recipe, so you aren't shopping on an empty stomach."

The indecision in her eyes stings. I grab the cloth, open the oven, and pull out the pot of warmed pancakes. The smell from them is heavenly, and my mouth waters. I set them on the table and pour her a glass of orange juice. "I said it last night, and I know me telling you that you're safe doesn't mean shit to you right now. But you are with me. I promise."

I set about doing normal things. Grabbing a cup, pouring her a coffee without asking, because I don't want to interrupt her while she's clearly thinking through what she needs to do.

After I place the cup on the table next to the orange juice, I take a seat. "Sit, Briar. You don't need to choose between the two. Eat breakfast, and then I'll take you for some clothes, yeah?"

She lets out a breath of air in a whoosh, like she's relieved I made the decision for her. The chair scrapes across the cheap-ass linoleum as she tugs it out from beneath the table. "Thank you," she says, reaching for the coffee. She hugs the mug for a moment, then sips. "Christ," she mutters after she takes a sip, blinking furiously as she winces. "That's . . . potent."

I can't help but laugh. "Sorry, I like it strong. You want me to add some water to your mug?"

"You got any sugar? Or cream? Anything to make it taste a little less bitter?"

"Sugar I can do," I say as I get up and grab the bag from the cupboard and a spoon from the drawer. "I can do milk, but no cream. Otherwise, we can grab a drive-through coffee on our way to the mall."

"Sugar's fine." She takes it from me and adds a spoonful to her cup before stirring it. "I didn't mean to sound ungrateful. Apologies if I did."

"You didn't." I sit back down opposite her.

In the sunlight, I can see how pretty, and young, she is. She speaks politely, smiles softly. But beneath the facade, I know she's still a terrified woman.

And I need to fix it.

6
———

BRIAR

As soon as I bite into the first sweet pancake, my stomach lets out a grateful rumble. Sticky syrup and butter are my weakness. Sugar and fat are my comfort, and I don't hold back.

"Sorry," I say between mouthfuls of food, keeping my eyes on my plate. "I wasn't fed the two days I was . . ."

I can't think about that place now. I take a deep breath, focus on the blue sky outside the window, and try to relax my grip on the table.

"Fuck," Saint mutters, putting his knife and fork down on his plate. "What do you need?"

I look down at the pancake on my fork. "I don't know. What you said last night about basic needs. I think I'm still there."

"So definitely no police?"

I shake my head. "I considered it, like you said. They said they had two police officers who could get them out of trouble. But what would they get charged with? Attempted abduction. Assault."

"Can I ask? Did they . . . were you raped?"

I pick up the fork and debate putting the pancake in my mouth. "I wasn't. The guy seemed happier smacking me around, but I was terrified he might. Even if he'd sexually assaulted me, there are so many cases where women report rapes and they aren't believed. Or the perpetrator gets some wishy-washy sentence. Did you know there was a research study done once? They gave over two hundred cops a police report of a rape. All the details were exactly the same, except in one version, the girl was a student, and in the others, they deliberately labelled her a 'hooker.' Not even a 'sex worker.' Just 'hooker.' Half the cops got one version; half got the other. In the 'hooker' version, the officers were more prominent in victim blaming and determined the consequences she suffered were far less, compared to the cops who reviewed the report from the student. Even when both reports of rape had the exact same data otherwise."

Saint chews a mouthful of pancake, but he narrows his eyes as if he's thinking. "Not all cops are—"

"Don't *not all cops* me," I say.

Saint holds his hands up in surrender. It finally dawns on me that he's shirtless. It makes me feel vulnerable. Even as I take in the shape of his arms and the ink that covers them.

"You're right. I know some cops are rotten to their core. I'm sorry."

The sincere and fast apology without defense catches me off guard. "I'm surprised a member of a motorcycle club would be so endorsing of them."

He nods and tips his chin toward my plate. "Eat some more. You want to talk about what happened?"

"Not really." I stab a pancake with a fork.

"Okay. Bottling it up won't help. If you don't trust me, you need to write it down. Every single detail. Every smell, every word spoken, every person you saw . . . all of it. It'll help you process it later, and you'll always have the details to come back to if there is ever a reason for evidence in the long-term."

Tears sting my eyes. "I can barely see past the end of breakfast right now. Long-term is an abstract concept."

Saint leans forward and lays his hand on the table. It's palm up, waiting for me to take it. I move towards it, my hand hovering in the air. Holding someone's hand is something I've done a million times. It suddenly feels like an incredibly personal and powerful act. I look at him; he's watching my hand.

Yet I can't place it in his.

I pull it back and place it above my heart, my fingers itching my skin.

"Briar, look at me."

I do as he says.

"You'll get to the end of breakfast. And the end of lunch. And dinner. You'll get through this day. And the next day. And soon enough, a year will have gone by, and you won't be thinking about what happened every moment of every day. You won't forget it. It'll shape you and change you in ways, both good and bad, that you don't understand right now. But one foot after the other, sweetheart. It's all you can do."

A tear spills over my lashes, and I sweep it away. "Thank you. For last night and for this."

"Even though I make shit coffee?"

I sniff and laugh at the same time. It's a funny sound. "Your pancakes make up for it."

"Good. Now eat a few more. And we can stop by somewhere for better coffee than this when we are done."

"Before we go, do you have a laptop I can use to request

a replacement bank card and perhaps transfer you some cash before we go shopping? Without my phone to pay, I can't access any funds."

Saint pauses for a moment, the fork halfway to his mouth. "You can use my phone. With me right here. There's shit you don't need to be seeing on it."

I almost forgot he was a member of an outlaw gang. He probably does all kinds of illegal shit. Would he want to punish me if—

"Don't look at me like that, Briar. It's club shit that doesn't involve you. As for the cash, you can run a tab."

After breakfast, I insist on cleaning up the dishes while Saint jumps in the shower. I gather the plates on the counter and turn on the tap to rinse them.

"*Briar*," he yells. "Turn the fucking tap off."

I quickly turn it off and bite back a grin. His tone is exasperated, not angry.

"Thank you," he shouts.

I wait until the shower stops before turning the tap on again. And I'm wiping down the table when he steps into the room. His presence is commanding. He's a man who knows he looks good in blue denim and a black T-shirt. "Sorry about the water thing."

Saint shrugs. "Normally here alone. Didn't know it would do that. Here." He hands me his phone. "Not going to watch while you enter your password and shit. Have your card sent here unless you wanna go home."

"I could move to a hotel," I say. I have the funds. But my voice sounds shaky even to me.

"I'll take you to a hotel if you like. But would it make you feel safer to stay here for a day or two, until you find your feet?"

I think about the answer to that. Would I feel safer? The

traffickers lost me in New Jersey to two bikers. They know my name, where I live. They probably know everything about me. If I check into a hotel in my own name, it might pop up on a search if they have access to such things.

Shit. I won't be safe. Here, I'm no one.

"I'll try not to be a pain in the ass."

Saint looks down at me. He must be close to six foot three or four. He's definitely older, which irrationally makes me feel safer. Plus, the age looks good on him. He smells nice, but as soon as I think it, my stomach flips in a bad way. I scrunch my eyes closed to shake the memory of the way the other man smelled.

"Hey," Saint says, his hands gripping my shoulders, but I shake them lose and bat them out of the way.

"Don't." The one word has him taking a step back. I focus on the fact that every time I've told him no, or panicked, or yelled, he's simply backed off and given me space to compose myself. "I'm sorry." The words are almost a whisper.

Saint shakes his head. "Don't be. You got nothing to be sorry for. I'm not sure I'm equipped to handle this right all the time, but I'll give it my best fucking shot."

I swallow deeply. My mouth is dry. I need a toothbrush.

"Let's order that card," he says, offering me his phone.

And I focus on that. Within minutes, I have a new card on its way. "It'll be here in two business days."

"Guess I have a roommate for four days, seeing it's the weekend," he says.

"If you're sure it's okay." I can't face anyone. Not yet. Not even the people I'm getting to know at the agency. Not when they'll rush around me, and crowd me, and ask me questions I'm not ready to answer.

"It's fine." He slides a leather vest over his shoulders with the logo of the Iron Outlaws on the back. It's a bit of a cliche. All skulls and flames.

But then, I don't know many men who would have readied a gun and shot at the people holding me against my will. None would have let me stay with them as their roommate.

"Go get cleaned up so we can get you some clothes that actually fit."

I look down at the clothes he loaned me to sleep in and smile. "I don't know. Loose fit is in, right?"

"Shit, you don't have shoes."

I shrug. "It'll look like a walk of shame. Just need some day-old mascara, and we'll be good."

Saint laughs. "Go do what you need to. We'll take my truck."

Once I've fixed my hair the best I can and rubbed some toothpaste over my teeth with my fingertips, I'm done.

I'll shower when I get back here with clean clothes and underwear to wear.

"I forgot you were barefoot last night," Saint says when I meet him in the hall.

I look down at my feet. "In the big scheme of things, losing my shoes seems like such a terrible thing to worry about, but they took my favorite red heels."

He grins. "You're a shoe girl?"

"Love them," I admit.

When we get to Target, Saint asks my shoe size, and then he jogs into the store and comes out with a pair of white sneakers. "It was either do this or carry you," he says as he slips them on my feet and ties the laces. "Sorry they aren't red heels, but I figured with all the cuts and bruises on your feet they'd be more comfortable."

I take the hand he offers to scramble out of the truck.

"People are staring," I mutter as we walk into the store. I have to hold the waistband of the joggers up as surplus fabric pools by my ankles.

"It's the cut," Saint says. "Can't decide if they're scared of me, hate me, or wanna be me."

"I'm pretty sure it's the fact I look like I'm wearing a diaper."

Saint tips his head back, looks down at my ass, then winks. "Definitely doesn't look like a diaper."

He's a patient shopper. I buy practical cotton underwear in bright colors to lift my mood and a bra without underwire because my body still hurts. While I glance at the citrus-colored summer dresses on sale as we slide into fall, I grab a pair of yoga pants and a pair of soft jeans. I throw in a couple of T-shirts in a multipack and a zip-up sweater. I toss in some socks, then agonize over sleep attire. On my own, I settle for a tank and shorts. But I'm in Saint's house. And the idea of feeling exposed still makes me feel ick.

I throw in a pair of plaid pajama bottoms and a long-sleeve T-shirt gloating about sweet dreams, then whip around the beauty department, grabbing the basics. And suddenly, I'm beat. I don't know if it's not sleeping, or not eating, or living in a constant state of fear.

Two boys are testing deodorant sprays. They're laughing, talking about a date one of them has. As I move closer to grab a deodorant of my own, they spray one that smells like the man who said I was his. It's sharp, harsh. My head starts to spin, my peripheral vison becoming blurred.

Suddenly, I'm chilled through to the bone.

"You good?" Saint asks, as he steers the cart to the checkout.

"I don't . . ." The words come out on a stutter as my teeth

chatter. Now people really are looking. "The smell . . . it . . . shit."

"Hey, come here," he says, engulfing me in his arms.

I'm shaking. Uncontrollably. I can't breathe.

"I'm right here, Briar. You're not under attack. You're safe. Slide your hand around my belt."

Through the fog, I hear his instruction and do as he says. I butt up against his gun.

"You feel that? Anyone comes near you, and they're gone. Let's pay for your things and get out of here."

He holds me long enough for me to ride out the worst of the panic attack. "I'm sorry," I whisper.

He cups my cheeks and forces me to look up at him. "Never say sorry for this. It's going to come in waves. Let it pass through you."

I take a deep breath while looking into his eyes. He breathes with me. One breath. Two breaths. Until I'm calm again.

I feel spacey.

And Saint takes care of me until I have the strength back to take care of myself.

7

SAINT

A scream pierces the night, and I jump up so fast, I fall off the sofa.

Fuck, I'm not in my own bed.

It's disorienting, but I hear sobbing punctuated with gasps of air.

Briar.

I hustle to the room, push the door open, and see her thrashing on the bed, still asleep. The sounds she makes are filled with pain.

They say you aren't meant to wake a person in the middle of dream like this. Not sure why. Probably some old wives' tale, like if you die in your dreams, you die in real life, which is total and utter bullshit. But seeing her jackknife on the bed, I know I can't leave her.

I turn on the small lamp, then crawl onto the bed and grab her shoulder. "Briar," I say softly, then repeat it more firmly. "Briar. Wake up."

She fights me, trying to throw my hands off. Her fear and panic get worse.

"Briar, you need to wake up, sweetheart." I try to keep

my voice gentle, but whatever she's dreaming about has an ice-cold grip on her. It doesn't take a rocket scientist to figure out what it is.

"Don't, don't, don't," she whimpers, pulling her hands up in front of her face.

"*Briar!*" I yell, shaking her too. And when she wakes up, her eyes immediately wide, her mouth in an O, she fights me for a second more before curling onto her side, facing away from me, and sobbing.

Jesus. I'm not equipped for this. I need to find some way to get her out of here and to someone who can actually help her properly. She deserves better than a broken ATF agent with the emotional range of a dead squirrel.

I place my hand on her hip softly. "Hey, it was a dream, Briar. You're safe."

Her body shakes and shivers. She tries to breathe through the sobs. I stand and head to the kitchen. Pouring her a glass of cool tap water, I compose myself, adrenaline still surging through my body at the alarming wake-up call. On the way back, I stop by the bathroom to grab the toilet roll. It's all I've got in the way of tissues. When I return to the bedroom, I sit on the opposite side of the bed so I can see her face. I place the glass of water on the bedside table and unwrap a length of paper.

"Here," I say.

Briar takes it, and I witness the struggle to compose herself. She breathes hard and deep, bites down on her lip, and blinks to clear the tears.

Sometimes she wins.

Sometimes she shudders and another fat tear leaks from the corner of her eye.

I nudge her hair back off her face. It's so soft, bits of it are stuck to the sweat on her forehead. I wrap a piece of tissue around my hand and dab her brow, her jaw, her neck.

"I'm okay," she whispers, her voice hoarse.

She's not, and we both know it. "There's a difference between pulling yourself together enough to function after reliving something traumatic, and truly coming out the other side of that experience. The work it requires to mentally and physically reset yourself takes time. I think what you mean is you're finding your feet back in the here and now after a hellish dream."

"That makes sense," she murmurs as I see the tension drain out of her body.

I'm proud of her for fighting back.

I see my friend Spark doing the same thing. We've shared rooms on runs occasionally. More than once, he's woken in the middle of the night, yelling some kind of unintelligible commands. And like Briar, he tried to convince me he was okay.

Her eyes are focused on mine now, and in the soft glow from the lamplight, I notice how big and wide they are. Her fingers sneak beneath my pinkie and wrap around it, squeezing it tightly as she closes her eyes and takes another deep breath.

I look down at where her fingers clutch mine. Hers are cut and bruised; her nails are a ripped mess of broken edges. She's injured, and I somehow need to convince her to document the evidence for later. Because right now, she's too churned up to think straight. Too hurt, stunned, and shocked to do anything more than function. But in time, she'll go through all the other stages of healing. And she'll get angry this was done to her. And maybe she'll decide to take action, to report it, and I want her to have every single piece of evidence at her disposal. She doesn't know that the night I helped patch her up, after I put her to bed in my clothes, I crept into the bathroom and scooped the single item of clothing she'd been wearing, let it dry out, and sealed it Ziplock bag. Who knows what kind of hair and body fluids and fibers could be on there?

But overpowering my thoughts of the next logical steps to help her is the utterly masculine satisfaction that it's my finger she's clinging to, like she's drowning in the ocean and I'm a piece of driftwood.

I remind myself she's too fucking young. I'll be forty-one next year. And only once did I try to combine being an undercover agent with having a girlfriend. Weicker warned me it wouldn't work. That the divorce rate is high.

He was right.

"You want some water?" I ask, and she nods.

I wish I'd never asked because she lets go of my finger and pushes herself into a seated position. But I grab the glass anyway and hand it to her.

"Thanks." She takes a few small sips.

"Feeling better?"

Briar nods, then rolls her neck like a boxer getting ready to fight. "I hate that they're in my head." Her voice is quiet in the dim room.

"Be open to the idea it might take professional help to get them out."

She shrugs. "Maybe."

We both sit there in silence, but I'm guessing her head is whirling like mine is. I want to push but doubt it's the best strategy. Everything is too raw for her to be objective.

"Thank you for this, for being here. I'm good now." When she looks at me, I know she's not. Fear ices her features.

"You'll get through this, Briar."

She nods once, and I can see from the vacant look in her eyes that she's not here in the room, but off somewhere deep in her thoughts.

I leave and come back with the bedding and cushions off the sofa, then throw them onto the floor.

"What are you doing?" she asks, peering over the edge of the bed.

"Will you sleep better knowing I'm right down here?" I ask.

Her shoulders leave her ears, and she breathes. "I think I would. Thank you."

Sleeping on the floor is like camping. I'm at one with the discomfort of it. "Sleep, Briar," I say before pulling the blankets over me. "It'll all seem better in the morning."

8

SAINT

It's five in the morning before I fall back to sleep, and when the alarm on my phone goes off at nine, I'm in a foul mood. I turn it off quickly and lift myself from the floor to check on Briar. She murmurs in her sleep but rolls over away from me. I stand to give her space but can't help noticing the way her pajamas hug the curve of her ass.

Could I be more morally bankrupt? The last thing she needs is me noticing how fucking juicy her body is, even if that's God's honest truth of it. It would take nothing to lean forward and take a playful bite.

I get up and head to the kitchen to make coffee. Outside the window, the yard is a mess. It represents everything I'm not. It's disorganized and chaotic. There's nothing good about it.

Maybe I'll ask King if I can get a handful of the prospects to come over one weekend and give it a makeover. If all they did was deal with the junk, edge the borders, and repair the fence, it would be less of an eyesore.

But then I remember I have Briar here.

For now, I remind myself.

I have a feeling that when she leaves, I'm gonna need to know she's okay. Last night she was . . . vulnerable. That dream really shook her. I don't know her well enough to know if death by suicide is something that would ever be on her mind. Hell, there are two people I knew their entire lives, people I'd swear would never make that choice, but then they devastated the fuck out of me by doing just that.

As I sip my piping hot coffee, I think about my former ATF friend Johnny.

At his funeral, people were talking about how the night before, he'd been laughing and smiling and throwing back whiskey.

I climb in the shower and shave my chest. Whenever Spark and I have to share a room, he always rips me for my manscaping. But how could I tell him I do it because the tape of the mic I sometimes wear sticks better?

I apply it today. Weicker has been on my ass for not capturing more evidence of the money laundering that goes through the club, and today is the day someone will be dropping off the cash.

I pray it's not Spark or King. Not that I want any of the guys to go down.

I need to go.

I scribble a quick note on a piece of paper with my details and leave it near the coffee machine. I tell Briar to help herself to whatever's in the fridge. And to let me know if she decides to leave so I don't worry about her.

The ride to the strip club is brief and gloomy. The fall weather in full effect. I'm not usually here this early, but I'm also interviewing a woman this morning.

When I open the rear door to the club, I see it with

different eyes. King gave me the club to run, thought I'd be kinder, as a former army chaplain, to some of the women. And I'd like to think I have been. But last night I started wondering about the girls who work here. How many have gone into those private rooms, only for something unexpected, unplanned, and unwanted to happen? Did they feel like they could come talk to me about it? Did they know *I* would take them seriously?

How many of them have woken up in the middle of the night like Briar did, reliving some horrific moment?

I make a promise right there, under the neon sign with the strip club's cheesy name, the Gold Pole, on it: *No girl is going to get abused in my club.*

I'm going to increase precautions every step of the way. From how I hire, to the security in the building, to making sure the girls know their word will be taken over any punter. We'll make a formal protocol for reporting any jackass who tried to hurt them. I'm gonna clean this place up so tight.

And here I go again with the false belief that I am actually Saint, a member of the Iron Outlaws, and this club is mine to run forever. I'm just an ATF agent currently losing his grip on reality, who will be undercover with some other group twelve months from now.

I scrub my hand over my face, pressing hard.

This simply means my goals have a time limit. I want to leave the club safer than when I joined it.

I've done shit I should never have done as an Outlaw. There are ATF rules. You're not supposed to do drugs. Ever. If you do, you're meant to call it in and act the same way as if you'd been shot. You're considered medically compromised.

Six months ago, at the big cross-country MC meet-up, Spunk, a brute of a man from the LA chapter, put me in a situation where I felt I had no choice but to do a line of coke.

I did it but was really fucking grateful when King stepped in explaining why, as a chaplain, I got a pass.

And, like the Bible says, thou shalt not kill. As an ATF agent, you're meant to get the hell out of Dodge. Defend but never attack. Not pour what a guy thinks is arsenic into red wine and make him drink it. Sure, the dude was a pedophile. He touched up Whip's niece's thirteen-year-old kid, Laney, but the cops had let him go. Lack of evidence.

So Vex helped Whip set up an online sting. The guy thought he was meeting a young girl. Instead, he met thirteen Iron Outlaws, one for each year of Laney's life that he'd ruined. And my defense? Everyone had to do something fucking awful to him. Clutch and King were going to take his fingers so he couldn't touch another kid. Bates, his testicles. But I was to go first. I got an old chalice and told everyone it was arsenic when really it was heavy-duty morphine and codeine in red wine. Wasn't sure the pain relief would help all that much, given what the guy was facing, but it was the best I could come up with. Showing up was an order from King, participation was not optional. Whip went last and put a bullet square between the guy's eyes.

Then I uttered the Rite of Committal as he was buried in the Pines because I was expected to by those who think I'm a preacher.

And there's my other dichotomy. I had always believed innocent until proven guilty, that the courts were the right legal process. Now I'm a vigilante, however I decide to wash it. Because, honestly, I was happy to bury that fucker.

When I open the front door of the strip club, I'm greeted by a young woman I think is the person I'm here to interview. "Heather?" I ask.

"Yes. Great to meet you, Saint." We shake hands and I show her the club before giving her some privacy to set up.

She reminds me of Briar—pretty face, great body—and she triggers my usual internal debate of how young is too young for my tired ass. Not in the pedo way . . . but as a man freshly in his forties, is twenty-five too young? Thirty? The girls who hang around the club will literally bang any brother, but I'm not taking a nineteen-year-old anywhere near my room. Legal or not.

Halo? He'll take a girl's word for her age.

Niro is used to asking for ID at the tattoo parlor and can usually tell when they're lying.

Personally, if they could pass for my daughter, they're too fucking young.

Twenty minutes into the interview, there is no doubt in my mind. Heather is going to be a great acquisition to the club. She's taken pole dancing classes, which—who knew—some women do as exercise. And she's amazing at it.

A large body drops into the seat next to me, and I see Spark checking out the girl on stage. Shit, the very man I didn't want to see. He tips his head in appreciation at Heather's moves.

"College student. Wants a quick way to make cash with minimum impact to her studies," I say. I emphasize the college student part, but it flies straight over Spark's head.

King stands next to him, his eyes on her too. I know they've dropped the cash in the office for me to clean. I've recorded every dollar—how much illegal money they've laundered through the strip club. It disappears into the take with the bar bills and cover fees and private dances.

The accounting is on my laptop. But I haven't submitted the evidence yet.

I want to say I don't know why.

But I do.

"Body like that, she'll cash in quick," Spark says. "Put her on Friday and Saturdays, and she'll make enough. She up for the private shit?"

I think about the girls in those rooms again and wonder if I should have panic alarms installed in them for emergencies.

"Says she is," I reply. "Wants to graduate without any loans. Wanna give her a road test?" The sentence catches in my throat. But Heather knows why she's here and what her limits are. I asked her about them, and she was candid. She enjoys sex, and if it helps her pay her bills, then she's cool. And, honestly, I trust Spark not to do anything she doesn't want, as he's a believer in consent and safe words. With his Viking looks and long blond hair, he gets enough pussy without trying, so he doesn't need to force anyone to do something they don't want to.

I'm meant to ask questions about the drop. I'm meant to ask them how much it is. I'm meant to get them to talk about where it came from. But the words escape me. These two men are my friends.

I can't do it.

"No, he doesn't," King says, slapping Spark's shoulder. "We got important shit to do."

"We do?" Spark asks. "Because my dick's saying the important shit I got to do is up there flashing her cunt at me."

Despite the tension gripping my chest, I can't help but laugh. "I'll get her number. Tell you when she's in."

I watch the two of them leave, then gesture for Heather to stop.

As she dresses, I put in an order to Vex for those alarms.

By the time she leaves, I've stepped into the alleyway behind the club, ripped off my wire, crushed it beneath my boot, and buried it in the trash of a neighboring establishment.

9

BRIAR

The back garden of Saint's single-level home is derelict.

And if my pop were here, it would break his heart. *Briar*, he used to say, *even cracks in the sidewalk can be home to flowers.*

And he was right.

Pop's garden was a riot of hues. Vibrant for as many months as he could eke out of the season. I think that's why my design work is so good. My professors always commented on my color combinations.

This is a sea of brown with a touch of burnt grass.

There's an old shed with a busted door and cracked glass windows. I tug on the rusted handle, and the hinges groan as I pull the remains of the door open. The inside smells damp and musty. Large cobwebs hang in the corners. Usually, I'd run screaming from them, but I've met the real monsters now, and these little things no longer have the power to frighten me.

Inside is a collection of old tools. "Well, I'm rusty at gardening," I say to the trowel with rust spots but a solid handle. "Haven't touched one of you guys since Pop died, but how hard can it be?"

There isn't a good place to begin. But I start with the patio. I use a small cushion off the sofa placed inside one of the bags we got from Target as a makeshift kneeling pad.

I'm slow and methodical, shoving the trowel down between the gaps, loosening the dirt and weeds and moss. I can hear Pop telling me to not lose the roots or else I'm asking for the weeds to grow back. I tease and wiggle, easing the roots from the tight and difficult places.

My spine groans as I sit up and run the back of my hand across my damp brow. I've only completed two rows of stones, but I realize I've not thought about what happened in the time it took me. And when the realization brings Joe's face to mind, I force it back down.

Saint's right. I need to process what happened. I need moments of peace when it doesn't feel as though my whole life is falling apart. I have a small nest egg; the savings will last me, but eventually I'll need to go back to my life. I have client work I need to get on with.

I take a deep breath and focus on another row of stones. Some of the weeds are a foot high. I haven't thought about where I am going to put them when I'm done.

Burn them perhaps.

Along with that stupid black slip I was wearing when . . .

I haven't seen it since the night I took it off in Saint's bathroom. He must have dealt with it, knowing I wouldn't want to see it again.

I should ask him so I can add it to my bonfire.

"You need some gloves, girl." As the gnarled old voice finishes the sentence, a pair of weathered gardening gloves with faded pink roses on them lands with a splat next to me.

When I look up, a short elderly gentleman as weathered

as the gloves, with skin like old leather, has his arms folded on the fence. His wispy white hair is too long, and it's pulled back in an elastic, all ratty ends. He's the first person I've spoken to other than Saint since . . . well, since I got on the back of his bike. While my heart races, I realize I'm not at immediate risk. There's a fence between us. Busted up as it is, it's protection enough; the old man looks like a gentle breeze could blow him over.

I pick up the gloves and slide them on. "Thank you so much. That's so thoughtful of you."

"Yup. Gonna take commitment to bring that place back from the dead." His gaze takes in the yard.

"Well, my pop used to say that a garden is its own reward. Maybe I'll feel like that when I watch the sun go down today from a clear patio."

The old man chuckles. "What're you gonna be sitting on?"

I look around. There is some wood and two old terracotta planters with nothing in them but cigarette butts and old soil. "I'm sure I'll be able to create something."

"I'm Harold. But my friends call me Hap."

I climb to my feet, pull off a glove, and offer him my hand. "I'm . . . Briar."

We shake, and I feel the curve of bent knuckles and swollen fingers. Like the arthritis Pop had.

"Are you living with the man who lives here?"

I guess Saint hasn't shared much of himself with his neighbor, and it's not my place to do so. If he doesn't want Hap to know his name, it's not for me to tell him. "I'm staying for a little while. Figured I'd earn my keep by doing some puttering around out here."

"Well, don't let me stop you. Shout if you need any tools. I have a garage full of 'em."

"Thanks, Hap. I will."

And with that, my new friend disappears into his house.

It takes another hour to finish the stones that pave the area by the rear of the house. When I'm done dumping all the weeds, I notice a hard-bristle sweeping brush has appeared on my side of the fence. With a smile, I peer over the fence and look around his garden. It's beautiful. A riot of fall color and blooms in shades of burnt orange and deep burgundy, given it's the beginning of October. There's a weathered shed and canes for beans and peas. "Thanks, Hap," I yell.

"You're welcome." The voice comes from within a small greenhouse in the far corner.

With a sturdy broom, I'm able to clean up the dirt and dust. It really needs an industrial power wash, but maybe that's something I can do . . .

"Stay in the now," I mutter.

I clean out the two large terra-cotta pots and put them upside down on the patio. The piece of wood that looked like a cutting from an old railway sleeper is harder to maneuver.

Once I'm confident it's free of critters, I drag it to the pots and manhandle it until it is centered across them.

I sit on it, and it wobbles a little. But I realize it's not going to tip or break. As I raise my head, the sun hits my face and the heat caresses my cheeks. It warms me from the outside in, reaching my bones and taking away the last of the chill that lingers.

"Here," Hap says from over the fence.

I turn to look at him, and he's holding a container with a small, bright yellow plant in it. "Can't have a pretty spot like that to sit in and no flowers."

The gesture brings tears to my eyes.

Chrysanthemums.

Flowers, like Pop would have given me.

Maybe he's watching out for me.

"It's beautiful, Hap, but I can't take it from you."

He grins and tips his head in the direction of his yard. "Hadn't planted it yet. Don't know why. Perhaps I was keeping it for someone who'd bring a little ray of sunshine to an otherwise lonely day."

I take the plant from him because it would insult him otherwise. "Thank you, Hap. It's beautiful." I place it in front of the bench so we'll be able to see it when we sit. "See how perfect it looks."

"A rose amongst thorns," he says, gesturing to the rest of the yard. "The rest is going to take a lot more effort."

"I think I'll save the rest of it for tomorrow."

Hap smiles, as if he knows some magic secret. "Until tomorrow then, if I'm so blessed," Hap says, before stepping back into his house.

Eventually, I do the same.

Home means something altogether different to me right now. It's not the comforts of my own bed and the smells I'm used to. It's a feeling of safety.

I look around and realize there are no personal touches here. No colorful cushions on the sofa, no artwork or photographs on the walls. There is a bookshelf with barely anything on it beyond a couple of miscellaneous cables and a manual for the microwave that's creased and has a stain that looks like it came from a pizza.

Yet, despite how sparse it looks, it feels more like home than my own.

In the bathroom, I look at myself in the mirror. My cheeks are flushed from the exertion outside. Two large smudges grace my forehead. The scratches on my face are properly scabbed over, no longer red after I diligently applied ointment for the last two days.

Once in the shower, I let the hot water wash over me as my mind drifts from the scabs to the man who caused them.

What kind of freak suggests that you can make a good life with the person who abducted you? From his words and his actions, I realize he thought kidnapping me was a small blip on the way to us having a meaningful relationship.

And the shame I feel about that is overwhelming, even though it's not my fault.

Bodies are meant to be mutually enjoyed, with boundaries of course.

I hate the idea that the man thought my body was meant to be his.

As steam swirls around me, I place my fingertips between my legs. My clit is hidden, my lips soft. I take a moment to appreciate how I escaped being raped.

I steal my hand away and wash up quickly.

There's a life waiting for me in New York. It's literally an hour away, yet it feels like a million miles and a billion hours. The idea of walking down my block, then pausing in the entryway to let myself in? That feels like the most impossible of moments.

How can I do that again after being abducted right outside my own home?

And for as long as I don't go back, I can pretend it didn't happen while adjusting to the fact it did.

The air is cooler when I sit back outside thirty minutes later, but I don't move, even when I hear the throaty roar of a bike approaching and then the silence after the engine's cut.

"Briar," he shouts as he comes through the front door.

"Out here," I yell.

He steps out, then stops. "What did you do?"

I shrug. "I couldn't just sit inside all day. Hap loaned me some tools."

"Hap?"

"Your neighbor."

Saint sits next to me on the plank of wood, and it wobbles back and forth a little while as he gets comfortable. "My neighbor is called Hap?"

"How can you not know your neighbor's name?"

He glances over the fence. "Guess it never really came up."

"Have you even spoken to him?"

Saint shakes his head. "In all honesty, no. I'm usually at the club."

"Is the club your job?" I ask. "How does it work?"

Saint pulls out a packet of cigarettes and offers me one. I shake my head, and he puts one to his lips and lights it up.

I try to remind myself that smoking is not sexy. It smells, which might even be worse than the fact that it's killing you. Nobody has to put up with your scent when you're six feet under.

But I feel a flicker of attraction for the very masculine way he does it. If I'm honest with myself, it's the masculine way he does everything.

He rests his elbows on his knees as he looks around the garden. "I manage our strip club. Was there today."

"Oh." It's all I can think to say. I'm never gonna judge a woman for the way she chooses to make a living. In fact, I wish I had their confidence. It's more that I feel a sting that I have no business feeling, that Saint has been around naked women all day.

"I thought about you," he says gruffly, glancing in my direction.

Shit. I shouldn't be feeling the spark of excitement that he thought about me either. "You did?"

I lick my dry lips and notice he follows the action before looking away.

"Yeah. I was thinking about the women who work for me. If they feel safe reporting customers of the club. I wondered if they knew I'd take their concerns seriously and shit. So I placed an order for panic alarms in the private rooms and spent the afternoon making some policies to make sure they're all safe."

I throw my arms around his neck and hug him. The action catches him off guard, and he fumbles to move the cigarette out of the way before catching me with one arm.

"Thank you," I say into the warm crook of his neck. He smells good. Leather. Soap. Fresh air.

He palms my back, rubbing circles gently. "You're welcome." His words whisper against my ear, his tone rough.

It feels comfortable, having his hands on me. Neither of us move.

I thought I'd be scared.

But I'm not.

I'm comforted.

Or maybe I'm more than that. I swear my heart skips a beat.

I panic internally and pull away.

Lust is one set of feelings. And I'd be lying if I said I didn't feel something more than gratitude for Saint's care.

But someone thinking about me. Caring about what I say enough to act on it and do something positive in the world. That's the kind of thing that inspires real feelings. And romantic love doesn't exist. I'm certain of it.

"I left you some dinner in the oven," I say hastily, then

get up from the bench. I'm worried about what I might do or say next in gratitude. And I'm conflicted in that I both want and dread what might follow. "I'm going to get an early night."

Leaving confusion in his eyes and in my stomach, I hurry inside.

10

BRIAR

W hen I step out into the living room the following morning, Saint is asleep on the sofa. He's not wearing a shirt; the blanket sits low on his hips. For a moment I wonder if he's naked beneath until I see the ivory of a drawstring from shorts or joggers peeking out over the blanket.

His body is a masterpiece, and I allow myself to look for a moment. His arms and chest are muscled. His hair is back off his face, and I can see the shape of his high cheekbones more clearly. There is a scar on his forearm, and I wonder how he got it.

The cut lying over the back of the sofa makes me wonder if it happened while he was doing something dangerous.

Something illegal.

But even that can't make me feel bad about my guardian angel.

I'm embarrassed by my physical reaction to our conversation the previous evening. But maybe it's the sign I needed to get back to my life. The respite of being here, of not having to make any major decisions about what to do next, to simply be and adapt to this new version of my life, has been vital.

"You done staring?" he asks. His voice is layered with gravel and likely some Jack from the bottle that sits close to the sofa, but his eyes remain closed.

"How did you know?"

"Army. Bomb disposal. I worked in silent high pressure. Plus, the bedroom door creaked when you opened it." Now he does open his eyes. "Did you need something, Briar?"

I love the way my nickname rolls off his tongue. "I need to go back to my apartment. See what those men may or may not have done. I need to start to put the pieces of myself back together. I've got work for clients that I've put off for too long, and I need my equipment to do it. I know I arranged for my bank card to come here, but I think I should go home."

And, as I decided somewhere around two in the morning, I need to put some distance between me and him. Before I make a fool out of myself.

Saint rubs a hand across his face, then sits up slowly. "Give me thirty minutes to shower and deal with some shit. We can have breakfast on the way. And I can drop your bank card over when it arrives."

"Maybe you'll let me buy breakfast or brunch or whatever. Given you've been so generous. Put it on my tab."

Saint stands and moves closer to me. It doesn't freak me out. He runs a knuckle down my cheek, and for a moment, I think I see something more than friendship in his eyes. "Nice try, but not gonna happen."

While Saint showers, I pull what few belongings I have together and stuff them in the bags from Target.

When he steps out of his room, he's dressed in jeans and

a T-shirt that stretches perfectly across his chest, but instead of his leather cut, he's wearing an unzipped sweater. And on his feet are sneakers, not boots. His hair is tucked beneath a ball cap.

This isn't the biker I'm used to seeing. I don't know which version of him I like better.

He grins as if he can read my thoughts and drops the bag he's holding to the floor. "Thought a little bit of disguise might not go amiss. Those guys were watching your place. If they really want you, they may be watching still. We'll take the truck, not the bike. I'll wear this instead of my cut." He plops a ball cap on my head at a funny angle.

While he says the words kindly, my heart drops. What if he's right? What if it's too soon to go back? What if they are waiting for—

"Briar," Saint says as he reaches for my biceps. "Look at me, sweetheart."

I do as he says, acknowledging the tension that has my shoulders up by my ears. I take a deep breath and force them to lower. As I stare into the bluest eyes, I relax.

"Good girl," he says. "I'm armed. We'll drive around once first. Then we'll figure out how close we can get the truck to the fire escape. We'll go in the front and out the back. If you don't want to go in when you get there, you don't go in."

The words were a relief.

"Thank you." I step up to him and put my arms around his waist, allowing myself the luxury of his heat. I'm chilled by the idea they'll be watching. And there is a part of me that doesn't want to leave here. Doesn't want to leave him.

With his broad shoulders and quiet confidence, I feel safe around him.

I hear my Pop's warning again. *You have the beauty of a*

wild rose but need to use your thorns to stop your petals from getting stomped on.

He wraps his arms around me and holds me close. He smells of his shower gel, as do I. It gives me comfort to smell the same. Lips brush the top of my head, a gesture that tilts my world a little. "You're going to be okay, Briar," he mutters.

"It's Rose," I tell him. "Rose Whittaker." He's about to know where I live. He cares. He should know whose life he saved.

He places his hands on my biceps. "Rose. It's pretty. Why Briar?"

"Because my pop, my grandfather, used to call me that. It felt safer giving you that name until I knew you weren't going to hurt me."

Saint studies me for a good long while before he speaks again. "If I tell you my name, you must promise to never mention it again. Not out loud. Don't write it in a journal or text your best friend."

"Is this because of the motorcycle club you're part of?"

He nods. "Something like that."

"I swear."

He takes my hand and kisses the back of it. We both ignore the ugly scabs around my wrists where I was tied up. "It's a pleasure to meet you Rose. My name is Ryker." He rubs his thumb over the back of my hand.

"Ryker," I say, realizing it comes out on a breath. "I like it."

Dimples pop in his cheeks as he smiles. "I like that you like it. But for everyone's safety, let's let that be the last time we use each other's real names. You're Briar. And I'm Saint. Got it?"

"Got it. What's in the bag?"

"Shit you're gonna need," he says cryptically.

My mind drifts to work as Saint drives. If any client is frustrated with a lack of response, I could tell them I had food poisoning or something. It sounds a little pathetic, that I could go missing and no one would care. I've always been more of a loner. My hobbies have always been solitary. Painting. Drawing. Reading. Happy in my own company, Pop used to say.

On the way, we stop at a diner, where Saint downs a plate of steak and eggs and I opt for waffles. I'm embarrassed I can't pay, but Saint reminds me it's okay. When we leave and a car backfires, I jump. Saint takes my hand until we're at the truck and he lets go to help me inside.

It's hard not to think about the way our clasped hands felt as we drive to my place on the southern end of the Upper East Side. It's right on the edge of Lenox Hill, and Saint does everything he said he would do. We circle the place twice before parking near a side street that leads to the fire escape.

"What is it you do that you can afford a place like this?" he asks as we enter the building.

"I am a graphic artist. And I hustle," I say as I hit the elevator button. "And as you're about to see, my apartment is quite possibly the smallest studio in the place."

"Never understood why someone would want to live in a shoebox like this, even if it is fancy as fuck," Saint says.

There are two of us plus Saint's bag in the elevator, and it already feels full, even though the sign says the elevator can take eight. I wonder if the men who took me have been up here. I wonder if I'm breathing their air. I start to freak out as my heart races.

"And what do you mean by *hustle*?"

I try to distract myself by considering the answer. "I have a lucrative contract as a graphic designer for a large ad agency, but then I do other freelance work in my spare time. Like book covers and indie movie posters. This spot is as close to suburbia as you get in the city. I mean, there are trees on the sidewalk. I can walk to Central Park and Midtown if I want to. I've barely scratched the surface of figuring out the neighborhood, but there is already so much I want to explore." The elevator dings for my floor, but I keep spewing words. "And I like walking. So even though the apartment is only three hundred square feet, it's my mansion." I suck in air. I feel like that monologue came out in one long breath and probably an octave higher than normal.

My palms sweat.

Saint's strong and calloused hand reaches for mine and squeezes, in spite of their dampness. "You're okay, Briar."

His words echo through me. "I'm rambling."

"You are," he says, encouraging me out into the hallway. "It's nerves. And it's okay to have them."

I try to shake free of Saint, but he doesn't let me. A part of me is relieved. There's a comfort and safety in his grasp.

Wide blue eyes with long lashes focus on me. "Just breathe, sweetheart."

"Who's going to remind me to breathe tomorrow?" I say, trying to ease the tension I feel in my chest.

He smiles. "You need me to text you a reminder? Send me your new phone number when you get one."

Urgh. The idea of being in my room without a phone . . . What if they come back? What if I cry for help and no one hears? What if—

"We'll go get you a new phone before I leave."

"You need to stop reading my mind."

Saint simply winks.

I knock on the door of my elderly neighbor, Mrs. Mantle.

"It'll take her a minute," I whisper, even though the volume of the TV show playing in her apartment reveals she's going deaf.

"Rose, sweetheart." She looks up at Saint, then back to me. "Is everything okay?"

"I locked myself out of my apartment and wondered if I could have my spare key."

"Of course. Of course."

She shuffles down the hallway to a dresser.

I feel Saint step up behind me. "Smart idea giving her your key." His breath tickles my ear and neck, making me shiver. The warmth of his chest seeps through to my back as I wrestle with fledgling feelings I'm uncertain I'm ready to act on.

"It can sometimes take ages to get the superintendent of the building to show up and let you in. I didn't want to be caught without other options."

Mrs. Mantle walks slowly back to the door. "There you go, sweetie."

When I open my door and move to step inside, Saint places his hand against my stomach and pulls the gun out from the holster beneath his zip-up sweater.

"Wait a minute," he whispers.

Cautiously, he nudges the door open as I eye the hallway nervously. Am I better inside where Saint has a gun? Or in the hallway where anyone can appear?

I wait for a minute like he asked, and then I follow him in. Being alone out here scares me more than being inside with him, even if someone else is there.

"Jesus Christ, Briar. I said to wait outside." He holsters his gun and walks over to me. "There's no one here."

I glance around my home, taking in the placement of items on my desk, on my shelves. The cutlery drawer that is a pain in the ass to close, unless you know the trick about sliding it to the left as you shut it, sits ever so slightly ajar.

"Is everything okay?" Saint asks.

I shake my head. "Someone has been here. Quietly. They haven't destroyed the place. But nothing is where I left it."

He looks around the room with another set of eyes. "I'm guessing you keep those cushions in a particular order."

I look over to the sofa, where the cushions aren't how I like them. "You're correct."

"They've been through your apartment but didn't want to draw attention to themselves or give your neighbors a reason to call the police." His arm slips over my shoulder, and I lean into him, taking comfort from his strength. "What do you need to make it right?"

It feels a little hopeless. "I don't know. I'm not sure it will ever feel right again."

11

SAINT

I see the sadness in Briar's eyes.

Rose's eyes.

Shit, I like Briar better. No, Rose suits her.

Fuck.

Whichever name . . . I want to make this right.

"You got cleaning supplies?" I ask.

"Yes. Why?"

"We're gonna clean this place up. Pull your supplies together; I'm going to start on your lock."

"My what?" Briar asks, looking up at me. I like the way she fits beneath my arm. I'm a solid six three, and she's not short either, but we fit just right. Fit better than I probably should be thinking about. The hug we shared on the bench outside last night was the first real affection I've received in a while. I'd like to believe that was all it was, not that I liked her hands on me and spent most of the night thinking about what her lips would feel like against mine.

I let go of her before I can act on those thoughts and return with my bag. I unzip it and show her. "Window locks, new front door lock, dead bolt, and a security camera."

I told Vex I needed them for a veteran friend whose house had been broken in to. Because he's a good guy and my brother, he offered them right up for free, even when I offered to pay. Said it was on the club. He also offered to come help, but I told him I could do it.

"You got all this for me?" Briar asks, running her hands over the locks like I gave her fucking diamonds.

"I did." I take off my sweater, place it on a hook by the door with my holster and gun. There's a two-tiered rack below with ten pairs of shoes in different colors. Guess she really is a shoe girl.

"How much do I owe you? I might need to pay you back in two payments if that's okay with you."

I think about the money I used. The last brown envelope of cash King gave me contained twenty grand. I'm gonna tell Weicker it was ten. I've often wondered about all the money and weapons and explosives the ATF seizes. They say the Asset Forfeiture Program means items get auctioned or sold, and a chunk of the money goes back to the victims of crime. It's easy to justify my actions. This way, I'm simply bypassing the program and giving it straight to Briar.

"You don't owe me a cent, sweetheart. It's what friends do. Like how you tidied my garden for me. Let's get on with it."

For a moment, I think about all the help I'd be able to call in if I were really a member of the Iron Outlaws. I could call Gwen and the old ladies. They'd clean up within the hour and offer Briar a female kind of comfort I can't provide.

I could take Vex up on his offer of help. Because while I'm half decent at this shit, Vex is a pro. He might see security risks I hadn't even thought of.

I consider calling Spark. He's the one I'm closest to, and I wonder if I could trust him knowing about Briar. He was there when we found her. Hell, if Spark saw me around Briar, he might even read between the lines and see the truth I'm not willing to accept. That I have feelings for her, even if I can never act on them. When the shit hits the fan—which it will because I'm not staying undercover in the club forever—I know he'll be torn between doing the right thing by standing with the club and looking out for me to save another life. The man already carries too many burdens in that head of his. There's no way in hell I'm going to add to it. He's been less open recently. More secretive. Like King, I have a suspicion it's to do with Iris.

And then I remember why I can't call anyone. Because the club will be ruthless if they ever find out how I came to be one of them. Then, if they saw me with Briar, if they knew where she lived, if they even suspected the feelings I'm catching for her, they'd come find her to get to me.

Which is why no matter how tempting Briar is, I need to keep my distance to avoid hurting her more than she has been. I've already told her more than I should. Riding the last dregs of sleep, I told her I was a bomb disposal expert. Not an army chaplain. My lock-tight ability to not trip up undercover is being tested by this woman.

I shake the thoughts from my head and start the process of fixing her door.

"Good news. They didn't take my work tools," she says, coming out of the bedroom with a laptop and tablet in her hand.

I rip the new lock from its packaging. "That doesn't make sense. If they wanted to know information about you, that would've been the first thing they took."

Briar places them on the table. "I hide them when I'm not home. Mrs. Mantle told me there was a break-in down the hall a few weeks before I moved in, using the fire escape and an open hallway window. They broke into the end apartment. Took some bills from a wallet and an old laptop. I've been paranoid ever since. I have a false bottom for one of my drawers and hide my expensive things there. I've always taken such good care of my things, especially things that are expensive or hard to replace. It seemed silly to keep doing it but—" She blows out a breath, and I notice the way her lips purse and her shoulders drop. "Shit. Shit. Shit."

I put the lock down and walk to her, then hold her biceps gently as she hugs her electronics to her chest. "It's not silly. Taking care of your belongings is important. Sends a message to the universe that you look after the things that are important to you. And the things you're not saying . . . the things that have got anxiety coursing through you right now, they are okay too."

She looks up at me with those wide brown eyes of hers. "What am I not saying?" The words come out on a broken whisper.

"That you take such good care of your things normally, but you feel like you didn't take good care of yourself."

Tears fill her lower lashes. "I know every single thing about street safety, Saint. I'm a woman. I know to not walk dark streets late at night, to keep my keys handy in my hand in case I need them. I even have a rape alarm. But everything happened so fast, and it was someone I thought I knew. How do you live in the world knowing that you can do everything in your power to be safe, and yet horrific things can happen to you anyway?"

A tear trickles down her cheek. A single straight line.

Breaks my heart more than any flood of tears.

I take her gadgets from her, place them on the table,

then tug her into my arms. Placing my hand on the back of her head, I hold her head to my chest while she cries.

Sobs rattle through her body.

I stroke her hair, kissing the top of her head occasionally. My other hand holds her tightly against me, and I bite down on the obvious reaction to her warmth and curves. She fists my T-shirt, her knuckles white.

There is fear and comfort in the grasp.

As her tears subside, there's recurring hitch in her breath as she tries to calm.

"I'm sorry," she whispers, and I feel the heat of her words through the cotton of my shirt.

"Never apologize for the ways you experience and express your trauma, Briar. That's rule one." I tip her chin with my thumb and forefinger so she can look at me. I wish I could let myself drown in those brown eyes of hers. Just for a moment, I want to be more than her friend. "Rule two, anyone who tries to dismiss it, tells you to get over it, tells you it's time to move on, tells you you're overreacting . . . they aren't worth your time. You got me?"

Briar nods. "I bet you're wishing you weren't in that parking lot that night, aren't you?" A hint of color is returning to her cheeks. "It's been a lot of work having me around."

With her eyes fixed on me, I struggle to consolidate the thoughts I'm having, but I try. "Throughout the rest of my life, there'll probably never be a better example of me being in the right place at the right time."

She steps up onto her toes and presses her lips to mine. It's soft. Sweet. Utterly perfect.

God, how I want to lean into it. To kiss her like this is normal. Like we aren't relegated to using fake names for each other. I've told her an ocean of lies while trying to show her who I really am. If only I weren't in danger every day, danger that might follow her if I were to get involved with her.

Instead, I cup her cheeks and pull away before placing a chaste kiss on her forehead. "Let's get the rest of this place cleaned up."

I let go of her and walk back to the lock I put on the floor. She doesn't move. I hear no footsteps. I'm guessing she's looking at me, wondering what the hell she did wrong. The answer is it was all me. I'll set her straight before I leave. Because if I turn around and look at her now, with that look of total vulnerability on her tearstained face, I'm gonna fall so fucking hard, my ass won't know which way is up.

And I try to remind myself of the things I've learned while being an Iron Outlaw. I like the kind of sex Briar doesn't deserve. And I like lots of it. What kind of asshole would I be to unleash that kind of shit on a woman who went through such a traumatic experience?

A weighty silence falls over us as we go about our tasks.

We both know that kiss could have been more.

My dick knows it best of all, and I'm grateful I'm facing away from her as I work until the boner I'm sporting disappears.

By the time I'm done with the lock, she's finished in the bedroom. There is a pile of bedding by the door.

And she manages to whip through the tiny corner kitchen in the time it takes me to fit the window locks.

The rest is done by the time I've wired the camera into the corner of her living room, pointed at her front door. It covers enough area that she could check there is no one in her apartment before even getting in the elevator.

It's been hours, but we've barely spoken, apart from the occasional polite pleasantry.

I pack up. "Want me to come with you to get that phone?" I ask. Perhaps it's best that I leave sooner or later, before I allow myself to do something stupid. Like sit her on that desk and let my tongue get busy wherever she'll let me put it.

"You've done more than enough. I can take it from here," she says. Her tone is clipped, but she crosses her arms across her chest, not in an act of anger or defiance, but as if she's hugging herself.

Like she's holding herself together so she doesn't fall apart.

I step towards her to hug her but then stop myself.

If Spark is looking out for Iris, I get it. Because I feel the same way about Briar. It's hard to walk away.

"You sure you're okay?" I ask, rather than share any of my thoughts with her.

She nods. "Fine. I need to get back to my normal life, right?"

I shake my head. "Briar, there's no time limit. You need to process what happened. I brought something for you." I pull the final item out of my bag. She gasps at the sight of it.

It's a bag with the slip of a dress she was wearing when she ran to me. "I picked it up and bagged it the very first night. There's evidence on it. And they can test DNA for years after. You don't need to deal with it now. But if you decide to, you've got it."

I offer it to her, but she won't take it.

"I can't," she says, pushing it away.

"I know. And I understand your reasons. But—"

"I mean, I can't do this. I know we cleaned the apartment. I know you made it secure. I just . . . I'm not ready to be here yet. I've barely stepped outside your house, and now there are millions of people out there who I walk by every day and one of them could be . . . one of them could grab . . . I can't . . . I just . . . I—"

"Fuck," I grunt as I drop the bag on the sofa before stepping right into her space and tugging her to me. "It's a really bad idea to stay with me, Briar. There's shit going you can't know. I don't know if you're safer with me or here."

She tips her head, in tears again, her eyes wide. "Please don't make me stay here, Saint. I'm begging you."

Her words whisper through me, mingling with Matthew 7:7. "Ask, and it shall be given unto you; seek, and ye shall find; knock and it shall be opened unto you."

"What?" she asks, her words muffled against my chest, and I realize I spoke the verse out loud.

"Briar, look at me."

She does as I ask, and my heart trips.

I cup her cheeks and catch her tears with my thumbs. "My world is messy, sweetheart. But you want to come home with me and stay for a little while, I've got you."

"If I kissed you again, would that make it weird?" she asks.

"Trying not to think about kissing you, sweetheart. Nothing but trouble will come of it."

"What if I wanted you to show me I'm still okay? Is it the age thing?"

I huff. "No. It's not even the age thing."

"Then please show me that I'm not totally broken after what happened." The word *broken* comes out on a hitch.

"Briar," I say, before claiming her lips with mine.

And when I do, I realize there's nothing broken about this sweet young woman. Her lips match mine as I drag her much deeper than the gentle kiss earlier. If she wants this, if she wants the trouble and the risk, then she needs to see what she's getting herself into. I grip a fistful of her hair in my hand as I tilt her head back, holding her exactly where I want her.

Her tongue is tentative against mine at first, all soft and smooth, and I wonder what it will look like licking its way along my cock.

My dick punches against my jeans; there's no doubt she can feel it as her greedy hips move against mine.

She wants to get off, I can help with that. I lift her and press her up against the wall, lining her pussy up so it drags against my cock. Fuck, it feels good. Even though denim and cotton separate us.

"You want it, Briar? You need to take it."

She rocks against my cock, and I shift from her mouth to her throat. Her fingers sink into my hair, holding me in place. She's like lightning in a bottle. I run my tongue along her neck, savoring the salty tang of her. She gasps when I nibble the soft spot behind her ear.

I palm her ass, holding her in place as I give her what she needs.

What she's asking for.

Her movements lose form. Her pace stutters as she comes on my dick, and it's everything I can do to not come in my jeans.

"Saint," she gasps. And I know I'm fucked.

12

SAINT

I feel like a total shit.

The look in Briar's eyes when I left my apartment for the clubhouse was disappointment. Well, maybe not, but something akin to *I need you, and I don't understand why you are leaving me.*

And it was impossible to tell her why I really needed to go.

I can't tell her I'm an ATF agent. At best, she thinks I'm off to the strip club. Maybe she gives me the benefit of the doubt that it's work. Worst case, she saw a biker pull on his cut and walk off to hang out with his friends. She saw an unreliable man. Probably a criminal.

Perhaps she knows what happens in an MC clubhouse, all the pussy and alcohol on tap.

It's chapping my ass that she doesn't know I can be counted on. That I have to put the job first. That the work I'm doing is important.

At least I thought it was.

As confused about that as I am about her, I climbed on my bike and told her I'd be back tomorrow.

She'd smiled when we'd thrown a large suitcase of her belongings into the back of the truck and driven home. She constructed a temporary workstation on the breakfast bar and was setting up her new phone when I told her I had to go. The two loaded guns I left for her were cold comfort. She's never fired a gun before. I gave her a quick primer and then had to leave her, with a pink blush to her cheeks and exhaustion in her eyes.

"Vex," I say, popping my head into his closet.

I say *closet* because he took a small room off the kitchen and set it up as our tech central.

He slips his glasses down his nose. "Preacher man. How goes it?"

"It goes," I say, taking a seat on the chair on the other side of the desk.

"You get your friend set up okay?"

"I did. Thanks for the help. What are you up to?"

"Spark and King got a bead on the truck you and Spark came up against the other night. They saw it again. We got a name from the plates. Joseph Hosea. Looks like he's affiliated with the Righteous Brotherhood."

"That's the name of the guy who grabbed"—I stop myself before I say Briar's name—"who grabbed the woman?"

"Yup. I'm thinking Spark's got a hard-on for the Irish chick. She was sitting outside a diner down by the shore, opposite the strip club. Spark spotted the dick who shot at you guys hitting on Iris. King wanted to ignore it. None of our business. But Spark went off like he always does when he sees someone in trouble."

"Was it after they did the drop at the club?"

"Yeah."

Fuck, I should have been there. They were so close. And I'd be a more credible future witness, because there's no way Spark or King will sign up to take the stand if it ever comes down to that. I could have taken photographs. Sent them to the FBI and the ATF and made use of facial recognition software.

Briar deserves some peace.

"They get any images?" I ask casually.

"Nah. Just the plates. I might have a way to get some though. There aren't too many organizations into running women. Russians, maybe. Some Eastern European groups. Maybe some incel shit. Think white alt-right groups."

"Those alt-right fuckers get everywhere," I mumble.

"As a Black man walking among 'em, I feel that," Vex says.

"I bet you do." My MO has always been laid-back, but I'm desperate for all the intel Vex has. "King gonna take action?"

Vex rubs a hand over his hair. "Depends on how they encroach, I guess. Two sightings in a handful of days aren't a trend. I think he's gonna take a ride out to Bethlehem, see if he can't figure shit out."

I pat my pockets. "Shit, I'm out of smokes. Gonna pop to the store and grab some."

"Later," Vex says, turning his attention back to his laptop.

Keeping from running is hard. I head out of the compound on my bike and pull up at the first bar I know has a phone. After dialing the number I know off the top of my head, I wait until Weicker answers.

I try to think of reasons why I'm about to tell Weicker all this shit. But there's only one.

Briar.

I want to use every possible resource at my disposal to keep her safe.

Thankfully he answers before I have to face the reasons why keeping her from harm matters to me so much.

Quickly I fill him in on what has happened to date, without telling him Briar is still with me.

"So we got a lead on the woman's abductors," I say, finally. "We're headed to Bethlehem; letting you know in case you need to get me out of trouble with their PD later tonight."

"What's that got to do with the case against the Outlaws?" he asks.

Weicker's words hit me hard upside the head. "What do you mean? There's a possible trafficking ring in Jersey. We need to shut it down."

"And you need to remember which government agency you work for. We need intel to incriminate the club. Not to lose you in the crosshairs of some side investigation. Tell me what you know, and I'll feed it to the Feebs. Then you keep the hell away, and what goes down, goes down. Stay where the club action is, unless it's impossible."

I want to agree. The soldier in me who knows how to take orders flexes inside. But I can't. I rebel. If there is an organization picking up women, and Briar wasn't a fucking awful one-off, this is where I need to be.

"I'll see what I can do," I say noncommittedly.

"The girl, the one you helped. Where did you leave her?" Weicker asks.

"Her place."

It's not true. She's at my home.

Oh what a tangled web we weave when first we practice to deceive.

The lies are starting to mount. It's going to be hard to keep them straight.

"Keep your head on straight," Weicker says, echoing my thoughts.

"Will do."

I hang up and buy some smokes from the store so I have a pack and a receipt in case anyone gets suspicious. When I quit the army, I figured I should do the right thing and quit the smokes. Managed to pull it off after a couple of false starts.

But living amongst my brothers, I've started again. I'd forgotten how good a nicotine hit feels.

I drive back to the clubhouse and am about to take a seat next to Track at the bar when King opens the door and shouts my name.

"What's up, Prez?" I ask as I walk toward him.

"We're going to Bethlehem. Sounds like the kind of place you belong," King says with a grin.

Spark's laughter booms from inside the office and I force a smile. "Did you know Bethlehem means 'house of bread' in Hebrew?"

King shakes his head. "I didn't know that, but those new scum that were in town this weekend are from there. Thought we'd go check it out."

I don't want to appear too keen, but this has become personal. Rules and laws are falling by the wayside, being replaced by the things I know are morally right for my own personal code. Do I want to fight for a safer America? Of course I do. I already have in some of the harshest places on earth. But I'm starting to feel like I'm here to stop women from being trafficked, not to stop a weapons delivery that will be a drop in the ocean when I think of all the guns that exist in the world.

Instead of saying all that, I scroll through my mental rolodex for the right quote. "Then, when Herod saw that he had been tricked by the magi, he became very enraged, and sent and slew all the male children who were in Bethlehem. Matthew 2:16. Are we slewing because we haven't slewed in a while?"

King laughs as I intended. "No slewing, which I assume means killing the miserable fuckers. Just intel. But the day for slewing may well come."

I nod. "Fair deal. Let me get my shit together."

We arrange to head out at ten p.m. Spark heads to Vex's closet to get the tech we need. King wants a tracker on the truck so we know when they come close. Vex is going to program some kind of alert so we know when they're in Jersey.

"You really worried about them from a club perspective?" I ask King when it's the two of us. I need to feel out how far he's willing to go to help Briar without ever asking.

King sits down in the big chair at the head of the table. He still appears uncomfortable in it because it took losing his father to be in a position to claim it. When King's father had lied to the club to save Clutch's father, he set about a chain of events that would lead to his own demise. I know King would have preferred to earn the seat any other way but that. He lights a cigarette, then shakes his head.

"I don't know yet. Maybe they're small fry, the girl you freed a one-off. Our good deed is done, and we move on. Or maybe they're big, bring police attention with them. I don't want another group to fight. The Los Reyes shit recently was enough. We don't need another reason to watch over our shoulder."

The group that killed King's father also killed his mother

and attempted to kill his twin sister, Gwen, until the club had figured out what was going on.

"I've got a sister," I say, before I can stop the words. Now I have to roll with it as if it's no big deal. "Can't help but think about her and want to know she's safe from these jackasses."

King nods. "I understand that feeling. Having Gwen back has put things into perspective."

"You guys getting along after her being gone for so long?" I ask. It changes the subject. Puts the spotlight on King instead of me. Then maybe I can get out of this room before I get asked any questions.

King huffs and draws on his cigarette. "You see Clutch?" he gestures around the room.

I look around in case it's a trick question. "No."

He flops back in the chair. "Yeah, me neither. Told me he was taking the day to do something with Gwen, seeing as it's her day off, which I'm pretty sure is code for stay-at-home fucking. And if you tell me they're consenting adults, I might just punch you in the face."

I can't help but laugh. "Older brothers, huh? Wait, are you the oldest?"

"Yeah, by minutes. Before midnight for me, just after midnight for her. We're twins with different birth dates."

"You two have the twin thing?"

King looks thoughtful for a moment. "When we were kids? All the time. Once, she was at a party and I was out with Dad, and I swear I could taste the ice cream she was eating. And there are moments while we were apart when I felt things, almost like I was experiencing a life that wasn't mine. Think she did too. And now that she's back, I can't really explain it, but there's a peace to it." He smiles softly to himself, like he's recalling good memories.

I let him for a moment. Because I felt that same sense of peace once I got Rae out of Dad's clutches.

"You cool with what happened? How it all went down in the past?" These are the kind of things Phillip, the battalion's military chaplain, would ask me in the quiet moments. He'd ask how I was processing things when we were in the field. I believe he's why I came home a better man, while Spark brought home fractured pieces of himself.

"Intellectually, yeah. Dad never made a wrong decision. Always had things under control. But what he did to avoid the death of his friend brought about the death of Mom, himself, and nearly Gwen."

"Would you have done the same?" I ask. I can't help but ask the question. I want to know my fate. "Was there any room for absolution in the chaos?"

King shakes his head. "Lesson learned. I'll kill any motherfucker who screws me or the club."

"You don't believe in the concept of a redemption arc?"

"You're losing me, preacher."

I wish I could tell him who I really am. I want to stand up and set him straight and show him why I'm a rock-solid choice for this MC in spite of what I do. Instead, I explain, "In storytelling, there's often a redemption arc. The person who is perceived as bad in some way goes through a transformation to become a force of good. I gotta believe we're all at some point in our own redemption arc."

King blows a plume of smoke into the air. "That's because of all that God stuff you believe in. Bet there's a billion quotes in the Bible about that shit, right?"

"I have brushed away your offences like a cloud, your sins like a mist; return to me, for I have redeemed you. Isaiah 44:22." It's the best I can do as I feel a wave of sorrow, an emotion I'm highly unused to, flood through me. I want to use my own words, not the words from a Bible that King doesn't believe in but is expecting from me.

King grins. "See. That's my point. It's gotta be bullshit, right? You do everything wrong in your life, and at the eleventh hour, you ask some mystical man on a cloud to forgive you, and he replies, 'Sure, let me wipe the slate clean for you because deep down you're a good person.' Me? I'd let them 'fess that shit, then put a bullet between their eyes and watch them fall off that damn cloud. Hopefully you can watch where they end up in hell. Like, lying there while crows peck at their eyeballs or something."

My brain attempts to focus on his words as my gut processes the fact there is no redemption arc for me. "That's pretty specific."

He takes a final drag on his cigarette. "Maybe. But I'll say this . . . there's something really fucked up about how cyclical everything that has happened is."

"You believe in karma?"

"That's a deep question and requires way more whiskey than I've drunk today," King says, stubbing out his cigarette in the ashtray. "You cool coming on the ride?"

I nod, knowing our conversation is over, as King stands to leave his office. "Wouldn't miss it."

At ten o'clock, Spark, King, and Kieran—one of the prospects—and I hit the road. It's cool for early October, and I've layered up beneath my leather. We wind our way south of the Lehigh River, and the properties begin to space out a little.

We park a block or so from our final target and leave Kieran watching the bikes. He knows to call if he sees trouble.

"You doing okay?" I ask Spark quietly as I straighten my skull cap.

He glances ahead to King, then turns to me. "He and I had words before we left. He's overstepping."

"Is this about Iris?"

Spark shoves his hands into his pockets. "We got her into this mess. I can't . . . fuck. I can't just leave her to the wolves."

King is getting farther ahead of us, and I slow our pace. "If whatever is going on between the two of you is bringing you peace, you should cling to it."

Spark shrugs. "Or I should do what my president asks and get over it. I'm taking a long ride when we're done here. See if I can't clear my head."

King waits until we reach him, cutting off another conversation today.

"Which one is the truck registered to?" Spark whispers as if he wasn't just confiding in me.

Our conversation is forgotten.

"Number forty-eight." King tips his chin up the hill. It's late and dark. The house looks deserted but the black truck sits in the driveway. I feel a wave of revulsion seeing it again, wishing I had been able to convince Briar to report it to the police. The windows have been replaced, but there's a bullet hole in the hood.

Briar could identify the truck *and* the man who owns it.

Anger pulses through me, even as I see Spark place a tracker beneath the wheel arch. Fucker deserves some explosives set to detonate when he turns the engine on.

It's the first time I've ever considered using what I know to kill instead of save, and the feeling is . . . heady. Maybe my redemption arc is going in reverse.

I head around back with King. Wrought iron bars cover every opening.

"Guess they don't want uninvited guests," I say.

King gestures to the outbuilding, an old wooden shed, but there's nothing of note inside when I check it out.

"Nothing," I whisper.

"We should get out of here," King says.

We walk back to the bikes, where King tugs Spark into a fierce hug. "Ride well, brother."

Spark nods and climbs on his bike.

As his lights disappear, King runs his hand over the front of his bike. "Hope the road breaks the hold the Irish chick has over him. Let's ride."

My president is telling us to leave. My ATF boss doesn't even want me to be here.

But as I mount my bike, I vow that I'm going to get revenge for Briar and for every woman who may have come before.

13

BRIAR

I thought I'd sleep easier here, in the safety of Saint's house. After our trip to the apartment, I couldn't imagine staying anywhere else. And when he lifted me into his arms and made me come against the wall, I thought . . . shit, I don't know what I thought. It's all muddled.

But one thing is clear. I realize the feeling of safety was coming from the man. Not the place. It's three in the morning, I can barely keep my eyes open, and I'm sitting huddled in a blanket in the middle of the sofa.

The weapons Saint left in two different parts of the house for easy access should I need them are sitting on the ugly coffee table in front of me.

Every pipe gurgle, car sound, and otherwise totally normal noise outside the window makes my heart race to levels I didn't know it was capable of. I've lived alone before, heard these kinds of noises, but now my fear of them feels amplified.

When we got back from the apartment, I tried to make things feel normal. I unpacked, showered, and pulled on my loose-fitting navy overalls and paired them with a bright tangerine T-shirt. The color boosted my mood, and my deathly pale complexion.

Five pairs of shoes now sat in Saint's hallway.

I was doing okay until Saint told me he was going to the strip club and then the clubhouse. I've had boyfriends before, and I've always been a huge fan of having my own hobbies and interests. So it wasn't that he was leaving. It wasn't even where he was going.

It was that he was gone, and I was scared to be alone.

I got online and was able to catch up on the work I missed. Then I'd tried to distract myself and start the label design for a new botanical-infused sparkling water brand. I captured a handful of concepts. I loved the idea of the wildly colorful houses of Burano, a small Venetian island. Everyone has been doing neutrals recently, and I'm kinda over it.

The flavors are so crisp and bright that I feel simple images of the botanicals would make them seem a little insipid.

Saint told me to help myself to the food in his fridge for dinner. There was more nutrition in there than I antici-pated, and I was able to pull together a veggie-filled pasta sauce to go over some bow-tie pasta.

It seemed like the absolute wrong pasta for a man like Saint. It's too formal, too stuffy.

I managed to cope until sunset when I felt compelled to check if there were any other missing women in New York. The idea that not reporting my abduction brought harm to others makes me feel ill.

As the street settled into the darkness of evening, fear and anxiety started to creep a little closer.

Once in bed, I lay rigidly flat on my back, with the

comforter pulled up to my chin like a safety blanket. Relent-lessly, I scanned for noises.

When I rolled onto one side for comfort, the pillow blocked one of my ears, which made me feel exposed.

So I moved to the sofa after putting on the television, to see if drowning out the noises would help.

It didn't.

I'm currently sitting in silence.

That isn't helping either.

Knowing someone had their hands all over my stuff is making me ill. I don't know how I'll ever go back.

I rethink going to the police. Like what if I went out of state, to a different police force? Would there be some over-sight to make sure I didn't end up transferred to the two cops my abductors mentioned? What if they didn't take me seriously and the two cops showed up at my home on the pretext of helping?

They'd know my address.

Shit, I'm not processing things properly. I already have proof they know my address.

They've been in my space.

Urgh.

I flop my head back.

But for the first time in days, it's not just fear I feel. Anger is starting to simmer. I'm mad this happened to me. I'm mad the system isn't designed to help. I'm mad that I'm in a virtual stranger's home, reliant on his good nature. But there is no way I can afford to walk out on my lease to get a new place.

Maybe I can sublet it and move out.

I'll have to check my agreement.

But then what? Do I move home with my tail between my legs and confirm that my dad was right when he said I was biting off more than I could chew when I moved?

I guess I bought into the famous theme itself, the song sung by Liza Minnelli before Frank Sinatra, that if you can make it in New York, you can make it anywhere. Well, what happens if you *don't* make it? What happens if you try and fail? What happens next? Where's the next place you go?

I hate the idea that my dad was right almost as much as I wonder if all those conversations—all those hours begging me not to move to a big city because bad things happen in big cities—actually manifested this for me.

And I hate the idea that I threw myself at Saint, came in his arms, and that when we got home after barely talking about what happened, he packed up and went to the clubhouse. And I may not know much about MC life, but I know it involves absolute disregard for society's rules and a whole lot of sex on demand.

I mean, he runs a strip club.

Am I being stupid imagining there's more to what happened than sex?

I think back to Josh, a man I was dating two years ago. I thought we were on the same page. After five months of dating, I just assumed we were monogamous, that we were a couple. I was foolishly letting myself fall in love with him while he was sleeping around.

I got tested for STDs and then shored up my heart.

The sound of a trash can lid dropping makes me jump. I place my hand over my heart and feel it race. "Probably a cat," I say out loud to no one. "And it isn't just sex either."

I've learned that dirty talk and sex and no demonstration of care beyond making sure you get off is just sex. But if they're falling for you, you can see it in their actions outside of the bedroom.

Saint's words and actions *show* me that. I see it in the new door locks and bagged evidence and cupped cheeks.

I worry I'm about to let go of my rules, my shield and give my heart to another man who either doesn't deserve it or won't cherish it. The temptation to push him away is there even as my feelings for him grow.

The mouthy growl of a motorbike grows louder outside, and my chest expands at the idea Saint is nearly here.

When he unlocks the door and steps inside, I fly off the sofa and into his surprised arms.

"Hey," he says gruffly, as he kicks the door shut with the heel of his boot. "You okay?"

He smells like fresh air and the faintest trace of his after-shave. I bury my head into the side of his neck when he lifts me higher and places his hands beneath my butt before carrying me to the bedroom, where he puts my feet on the ground. "Sorry," I say quietly.

Cold fingers push the hair back from my face. "Not going to complain when an attractive woman throws herself into my arms when I come home at night. But why are you not in bed fast asleep?"

I look over at the sheets, all crumpled, a testament to my attempts to settle. "I was scared." Tears sting my eyes, but I push through. "I kept telling myself I was safe. That no one knew where I was. But I couldn't stop the freight train of fearful thoughts rattling through my head."

"That's understandable. You're safe here," he says. "You know that, right?"

I nod. "Intellectually yes. Emotionally . . . a solid maybe."

"Do you feel better now that I'm home?"

"I do. God, I am so fed up with crying. I'm like a leaking sieve."

Saint cups my cheeks and swipes his thumbs beneath

my eyes to brush away the tears. His hair is up in a wild and windswept man bun. It's hot. "Technically a sieve can't leak, given that by design, water was meant to pass through it."

"You're so funny. I'm tired of being scared. Tired of being tired. Tired of not knowing what to do next." I take a deep breath then glance over at the sheets. "Maybe a better night's sleep will bring a better day."

He grabs my hands. "Anything you need to help with that?"

Am I misreading signals? Maybe I'm tired, but I feel anchored back in my body when he holds me. I'm not sure I could handle another rejection, even after what we did in my apartment.

"You got any sleeping tablets?" I ask.

Saint shakes his head and grins. "No, but I hear whiskey works."

I think about it for a minute. "Thank you, but I'll pass. The last thing I need is an all-day hangover. It's partly my own fault I'm so unsettled."

"Why?" he asks.

"I started to research if there were more women abducted besides me. And, oh my God, there are so many missing women in general . . . all over the country. The FBI's website is filled with pictures, and each post has a section called *remarks* with details you might need to know to identify them. A surgical scar on a foot, a mole on the right cheek, a birthmark on the back. I started to think about what my mom would have supplied for me. A tragus piercing in my right ear that my dad didn't want me to get. A mole at the back of my neck, one Mom would always catch when she tied my hair up when I was a kid."

"That's a lot of ugly thoughts and images. Probably not the right time for you to be researching that."

"What if I'm not the only one, Saint? What if there are more than just me?"

Saint pauses. "We need to talk some more. But first, I need to shower. Use the time to get into bed. I'll come find you when I'm done."

I nod and look back at the bed, deciding to put myself out there. "Maybe you don't need to sleep on the couch tonight."

He tucks a piece of hair behind my ear. "You don't owe me anything, Briar."

"I know, but you asked if there was anything I needed help with to get a better night's sleep tonight. And I think maybe having you close will help."

14

SAINT

I told a fuck ton of lies today. To my president. To my friends and brothers. To Briar, although those are lies of omission rather than direct untruths. I lied to my boss, told him I wasn't going to go looking for the men who hurt Briar, but I did. And I'm going to lie to him again in the morning when I say King gave me no choice but to go.

But the biggest lie I've told today is to myself.

I look in the large mirror as I brace my hands on the sink.

The whole ride home tonight, I was trying to convince myself that Briar didn't matter. That she wasn't my business. That for both our sakes, I needed to send her home.

But I know I'm about to shower, then pull on a pair of joggers and no top because I want to climb into that bed with her and feel her all up in my space. Even though I'd rather be naked. I stand by what I said, that she should take the lead on the steps of her healing.

And I don't want to let her down again today. I know it's irrational to feel this way. But not finding the men who took her, not beating them to a lifeless pulp on their own front lawn weighs heavy. With the kind of persuasion my club can dish out, the kidnappers would tell everything they knew before their demise.

I don't have the energy to mentally debate the term *my club.*

Sometimes, I imagine paying my father a visit and doing the same things to him. Give to him the kind of pain he caused Rae, Mom, and me. Violence begets violence. Part of me wants to stop the cycle, and part of me screams for justice.

It builds up inside me, seeking an outlet.

Steam swirls around, and I draw my attention back to the shower. I step in and close the door behind me, letting the heat soothe my tired muscles. I place both hands on the wall in front of me and allow the water to pound on the back of my neck.

When I look down, I can see my cock, still hard.

It's been like that periodically today. Thoughts of the way Briar gasped my name, the feel of her hot pussy pushed up against my erection, the way her puffs of breath felt against the side of my neck.

I place my hand on my cock and pump it once, twice. It feels good. Not as good as Briar felt, but the last thing she needs when she's so terrified that she can't sleep is my boner. I close my eyes and bring a picture of her face into my mind. In the visual, I strip her. Tits that are more than a handful, a wet pussy I can thrust into, and a juicy ass I can watch move as I fuck her. In my imagination, she's horny and desperate for me.

I visualize those plump lips of hers dragging along my cock. I imagine the way her tongue feels brushing my balls.

I huff out a breath.

And another.

Running my tongue along my lips, I wonder what she tastes like. If I pulled the lips of her pussy apart and lapped her, would it be sweet or musky? Does she like coming by a man's mouth or his fingers? Or both?

I'd start with one finger, then two. Fuck, I'd try three. As many as she'd let me.

I don't want to rush, but I also don't need Briar figuring out I was jacking one out in the shower that shares a wall with the bedroom.

The idea she's nearby nudges me closer. I focus nearer the head of my cock and stand up straight so I can tug on my balls.

I close my eyes and think about how she'd feel on top of me, riding me. Would she coat me with her cream, or does she need help getting wet? Would the orgasm I give her with my mouth ease the slow slide and grind on my dick?

And that ass of hers . . . what would *that* look like as I pounded into her from behind. I wonder if she'll let me do dirty things to her, let me feast on her pussy, let me bang her against a glass window in a high-rise hotel where someone might see. Will she let me put my hand around her throat, let me hold her down, let me fuck her until we're both high from the sensation of it?

Can she give over her control to my safekeeping? Will she trust me to know what she needs? I imagine her on her knees, ass in the air and face on the sheets, hands tied behind her back while I fuck her into the mattress.

I feel the rush of the orgasm before I start to come.

"Fuck," I mouth. It comes out on a breath.

Stars spin in the corner of my eyes, and the hand that was tugging on my balls slams against the shower wall to keep me upright.

Even though she's not here with me, just thinking of Briar makes it one of the best orgasms I've ever had.

I milk every last sensation as my cock softens.

Perhaps I should have gone to the club, found one of the girls. Reminded myself why what I'm about to do is such an awful goddamn idea. Instead, I towel dry myself off, including my hair. Then I pull on the clean gray sweats I picked up on the way out of the bedroom.

I use the towel to wipe some of the steam from the bathroom mirror and look at myself.

One of the ways I keep myself level is looking the mirror and reminding myself of why the job I'm doing is so goddamn important. Tonight, I repeat the action, even as I know I'm going to walk straight out of here into the arms of Briar and fuck everything else up.

Even so, I go to her.

Briar is in bed, fussing with the sheets. "How old are you?" I ask.

"Twenty-eight. Why? How old are you?"

"Forty-one next birthday," I answer honestly. One of the best tips I ever got about doing undercover work was to keep as many details real as you can get away with.

"Practically an old man," she says, but there's humor on her lips and mischief in her eyes.

I glance down at the body I work hard to keep in shape. Some parts of military discipline are hard to let go of. "I like to think of it as maturing like a fine single malt." I rub my hands down my chest, over my abs, then back up again. Her eyes shamelessly follow the action. "Stop looking at me like a Popsicle, sweetheart."

Even though I really want to give you something to suck on.

She yawns as she pulls the sheet up to her chin. "Sorry."

I go to turn off her nightlight before placing my hands

on either side of her head. "I like you looking. So don't be sorry, even if I'm an old man."

She smiles sleepily, and after a day that contained tears and sadness, it looks especially good on her. I kiss her lips, softly. I don't want to rev anyone's engines. Hers or mine.

Instead, I walk to the other side of the bed and climb in before turning the light off.

"Where do you think people find courage, Ryker?"

The sound of my real name from her lips is sweet, even as I realize she shouldn't be saying it at all. If she gets in the habit, she might say it at the wrong time. But here in the dark, I don't have it in me to berate her for it. Not when it sounds so perfect. Not when I rarely hear my own name these days.

"There was an army chaplain I once knew." I shouldn't tell her about Phillip, the man whose name I'm using for cover, but the moment calls for it. "One day, while I was in Afghanistan, I'd been called to disarm a bomb. Pretty routine. I identified the detonator core that was going into the main charge, started to break down the explosive frame before I pulled the detonator cap out of the fuse well. All standard stuff. Then I found this other wire, and when I followed it, I realized I was standing in the middle of a daisy chain bomb. One bomb linked to another bomb and to another bomb. It was the only time in my life my courage wavered."

"Ryker," she whispers. Her hand slips into mine, and I close my fingers around hers as I put myself back in that day. In the heat of my bomb suit, sweating beneath it. Knowing that I didn't know where the other bombs were, only seeing the junction where the wires all met.

"That night, after I'd disarmed all those bombs, I found the army chaplain. He said there were two types of courage.

Faith-based courage. 'Be strong and of a good courage; be not afraid, blah, blah, for the Lord thy God is with thee whithersoever thou goest.' 'And the Lord is my light and my salvation . . . though war be waged against me, even then do I trust.' 'You of little faith, why are you so afraid?' Some people are bolstered in their faith that someone has their back, and if it is the end of their days, it was part of the plan of their lives."

"So you believe in God?"

"I'm the son of a Baptist preacher with a passion for brimstone, damnation, and alcohol. So, no. Not in the purist sense. But Phillip said something that stuck with me. It's possible to have that kind of faith in yourself. The words still work. I could be strong and be of good courage because I will always be with me. I can be my own light and salvation, even though war *was* waged against me, because I will always trust in myself to do what is best for me. There is no need to be afraid if I have faith in myself. And that bolstered me." I pause for a moment, the question getting stuck in my throat for a second. "When they took you, did you believe you were going to be saved?"

I hear her sigh. It's an intimate conversation. I almost wish I could see her face, but sometimes things are easier to discuss in the dark.

"At first, I was convinced I would be. I remember thinking someone will see this, they'll report it, they'll get license plates, and all that stuff you see on crime shows. I live in a city filled with cameras. But they put me in a room with walls of smooth gray concrete. And it was set up like a prison cell, only the bed was made up with soft bedding. There was a toilet in the corner. No windows. There were a couple of narrow vents that I assumed were heat and air ducts. That's when I struggled to remain positive. Nobody goes through that much trouble to create that kind of room for a one-off abduction. There must have been more women than me. That's why I searched tonight to see if I could find any of them."

The picture she paints in my head is terrifying. I don't know who'd want to destroy the spirit of someone so lovely. "But you found your courage again, the night we met."

"The night you saved me? Yeah. I guess . . . I knew it was my last chance. I was being transported to my final home. And I knew if they had a chamber like the one I'd been in, my hope wouldn't last long enough for me to be found."

I tug her arm and pull her close, spooning myself around her. "You were brave, sweetheart. You saved yourself. You had courage. Circumstances made it waver, but you overcame the doubts and kept the faith in yourself. That the timing was right. That your option was now. That you could escape two armed men. You had courage at the very worst of times."

"Says the man who faced down bombs."

I wrap my arms tight around her. "It was my choice. I was courageous in a situation I'd been trained for. *You* were courageous when being brave was all you had. Go to sleep, Rose," I say, planting a gentle kiss on her lips.

She called me Ryker, and I let her.

Because for one night, I want there to be nothing but truths between us.

15

BRIAR

The concrete is smooth beneath my fingers, and my hips ache from sitting on it for so long. The door creaks as it opens, and the man comes in.

The buyer, my captor tells me.

My stomach clenches. There's nothing in it to vomit. I can't remember the last time I ate. I don't even know what time it is. He walks towards me, and my breath starts to come in gasps. I push my heels against the concrete, sliding away from him toward the wall.

He keeps walking, smiling softly, like he's approaching a skittish kitten rather than an abducted woman.

I keep pushing with my heels, even though there is nowhere for me to go.

"My wife," he says.

"I'm not," I say.

"You have no choice." He reaches for the strap of the silk slip I was forced to change into and nudges it off my shoulder, but I grab it. Before I can put it back in place, the blow comes fast and hard, smashing the side of my face into the wall.

Everything aches. I taste blood in my mouth.

He says nothing, simply reaching for the strap to push it off my shoulder again.

I turn feral, smacking his hand away, shoving him hard with one of my feet, knocking him back onto his ass. And I know I'm beat when he grins. He pins me to the wall, rakes his fingers down my cheek and whispers, "I like it better when you fight."

I cry out and—

"Briar. Rose."

I don't know who's calling me, but I need to get out of this place. I need to—

Someone shakes my shoulders. "Briar. It's me. Wake up."

I suck in air as my eyelids flip open. I repeat the action of the room, pedaling my feet into the mattress to scramble up against the headboard and wrap my hands around my knees.

"Shit. Shit," I mutter. Everything is tense. My shoulders and spine. My fingernails dig into my palms.

Saint kneels in front of me. He's turned a lamp on. I focus on him, using him to bring me back to the present. His hair is thick and wild. His eyes are blue and clear. Tattoos cover his chest and arms, and I wonder what they all mean, what they are for.

"Breathe with me," he orders, and I do. Breathing in when he does. Breathing out when he does. I watch his pecs expand and contract. I watch his chest rise.

Slowly but surely, I leave the dream behind.

Slowly but surely, the cold I felt is replaced with warmth.

When I sigh and drop my shoulders from my ears, he reaches for my hand.

"There we go," he says.

I nod, embarrassed. I feel the color hit my cheeks and lower my gaze.

"Hey," he says, tipping my chin with his thumb and forefinger. "You don't do that. You had a bad dream. It's understandable. It's been less than a week since it happened. You're doing great."

He sits again, his back against the headboard. Then, in a move that surprises me, he tugs me onto his lap, so I sit astraddle, and holds me to his bare chest. "You want to talk about it?" His words are raspy as his wide palms stroke my back.

I shake my head. "A dream. About the obvious."

"This strategy of moving on by not taking action isn't working," Saint says.

I sit up fast. "What kind of a comment is that?"

"An honest one. Because I care about you. You haven't told the police. You haven't told your parents. You haven't told any friends that I know of. You haven't told a therapist. You haven't told work. You've barely told me. I know dreams are sometimes your subconscious helping you process things. And I know dreams don't always go away, even if you've done all the work."

I *haven't* told anyone. I want it all to disappear. I want to lock it all in a box and bury it in the woods. I don't want to process it. I don't want to think about it and direct it. I don't want people who know me to know about it. I can't face the looks of pity. Every time I'm ever spoken about in the future, they'll say, *You remember Rose, the one who was abducted.*

Worse, I can hear my dad telling me how right he was about my decision to move.

But Saint is correct. It's not working. "I want to be mad at you," I say, lying back against him.

"Why?" He slides his calloused palms up my arms.

"Because you're annoyingly observant. The dream started because I was worried there were other women who'd been taken."

Saint nods. "It's on your mind. And I'm sure checking out the missing women on the FBI website hit your subconscious."

"I feel like such a coward, but the man, he said he'd chosen wisely. Like I was picked as opposed to being snatched opportunistically. The fact I know two police officers are involved . . . I can't take a risk they'll come find me. I need to move. I realized last night that I'll never know a moment's safety back at my place, no matter how hard I try."

Saint glances out of the window. The moon is low. "What if you were able to feel safe another way?"

"Like what?"

He grabs my hips firmly and looks at me intently as if searching for something. Whatever he sees in my eyes answers his question. "Tonight, we drove to the house of the man who shot at us that night. That's why I left you here alone."

"You did what? Saint, you could have been killed."

"Love that your first thought is for my safety, sweetheart," he says. "I went with my brothers. We placed a tracker on his truck so we can see where he's going and what he's doing. He's over in Bethlehem, Pennsylvania. I know you're carrying guilt in case there are or were other women, but we're going to take them down."

I sigh, but my breath hitches. "How are you going to do that? How will you know where the other women are?"

"What we'll do is illegal. It's better you don't know."

I shake my head. "That doesn't fly with me. I need to know."

"There's more going on than I can ever tell you, Briar."

I shake my head again and fold my arms. "Meet me half-way. How will you find the women?"

"One of my brothers is a certified technical genius. There will be a digital trail. We're going to track them down, find the buyers, then find the women."

"By yourselves or with the police?"

Saint shrugs. "Bit of both. If it's local, we'll do it to make sure no one ever gets off with a technicality."

"I can't ask you to do that for me."

His eyes meet mine, his gaze intense. "You remember me telling you about the army chaplain I knew? He had this really interesting take on the Army Chaplain Corps motto. It was *Pro Deo et Patria*, for God and country. And he struggled with the idea that serving God *and* serving his country could be equal. Partly because, as a true believer in God, he believed he served God *above* all others. God first in all things. And the military doesn't expect theological answers to battalion questions. Like a day of repentance for shooting someone when it goes against *thou shalt not kill*."

His hands slip to my thighs, rough palms glancing up and down my skin. I get a feeling this answer isn't for me, and I don't know why. It's like he's thinking through a problem out loud, so I wait.

"I guess what I'm saying is sometimes what you believe in as a man has to take precedence over all other things. Like orders. And what others think." He squeezes my hips. "What was done to you was wrong. What was done to you also involves the police, who are supposed to serve and protect. Sometimes, the organizations that want to do good in the world actually do the worst."

His words ease my worry. "I should be appalled at what you're suggesting. And maybe it makes me a coward that I would rather the men who took me were dead instead of in prison, always with the potential of parole. Maybe it makes me an awful human that I can't stomach the process of being a witness. But I also can't bear the idea of you getting hurt for me. I couldn't live with that."

"The risk of getting hurt comes with the job," Saint says on a huff. And I get the feeling that there are layers to his words I don't understand. "I'll keep you safe, Briar. I promise."

The words are barely out of his mouth before I press my lips to his.

16

SAINT

I'm fucked.

That's my only thought when Briar kisses me like her life depends on it.

I'm sure in her eyes, it does.

I disassociate from every component of my life. I'm a man before I'm an ATF agent or an undercover MC member.

Right now, with those big brown eyes looking at me before they flicker shut, none of it really matters. Not when she's so soft and warm in my arms.

I want this brave, courageous woman more than I've ever wanted anything else.

"Fuck, Briar," I say, rolling us so she's beneath me.

Her hands sink into my hair, and she greedily guides me back to her lips. I love a woman who knows what she wants. And I'm the man to give it to her. She isn't holding back, so I'm not going to either.

Our tongues meet, and I savor the raw flavor of her. It's primal. I want to consume her, but I bury the urge I have to bite her.

I sink my hips between hers, settling my hard cock right at the seam of her pussy, grinding back and forth. I know I got her off like this already, but I want to explore so much more of what turns my sweet Briar Rose on.

Her hands shift from my hair to dig into my ass as she takes what she needs.

Heat bleeds through my sweats, and I push up onto my hands. "I want to taste you." I raise to my knees and slip her tank over her head. Her breasts are full, dusky nipples are pert and ready. I cup one and run my thumb over the stiff peak before bending down to suck it into my mouth.

"Saint," she gasps, her back arching.

I squeeze the other while I suck on her. She writhes beneath me, her legs bending and stretching as she seeks the relief she needs. The urge to bite returns, and I gently do, starting wide on her breast, then narrowing down to her nipple.

She cries out at the sensation.

I kiss my way down her stomach, deliberately ignoring the tugs on my head to get me to return to her tits or move down to her pussy. "Patience," I mumble against her soft skin.

I hear a chuckle, and it makes me smile.

My fingertips slip beneath the waistband of her shorts and ease them down her smooth legs. And then she's lying naked before me. She's beautiful and vulnerable, and there are still bruises on her body from what happened to her. My anger threatens to ignite all over again.

And I just bit her.

Jesus, I'm a freak.

"You sure you want this, sweetheart?" I ask, praying she doesn't say no. I can reel it in if she needs me to, but I want to fall into this with her.

"I want to feel normal," she says. "I want to reconnect with myself this way."

I lean forward and steal another kiss from her lush mouth. Despite our conversation, it's as hot as the first one. Then I return to her pussy because I need to know if it tastes as good as it feels. She pulls her knees up and opens her legs wide, exposing herself to me, and I love that she isn't shy.

I run two fingers between her lips, then drag them over her clit. She's already wet. And I follow them with my tongue. She tastes salty and sweet at the same time. All thoughts of easing her into this escape me. "Tell me if you need me to stop," I mumble against her pussy.

"Please. Just . . ."

I know what she needs. The steady tumble back into her own skin. To set the world back to normal. I used to feel the same way when I returned from duty overseas.

I lick as far inside her as I can reach. I can't wait to fuck her, but I want her to come first. I suck on her clit, nothing polite or pretty. Just a genuine appreciation for her cunt. Amazing what that thing can do. Maybe bring a life into the world, and definitely bring this man to his knees.

I flick my tongue over her clit and slide a finger deep inside her, followed by another. I drag my fingertips along her inner wall, reaching for the part of her guaranteed to set her world alight.

When I reach it, she arches off the bed. "Saint," she gasps, and I repeat the action as I suck her clit into my mouth.

Her heels dig into the mattress as she moves against my face.

My teeth clamp down on her clit, and she detonates with a cry.

I try to bring her down gently, but I can't wait. I grab a condom from the side table and tug it on before positioning myself between her legs. "You still good, Bri?"

Wide eyes look up at me as she nods.

"Fuck," I groan as I inch into her. Her knees come up by my hips, changing the angle so I slide in more easily until I'm fully seated.

It's like her body was meant for me. The curves, the way she fits, all of it feels so good, I can barely move. In a controlled detonation, you set everything up and then pray it works the way you want it to. Same with sex. Two people come together and hope there's magic. Sometimes it disappoints, sometimes it ends too soon, and sometimes it's simply fine. But other times? It's everything. It's as wild and reckless as an unconfined explosion, scorching everything it touches.

I begin to move, and her pussy clutches around me. She's greedy for more, for another release, and I want to give it to her.

Her hands clutch for something. My back. The sheets. I link my fingers with hers, holding them both gently above her head. The scars on her wrists are healing, and I don't want to make them worse.

I kiss her softly, feeling the soft gasps as her breath hitches. "You okay, sweetheart?"

I don't normally ask. Generally, I don't really care. Not that I'm an asshole. The kind of women I hook up with will tell me if they don't like what's going down. But with Briar . . .

"Don't stop," she begs. And I don't.

She's so wet, easing the slide. "God, you feel good," I gasp.

Our bodies intuitively rise and fall to meet each other. I feel my orgasm building. I put more pressure through my knees, hitting her harder with every stroke. "I need you to come. Come for me."

"Saint," she gasps, and frustration laces the word. She wants it as badly as I do.

Man, I try to stall. I think of the report I owe Weicker. But nothing can take away how good this is.

"Please," Briar shouts, slamming against me as hard as I'm hitting her. "God, yes."

Then she cries out as her body tenses, as though an electric charge is flowing through it. Even her pussy tightens around me, with fast flutters that clench and release.

And I'm done for.

I let myself go, losing pace as I sink deep into her. Feeling my cock throb in a glorious agony as I ride the high.

My lips meet hers, but it's barely a kiss. We breathe into each other's mouths as we ride out the ecstasy.

"So fucking good," I murmur against her skin. I kiss a trail to where damp hairs curl at the nape of her neck.

I release her wrists and stroke a hand down her body.

And then I realize the shudders aren't release—they're sobs.

"Babe. Briar." I take my weight in my elbows so I can look at her properly. "Shit." When I see the tears, I reach between us to grip the condom and slide out of her. I should remove it, but my only thought is Briar. "Talk to me, sweetheart. What's wrong?"

I fall to the side, taking her with me so I can hold her while she cries. I'd like to believe she had an earth-shattering orgasm that blew away all her defenses. But I know in my heart this is so much worse.

I hold her until her sobs subside. I stroke her hair away from her face, then I find the edges of the sheet and pull it over her, so she doesn't feel so exposed. "You need me to let go of you?" I ask.

She shakes her head and sniffs. "No. God, I'm sorry. I . . ."

"In your own time," I encourage.

It takes a few more minutes before she lifts her head to look at me. "I wanted that . . . but partway through, memories came back. And I wanted to chase them away with something more. With you. And I couldn't get there because of it, and then when I did . . . God, none of this is making any sense. I'm sorry. It was me, not you."

I cup her cheek and run my thumb beneath her lashes. I don't know what makes me catch one and put my thumb in my mouth. Her tears are salty. "Was it too soon?"

Briar shrugs. "Maybe. I don't think so. I needed this. I needed the feeling of connection. I've been in my head since it happened. I wanted to get back in my body. To reclaim it, if that makes sense."

"We can work on the connection thing without having sex." I can't believe the words are out of my mouth. Let alone that I actually believe them.

Her cheeks go a little pink. "I don't want to take a step back. I want to move forward."

I think of the men in my unit. How Phillip would counsel them after a shit day that we all knew would be followed with an equally shit day tomorrow. "Everything you feel right now is valid. Even if those feelings contradict each other. You can get aroused and want sex yet still feel traumatized. Those two things aren't mutually exclusive."

"I think it helped though. I feel better for crying and letting it out."

I think for a minute, wanting to be careful in what I say next. "I'm happy to be with you wherever you're at. And I'm happy to be with you if where you're at changes like the breeze."

"But it's not fair to you. To want sex. To not want sex. To want to hide from you. To want to fall asleep in your arms."

I lean forward and kiss her lips softly. "It's not about me, right now. And it's not about forever. It's about you finding your feet. And if you need me in some capacity to help you do that, I'm here. You want to sleep alone, you tell me. You want to sleep curled up with me like a burrito, I'm not going to complain. You want to jump me like a porn star, complete with cheesy dialogue and soundtrack, I'll give it the good old college try."

Her chuckle makes me smile. "Saint," she says, her eyes on me.

"I will say this, you focused when you were restrained. You were flailing a little until then. Is that something you've explored before?"

She lowers her gaze but nods.

"So, it's not something triggering given what you went through?"

"Maybe. But I don't want it to be."

"Then we talk. A lot. About what we're doing. And what you're feeling."

Briar shakes her head. "It'll feel awkward. I'm not big on sharing feelings. I lived in a family of emoters. Emoters of predominantly fear-based emotions. I said I was never going to become one of them."

"You don't have to be," I reassure. "But I think there's a reason people become led by fear as adults, and it's usually because they didn't process the trauma from childhood.

Processing things after a stressful situation is a lot different to remaining stuck for the rest of your adult life. Trust me, Briar. You're safe with me."

Even though you don't have a clue who I really am.

17

BRIAR

When I wake in the morning, the world comes back slowly.

I'm warm, the sheets wrapped tightly around me.

And as I open one eye, I realize I'm alone.

I open the other eye and see nothing but a pillow with a dent in it, where a head lay all night. But Ryker isn't here with me.

Closing my eyes, I allow the memory of last night to replay in my mind.

But I think there's a reason people become led by fear as adults, and it's usually because they didn't process the trauma from childhood. Processing things after a stressful situation is a lot different to remaining stuck for the rest of your adult life. Trust me, Briar. You're safe with me.

He wants me to trust him, but I wonder how much he's keeping from me.

I tug on some leggings and a T-shirt. I got a request from a design firm I occasionally work with to design a library card and new branding for the library's website. It's exciting.

I've loved libraries since I was a little girl. And I really like Janice, who I'll be working with. The rate is good. And it's time for me to begin filling my work calendar again.

I get out my tablet and begin to sketch out concepts. It has to include books, obviously. But maybe the spines are the name of the library. Fun colors for sure. I pause occasionally for research. The New York Public Library has a simple black-and-white outline of a lion. The British Library is a simple red background with the words *British Library*. Their websites are focused on the content. I want to focus on the joy.

Libraries are a whole new world. The smell of books. Where I grew up in Gary, Indiana, felt small, but books made the world feel huge.

And maybe that's it. Maybe it's not about the books but the places they'll take you. Brightly colored birds. Oceans and deserts. Landmarks.

I make notes of the ideas as they come. They're all worth consideration.

I'm adding comments about diversity and representation in the community when the front door opens. Saint walks in with a tray of coffee cups and a paper bag.

"You're up," he says, pressing a kiss on the top of my head before placing the things he carries down on the table.

"Trying to get some work done. You've been busy."

I open the bag, and inside are fat pastries. Pain au chocolat with two thick rows of chocolate inside. Croissants, still warm. My stomach rumbles.

"Here," he says, placing a plate in front of me. "Thought you'd be hungry." He hands me a large cup that smells nutty and delicious.

The first sip is heaven. "So good," I mumble against the lid.

Saint sits opposite me and rips the paper bag open. "You okay? After last night?" he asks.

"Do we have to talk about this?"

He takes a big bite of croissant. "Thought we agreed we'd talk this shit through. Breakfast feels like a safer place than in bed with my dick inside you."

I blush at his directness. "Fine. Yes. I'm good. Still a little embarrassed. But good."

Saint grins. "See. Not that hard, was it?"

"You know, last night, you said, 'You're safe with me.' But I don't even really know how dangerous your life is."

I bet Saint would make an exceptional poker player. Nothing super noticeable about him changes. Not in his posture or the creases in his eyes. Yet I can feel something change, even as he leans back in his chair and drinks some of his coffee.

"I mean. You've told me it's not safe. But how not safe is it?"

"You're safe with me."

I raise an eyebrow. "What did you say earlier? 'Thought we'd agreed to talk this shit through.' I think this is a prime example of you not keeping your side of the *talk about your shit* bargain."

The corners of Saint's lips twitch as if he's going to smile. "Fine. But there are lines. Things I'm never going to be able to tell you."

I decide to help him out a little. "Am I in more danger here than back in New York?"

"Definitely not. Let me think on how much I can say. I swear it'll be the most detail I can give you."

It's surprisingly honest and good enough for now.

When we're finished eating, he stands and throws the garbage away. "I got something for you." He offers me his hand, and when I take it, he leads me to the front of the house. "I figured you might want to make a start on the rest," he says.

In the back of the truck is an array of new tools and plants. There are a lot of shrubs and small trees, given it's October. One I recognize as a crab apple. There are three rose bushes, long since bloomed, but the hips are still present.

"I know it's probably the wrong time to plant them or something. But I figured it might make for a nicer view out the kitchen window. And my sister assures me the plants won't mind if we give them plenty of fertilizer and water."

"You called your sister to ask?"

He shrugs. "She loves plants, and I know shit about them. I took her for a video walk around the garden center, and she told me which pots to shove in the cart."

I'm speechless.

I throw my arms around his neck. "They're perfect."

It takes several trips to get everything around the back. I realize I'm timing every trip so I am there at the same time as Saint. I guess I'm not ready to be alone near the sidewalk yet. If Saint notices, he doesn't say anything.

"Do you have plan?" I ask Saint.

"A plan for what?" he asks, placing down two large pots.

"Where you want all the plants to go?"

"Babe, I don't even know what the fuck half of these are." He shakes his head and grins. "I'm the free labor. You tell me where you want them, and I'll lug them."

"You two need a hand?"

Hap looks even more like a hippie today. A thin brown leather lace ties his hair back off his face and he's wearing a pale green bandana.

"Hey, Hap," I say. "We'd love one. Have you properly met Saint?" I wave Saint over and the two men shake hands.

"Seen each other around often enough," Hap says.

"Sorry it's taken Briar's arrival to properly meet you," Saint says. "Thanks for the plant."

Hap nods once.

"Hap was in the Vietnam War. Had the deadliest job, checking the tunnels for traps and mines and things."

"Bomb disposal? Know a thing or two about that myself," Saint says. "Heard tunnel rats were volunteer specialists. How'd you end up doing that?"

Hap nods, his blue eyes watery. "The tunnel complexes were vast rooms connected by tiny tunnels. They'd have aid stations and sleeping chambers and storage caches. Even had wells. Bombing from above did little. Smoking them out even less. Because there were super narrow tunnels, they looked for men with my build. Just did my job."

Saint casually puts his arm over my shoulder. "Takes balls, crawling though those claustrophobic tunnels in life-or-death situations."

Hap takes a deep breath and looks up at the sky. "Part of the reason I spend so much time outside now. Hated tunnels of any kind since I got home."

"Thank you for your service, Hap," I say. "And yours." I look up to Saint. "Thank you."

Saint winks, and Hap brushes my thanks aside. "What can I do to help?" Hap asks.

Between the three of us, we manage to get some of the bigger pieces of crap littering the back yard into Saint's truck, and Saint takes them away to be disposed of while Hap and I dig farther around the border. Well, he digs, and I follow and turn the soil. He's wiry and strong. I place plants in their pots on the surface as we go.

At some point, Hap goes and brings his lawn mower around. It's amazing how much better the yard looks after four hours of hard work.

Saint has taken his shirt off, and he wipes sweat from his brow with the back of his arm. It's quite the distraction. I think about the way his chest felt against mine in bed last night. When he notices me looking, he gestures for me to get back on with the planting. Later, I catch him checking out my ass.

Eventually, Hap leaves to run errands, and it's just the two of us.

Saint steps into my space, his body all sweaty. I touch a drip on his chest. His lips touch my ear. "What would it take to persuade you to let me eat you for lunch?"

I think about yesterday. About my little freak-out. About the conversation that followed. About how I've fantasized about his hands on my body most of the morning.

"Hey," he says, tipping my chin and pressing a chaste kiss to my lips. "I was just teasing. We can go make ham sandwiches."

"No." I shake my head. "I was reliving embarrassment from last night. I've been watching you most of this morning. It's hot when you get physical."

Saint grins. "With you or just in general?"

I gaze at the empty space where most of the junk sat in the corner. "Both. I think it's your shoulders."

He looks down at them. "They're just shoulders."

Now I laugh. "There is nothing *just shoulders* about your shoulders."

Saint grins. "I know what you mean though. There is nothing *just pussy* about your—"

I slap my hand over his mouth before he can finish the

sentence. "Speaking of which. You aren't the only one who got hot and sweaty. How do you feel about a shower?"

"You. Wet. Steam. I'm in." He takes my hand and leads us into the bathroom where we strip each other at record speed.

I step in first and turn the water on, jumping a little as the initial cold spray hits me before warming up. The water rinses away the stickiness before Saint steps in behind me. He tosses a condom on the little shelf in the corner with the shampoos. "We need a fucking step in here or something," he grumbles.

"Is that because bending is tough on your back, old man?" I tease.

His palm playfully swats my ass. "I'll show you fucking old."

He is taller than me by enough of a margin and has to bend his knees to rub his dick along the crack of my ass.

A flicker of a memory of the first night here ripples through me. Of collapsing in the corner. Of Saint pleading with me to stop scrubbing at my skin. He's taken care of me from the first.

"Make good memories for me," I say. And without giving him more context, I let him touch me and it's like he knows what I mean.

He turns me in his arms and kisses me. It's passionate and lustful. It means more than just sex and we both know it. Yet I feel like he's holding back. "Saint," I say, holding his biceps.

Water runs over his head as he looks at me, and we both laugh as we step out of the spray. "I don't think I can do this if you aren't who you really are. Don't hold back. Whether it's the danger you're in at work or how you like to have sex. I don't think we'll work if you do."

He runs his hands over my breasts. "You telling me this because you think I'm holding back now?"

"Aren't you?" I ask.

"Fuck." It's the only word I get before he kisses me. This time it's with abandon. He grabs my hands in one of his behind my back as his tongue seeks mine. The other hand cups by breast then tugs at the nipple. Something in me switches completely.

I feel like I need more of this. Vanilla is sweet, but sometimes I need it spicy.

His hand trails down my body and slides between by legs, dipping between my lips. He pinches my clit, waking something inside of me. Slowly, he slides a finger into me, a steady back and forth until he's fully seated.

"Think I can make you come hard and fast, sweetheart?" he says against my ear.

His thumb teases my clit. My hips jerk forward, seeking more. I want him, and I know I'm going to get him. "Please," I beg.

"*Please* you want more of my fingers? Or *please* you want my cock?"

"Yes. Both."

Saint grins. "Good answer."

He lowers his lips to my breast and sucks hard on my nipple before biting it, harder than he did last night. The sensation takes me out of my body. I can barely breathe. His fingers are inside me, his thumb pressing hard on my clit. The sweet suction and pressure on my nipple. My hands held tight between my back. There's nothing I can do but take it.

Tension explodes at my very core. "Ryker," I gasp.

Before I have time to come down, he spins me around and places my palms on the wall. He tugs my ass out so I'm bent forward. "Remember you asked me for this?" he says, and I hear the rip of the condom wrapper. It flutters to the floor of the shower.

He slides into me. It's not gentle, but it's so deliciously good, I feel the need to step onto my tiptoes.

"Keep your palms on the wall." He grunts as he pulls out before sliding home. "Fuck, what your pussy does to me."

He speeds up. Faster and faster.

"You gonna come again?" he asks.

As much as I love this, I know I'm not. "I want to feel you come in me."

This spurs him on. I imagine what it must look like, his cock sliding out of me. How turned on he feels.

Turning my head, I see his side-profile in the shower door. I see the tensed muscles in his thigh and butt. He's watching where we're joined, his mouth open, his brow furrowed.

I feel it the moment he comes. He slams his palms down on my ass, his fingers digging deep into my skin, as his thrusts stay deep. "Briar, fuck. Yeah, milk me."

And I squeeze around him, smiling as he groans some more.

He cups my chin and pulls me as close to standing as we can get in this position.

"You want me?" he says. "You've got me."

18

SAINT

"It's a risk, me being here," I say, as Weicker sits down across from me in one of the New York offices of the Bureau of Alcohol, Tobacco, Firearms, and Explosives. Group II is responsible for firearms trafficking and violent crime.

When I was heading to the office, I circled back on myself three times before I was confident I wasn't being followed. Still had me peering over my shoulder as I pulled into the lot.

Weicker nods. "I understand. But we needed to get together. You haven't been checking in like you were supposed to."

I turn the cup in front of me slowly. At the coffee shop, they asked my name for the order. I said Saint without thinking, and they wrote it on the cup. Out of context, in this nondescript government office, the name looks out of place.

Davis walks in a moment later. "Miller," he says curtly.

They're both dressed in suits. Weicker removes his jacket and rolls up his sleeves. Davis nudges the gold-rimmed glasses back up his face, rubs a hand across the sweat on his forehead, and pulls out a chair.

I glance down at my dusty boots and my jeans, soft as butter. They suit me better than the jacket and pants I wore when I wasn't undercover. I'm underdressed compared to the two of them, but I've never felt more in my own skin.

I'm missing my cut. The last thing I need is for someone to identify an Iron Outlaw walking into a federal office. I'd be dead in a heartbeat.

Davis clears his throat. It's noisy. Phlegm. I feel sick at the sound of it. "When we picked you for this op, I said to Weicker we needed an agent with more balls than good sense. In many ways, he did good, but we're worried you're losing sight of the objective."

I'm ready for the first volley and don't let it rattle me. "You're going to have to expand on that. What's making you think I lost sight of the objective?"

Davis's eyes widen. There was no *sir* on the end. No *please*. I don't owe these guys any kind of hierarchical titles. We're all just men. In the club, respect is earned, not demanded. "Your attitude for a start," he says.

I rub my hands over my face. "When you asked me to do this two years ago, I worked my ass off to build a believable background. I've put myself in harm's way every day since. Forgive me if the stress of that gets to me when I get called into a well-known federal building while still undercover."

Davis leans back in his chair. "You know the deal here. It's not what you personally know. It's what we can actually prove. If your word were enough, we could have pulled you out of the OMG a year ago."

I shake my head. I know he couldn't.

The look on his face confirms it.

And I rankle at the acronym. Outlaw Motorcycle Gang.

As the ATF would call them, a highly structured criminal organization.

"Anyway, tell me what's happening. Let's start at the top. Uther 'King' Hills. How is he settling in as replacement president?" Davis holds up an image of King.

"I know what they all look like," I say, and he puts it down quickly.

"King was born for the job," I say. "His father was quick to explode. King has historically been more thoughtful, but his patience is being tested. He's been the brains behind many of the club's expansion efforts. Like the strip club, etc."

"Speaking of which, you've got the real books of what money is being laundered through there, right?" Davis asks.

"I've got a log of what I've been asked to clean, but it'll be my word against theirs. As you said, it's not what you know but what you can prove."

Davis smirks. "These guys are sloppy. Uneducated. How hard can it be?"

This even gets a rise out of Weicker, who looks at Davis like he had a frontal lobotomy.

I say, "You're wrong on several fronts. First, they are suspicious. They live on high alert. Cell phones are encrypted. They're paranoid. And they have tight leadership. A unanimously elected president and vice president. Rules. They aren't sloppy. And maybe they aren't educated in an academic way, but their street smarts are endless. Vex is the kind of technical wizard who makes our guys look like they're sleeping on the job. They have military guys: Halo was a goddamn Navy SEAL. Spark was in the Marines. They can plan a raid with precision the ATF can't replicate."

Davis raises his hands. "Obviously touched on a sore spot. What happened to the mic the other day? Thought you were going to get whoever did the drop-off to talk about the cash."

I glance out the window. The gray sky has cleared, and the sun is high, even if the early October weather is a little cooler than it has been. I wish I were outside on my bike. Spark texted and said he might be home tonight. Maybe I should message him and see where he's headed in from and—

"Miller?" Davis says, interrupting my line of thought.

I shake my head for a moment, trying to force my brain back in the game. Undercover has become natural. This feels forced. It takes a lot of emotional energy to walk these two lives in parallel and switch between them on demand. I've been doing this every day for two years, remembering every detail, real or false. Hell, the club would routinely test me on it during that first year. They'd question me on shit I'd told them two weeks previously. "You got to know how to read these guys. I'm starting to tell when they want to talk about shit and when they don't. And that day, they didn't. Not to me. There was no point risking being caught on that day for nothing when I could save it and record them another time."

Weicker nods, but I doubt Davis believes me.

"Did you follow up on the lead I gave you?" I ask Weicker before Davis can say anything else.

Davis perks up. "What lead?"

"I accompanied Tyler Hyatt to the docks—"

"Spark?" Davis says. And the way he says it chaps my ass. Like he's somehow down with the cool kids because he knows my friend's road name.

"Yes, Spark," I answer, trying to hold back my sarcasm. "And a girl escaped from a truck. She's been abducted and beaten. The club figured out where the guy lived from the license plate."

"You said the girl wouldn't file a report with the local police," Weicker says.

"She overheard one of the men say two police officers were helping them out. I'm thinking they were on the payroll. She didn't feel like she could." It's an oversimplification of everything Briar has been through.

"What are you hoping we'll do?" Davis asked. "Like before, it's not what you know but what you can prove. Can you prove any of this?"

I shake my head. "We have a name and an affiliation. Joseph Hosea, Righteous Brotherhood. We think he's part of a sex trafficking ring trying to find good American women to become their wives. And they're operating in or around New Jersey and the docks."

"You found this girl near the port?" Davis asks.

"Yeah, one night when Spark was dropping off payment to an informant at the docks."

Davis taps the table. "I'm not sure this is the best use of your time. Following up on missing girls."

I roll my eyes. "I know. That's why I gave the details to Weicker. This could be an op twofer. The club and the traffickers."

"I passed it to the FBI, but without a witness and proof, their hands are tied. You'd need to blow your cover to come forward. They are under-resourced for the work they're supposed to be doing without going off on a goose chase. The girl doesn't even want to give a testimony."

"So, the bottom line is you aren't going to do anything?"

Weicker puts his hands out. In surrender. "I didn't say that. I just said that without the woman, it's hard to make it a priority."

I close my mouth, refusing to give them details about Briar. Maybe it's from hanging around the club, but I'm becoming a paranoid fucker. If I tell them about her, that she's staying with me, they might find some way to get her out of there so I can focus.

And perhaps her presence is the only thing keeping me sane right now.

"I mean, we don't know if this woman was actually abducted or if she's one of those women who have a few drinks with a group of guys, lead them on, and then cry rape when they do what she went home with them for. She could be a pissed-off girlfriend for all we know."

I stand and shove the chair back. "Her hands were raw from being tied up. She was bruised."

"Miller," Weicker warns.

Davis straightens his shoulders. "Could be some kinky sex game gone wrong and the two of them have already made up, given she's not here right now as a witness."

"You better make sure I never hear you spouting that bullshit again. It's no wonder she doesn't want to come forward when a senior member of the ATF is wondering whether she was making it up. I'm leaving."

With that, I walk out of the building so I don't punch Davis in his bloated face.

I ride back to Asbury Park, everything churned up in my mind. I itch to see Briar. I want to reassure her that there are some good people who would believe her and center her in any conversation about her assault, but after today, I'll struggle. I believe Briar. I believe what she told me about hearing there are two police officers on the payroll. And I'm furious Davis believes there is a narrative where Briar brought this on herself.

Fucker is lucky I didn't punch that smug, sweaty face of his.

But I know I need to appease my bosses *and* use the club to help find the roots of the trafficking organization. They're like trip wires. Pull on one and you alert the others with the explosion.

There's a damaged car on the side of the road, and I see a woman helping Iris, the woman Spark is all messed up over, into a different vehicle.

I wonder if Spark knows.

I should message him, but then, I'm already on the wrong side of this conversation by even thinking about helping Spark and Iris like I'm cupid or some shit.

I don't need another reason for King to be pissed with me. I assume that he knows most of what happens on my phone through Vex.

Instead, I simply ride on to the club and hope I'll find my salvation along the way.

19

SAINT

The sharp wind cuts through my leather as we drive towards the Allentown clubhouse of the Iron Outlaws Pennsylvania chapter.

Briar has been in my life a week.

That's it.

And I hate that I had to leave her.

She's flipped my world around in seven days. I remember my sister going on a rant once about how the leading couples in suspense and action movies find the time to have sex in between saving the world and avoiding assassins. Her view was: if she were being chased or caught up in some life-threatening drama, sex would be the last thing on her mind. She created an adrenaline-stops-me-doing-it list that included showers and food shopping.

She also said guys wouldn't have time to be led around with their dicks.

I disagreed and said most men are led around by their dicks regardless of the situation.

Now I can prove it. Even at the very worst of times, when you know it is quite probably the most ridiculous thing you can do, you can still find yourself boning a woman you're building feelings for.

In just seven days.

I've never believed in love at first sight. Lust at first sight, I can totally get behind. But love? It takes effort and too much sacrifice.

Not that I'm thinking of Briar as the love of my life.

Not at all.

She's skewered right between a major inconvenience and . . . feeling so good against my body that I can't imagine not having more of her.

And if that were all there is to it, I wouldn't be so concerned she wasn't going to be home when I get back. That she might have decided to return to her life without saying goodbye.

As we pull up our bikes, a bunch of prospects head out of the clubhouse to keep an eye on them as a couple of brothers work with Halo and Niro to unload the weapons we brought. I haven't told Weicker.

If I had, the ATF could have hit the club on the road. Confiscated all the weapons.

And if I'd told them, then this gig would be over. And if it were over, I'd be out of the loop on what was being done to find the men who abducted Briar. This way, by staying, I can be a part of the solution.

Plus, I'm pissed at Davis. If they'd hit the club, it would have been a huge win for our department, and I don't want to see Davis's smug face taking credit.

Spark and I step into the clubhouse. Smoke hovers precariously close to the ceiling from all the cigarettes, and loud rock pounds through the speakers. There's food and drink, something that tells me the club's old ladies were here earlier setting all this up. But they aren't here now.

Tonight's for the boys.

Spark is reading something on his phone but looks up when Whip, the sergeant at arms of Allentown, calls his name and slaps his back. "Long time no see, brother," he says.

Spark grins. He told me they've been friends for years. "Way too long. I've not seen you since I got back from Afghanistan."

Whip studies Spark for a moment. "Don't envy you. That evac looked horrific. Heard about what happened. You good?"

It's a question I've been wanting Spark to answer honestly since I've grown to know him. I know too many good servicepeople who never conquer the demons they bring back from war with them. I don't like the idea that Spark could be one of them.

"Hits different when it goes that wrong," Spark says.

There is so much unspoken in his answer. He's never really spoken about the bombing at Abbey Gate in Kabul that he was involved in. I only know from the tattoos that cover his back. A guy doesn't get an altar to his friends inked on his skin if he doesn't feel that shit deep.

Whip grips Spark's shoulder. "That it does." Noticing me standing behind Spark, he extends his hand. "Saint. Good to see you. Hear you're busy saving trafficked women."

Briar's face flashes to mind. She's smiling. "I'll take it. Bastards had done a right fucking number on her. She shivered the whole time she was on the back of my bike."

"You know who it was?" Whip asks.

Spark nods. "We think it's the Righteous Brotherhood."

"Shit." Whip shakes his head as he finishes his beer. "Those fuckers are up in our faces too."

"Yeah, we tracked a truck back to Bethlehem," Spark says.

"Not surprised. I think they want to take the East, one state at a time. Keep getting caught up in territory disputes with them. We think they're getting close to a local Russian group, trying to cause instability. Real insurrectionist shit."

I can't help but think they might be bigger than we estimate. If they are insurrectionists, and partnering with the Russians, *and* trafficking women. Or perhaps that's part of the deal. Sex trafficking to and from Russia isn't infeasible. I make a mental note to follow that lead.

"You might want to hold on to some of those guns from the load we brought," Spark says.

And now I'm even more relieved I didn't tell Weicker. What most people don't realize is the work motorcycle clubs do to keep their towns peaceful. We don't want drug wars and turf wars and gun wars. We don't want pedos and traffickers. Because all those things bring police presence. The clubs work behind the scenes to deal with a large share of the unsavoriness.

"I think they might be trying to steal weapons to arm their endeavors," Spark continues. "Watch who you sell to if you sell on."

"Good to know, and I'll propose it. You guys taking them on for the trafficking?" Whip asks.

"Don't get me started on that shit," I say. I wish we could do so much more, and I need to convince King. "I'm hitting the shitter before I get mad."

"King doesn't give a shit about the women. Just wants to keep the Brotherhood out of Jersey because of what they stand for. Saint wants us to use our access to the docks to actually scout for the women being transported. King thinks that puts the advantage we currently have at risk," Spark says as I walk away.

I take a leak, then head outside. I need some air. I want to call Briar. My second phone is hidden in the false bottom of a saddlebag on my bike. The need to call her, to check in, burns. What I *should* do is pull myself together.

"You good?" King asks as he steps outside.

"Yeah. Gearing up for that," I say, tipping my chin in the direction of the clubhouse.

King laughs and leans against the wall next to me. He lights a cigarette and blows a ring of smoke into the sky. "Yeah, Wreck sure knows how to throw a party."

"I need to say something. I can't deal knowing those guys are trafficking women. I need to do something about it."

"We did something. We put a tracker on the truck. Vex is watching."

"It's not enough."

King turns to face me. "Are you questioning my judgment?"

I look up to the sky as I wonder how best to answer. "Your judgment? No. Your compassion, maybe."

He shakes his head. "Compassion in this game gets you nowhere. Especially not with women."

"You talking about Skylar?" I watched him put a bullet into the head of a woman he had feelings for, even if he never admitted them out loud.

"Not going there with you, preacher man."

"Some women let you down. But the majority are good fucking women. This feels like something we can do. The police at best are going to use due process. They're going to apply twenty percent of a cop or detective's time to it. And it will lead nowhere. We have Vex. The guy has dark web superpowers. He could help. We have access to the docks. You want these guys gone, we can do it."

"Were you always a religious man? Like, from being young, did you want to be an army chaplain?"

"Grew up in a religious home. Army seemed a good way to see the world. Sometimes you've got to do what you've gotta do, right?"

None of it is a lie. Yet it is. He doesn't seem to notice I didn't exactly answer the question or claim to be a chaplain.

"You have the power to do something about this, King. To stop women like your sister, Gwen, from being ripped from their families. You know what this feels like. To not see your sister for over a decade. Don't make someone else have to go through this." It's a shit move on my part to bring Gwen into it, given she reappeared in the summer after a decade missing. "You know something of those feelings of loss."

King scratches the side of his face, his fingertips rasping along his bristles. "You're not going to let this drop, are you?"

"Not while there's a chance you could change your mind."

He takes a drag on his cigarette. "Fine. If Vex agrees he wants to do it, you can start the recon to understand their organization, what they might be doing, etc. Action requires a club vote. Come to me when you have something worth sharing."

"You won't regret this," I say.

King shrugs. "It causes shit for the club, I'll kill you before they do."

And with that he goes inside.

I can't help the grin. Maybe this is my excuse with the ATF. They aren't going to like this, but this is the operation I'm here for. Right place at the right time to build a rock-solid case. And if all else fails, I can tell them I'm following my president's orders. It's a stretch, but it'll keep the heat off my back.

Perhaps I'll chat with Vex now. He's at the bar with Clutch.

"Vex, you got a sec?"

He lights a cigarette. "Sure thing, preacher man. What's up?"

"I want to dig deep on the Righteous Brotherhood. Treat it like an op. Reconnaissance. Intel. Where their funding is coming from, who their buyers are. There has to be a way in."

"Is King in?" he asks.

"All the way. Said to take anything to him that needed a vote."

Vex nods. "Good enough. Where do you want to start?"

By midnight, we have a plan. And by two in the morning, I'm drunk and in boisterous conversation with Halo, King, Spark, and Clutch. Because, thanks to my current actions and my meeting with Davis, I don't know how many nights with them I have left.

20

BRIAR

"You stuck there, Briar?"

I glance across the yard to where Hap is standing in a pair of old camp shorts and a T-shirt so faded, I can't make it out what was once on the front of it.

My hand is on the handle of Saint's truck, where it's probably been for the past ten minutes while I debated my life choices. I spent the morning doing what Saint suggested. I wrote everything down about what happened. Every sound, word, feeling, action. I even sketched all their faces and ink. It put me back there, and now I feel emotionally adrift. Untethered.

"Maybe a little," I say, walking toward him.

"What's got you bamboozled?"

I can't help but smile. "Do people still even say *bamboozled*, Hap?"

He shrugs. "This old fella does. What's got you so you can't move forward or backward?"

I study his clear blue eyes and imagine that's how Saint's eyes will look when he's older. And I think of Saint telling me how I haven't told anyone what happened. "I was abducted. Saint saved me. And I've been hiding here ever since."

Hap's eyes widen in horror. "Jesus. I had no idea. Are you . . . ?"

"I'm fine. Well, physically at least. Mentally though? I'm a wreck. Haven't been past the end of the driveway without Saint going with me."

"Poor thing. Is he away?"

"Yeah. And he's back today from a trip. I thought it would be nice to clean the house and cook him a nice meal tonight. To say thank you. Then I debated if he'd mind me borrowing his truck. Then I debated if I could drive there without freaking out. Then, I—"

"Okay. I get the idea. Let's go." Hap turns and stomps over his lawn.

"Go where, Hap?"

"I'll drive. I need to grab some groceries and run a couple of errands myself."

Relief floods through me. I told someone, and they didn't freak out. I jog after him, and we drive to the store.

"You need me to come with you?" Hap asks.

I'm feeling bolstered by his presence, that he helped me get here. And the mall is plenty busy, so I don't feel quite as scared. "I think I've got this, Hap."

He awkwardly pats my shoulder. "I'm glad."

With my phone and the new card from my bank, I'm all set. Hap and I agree to meet back at his car in an hour. My first stop is to grab some new underwear. All I brought with me from my house is the practical stuff, but it might be nice to surprise Saint with something a little more enticing. I grab a new body cream and spray because I found out this morning that the ad agency decided to go with my graphics for the botanicals ad. They want to see me in person next week with some minor revisions and proposals for more work.

I surprise myself by walking by a shoe store. If I go in there, I'll be late to meet Hap.

Then I whizz around the store. I grab all the things Saint likes, including two new bags of bow-tie pasta. But I also throw in a couple of steaks to grill and chicken to make a casserole. At Christmas, my mom used to make the most delicious potatoes, and I wonder how she made them. There was cream and potatoes, and maybe nutmeg. I debate messaging her for the recipe.

But a recipe request will lead to questions I don't want to answer. Certainly not in the middle of a grocery store. We've never really understood each other. I was too quiet as a child; she was too quiet of a parent.

So I tap the dish into my phone and find a similar recipe online.

When I've found and paid for everything, I push the cart into the lot and wait for Hap. I'm relieved when I see him.

His eyes remain stern. "Now that I know, I see it. I'm pissed someone took advantage of you."

"I'm okay, Hap. Saint helps."

Hap pauses as he opens the trunk of his car. "That's another thing. A veteran knows when another vet has seen things. Saint has seen things. It ages the soul and puts the whisper of a ghost in their eyes. I'm an old man. Perhaps I don't know what I'm saying. But be careful, Briar. It's easy to confuse safety with something else. I've seen the way that man looks at you. I don't think he's a risk to you. But there's obviously a much bigger story."

We dump my bags into the trunk as I think about what

he's said. "He's done nothing but care for me, Hap. I think he might be the first person since my pop who really has."

Hap adds his own bags and closes the trunk. "Just be careful. That's all I'm saying."

I think about what Hap said for the next couple of hours, as I clean and prepare a chicken casserole that will come together quickly with the fresh bread I bought. While I'm in the shower, I conclude one thing. I'm letting an elderly neighbor who likely doesn't have a lot of excitement in his life make me doubt my developing feelings for Saint.

There will be time for serious conversations between the two of us, but this is all so new. And I am the worst for falling irrevocably and quickly. I do need to learn to slow down. To throttle those feelings so I don't fall back into my old ways of giving my heart to men who don't deserve it.

Instead, I decide I'm simply going to seduce Saint.

When I wrote down the events of what happened to me this morning, it put some things into perspective for me. I've been acting and thinking like a victim. And I realize I don't like that word. It makes me feel like I have no control over the narrative. I obviously carry baggage about the word because a victim, to me, is someone who can't get out of the cycle.

I want to be a survivor.

No, a thriver. And I don't even care if that's a real word.

I'm going to fake it until I make it.

And I want to enjoy the feel of this man's hands on my body because I've always enjoyed sex.

I wasn't raped. I wasn't sexually assaulted.

I was abused, yes.

He touched me without consent. He beat me.

And I'm incredibly fortunate my journey ended where it did.

It's time to focus on that.

When I finished writing, I wrote fifty things I'm grateful for since I escaped in that lot. Shoes, because those stones had cut my feet when I ran. Coffee made how I like it, because who knows if I would ever have been given coffee again if I hadn't escaped. It reframed so much for me. Every reason I was grateful for something, it was because I had enough agency to escape.

And that was perhaps the most empowering revelation of all.

After I shower, I use all the goodies I bought on my skin. Then I pull on the new underwear. It all helps, grounding me back in my body. I focus on the slide of my hands over my skin. I cup my own breasts, feeling their weight. I press my palm over my underwear and feel my own heat.

It's a sensual experience just to soothe myself.

When the door slams, I jump but refocus on my goal. Saint is home, and I want to give him a welcome to remember.

"Briar," he shouts from the hallway. "It's me."

"Like I wouldn't know your voice," I say and lean against the wall.

He looks up with a smile, then looks away but does a double take. "Holy shit, you look good."

Dropping whatever was in his hands, he walks toward me. His gaze slides down my body and back up. "This all for me?" he asks.

I nod. "Welcome home."

He shamelessly reaches for his cock and adjusts it in his denim. When he stands inches away from me, the energy between us is palpable. A hiss and fizz of tension. Anticipation. He slides a single finger beneath the shoulder strap of my bra, his knuckle scorching my skin. "You know, last night, there was a more pussy on hand than you can count. And usually, I'd partake. But . . . you were on my mind, Bri. Couldn't stop thinking about the way it felt when I sank into you. Couldn't stop thinking about the way you felt against me. The way you smell. The way you smile."

And I do just that—I smile at his words. "Well, because you were such a good boy . . ." I reach for the zipper of his jeans and lower it slowly. When I reach inside and grip him through his boxer briefs, he grunts.

I slip to my knees and take off his boots and socks before lowering his jeans and boxer briefs. His cock is hard, standing proudly against his equally hard body. I lick my way down the V-shaped muscles to his groin. As I do so, Saint tugs off his cut and pulls his long-sleeved Henley over his head.

I lick along the thick vein on the underside, and his cock twitches in my hand. When I get to the head, running saliva over his slit, he thrusts his hand into my hair and grips it firmly. I love the sting of it. He's thick, and I stretch my mouth wide to suck him inside.

"Fuck, sweetheart," he gasps and places his other palm on the wall behind him. His hips begin to move, not enough that he's thrusting down my throat, although I do wonder what that will feel like. I'm about to take him deeper when he tugs my head away and grabs me beneath my arms. "Don't want to come down your throat today. It's been a really long ride, and I spent most of it thinking about your pussy."

He grabs a condom from his wallet, then leads me to the sofa where he sits. "Kneel between my legs while I put this on," he says, and I do as he says. I'm not submissive, but I used to love role-play and fantasy. I'm happy to give him the mood and visual he wants.

I stroke his cock up and down while he opens the condom packet, and I watch as he confidently rolls it on. "Now get up here and welcome me home," he says.

I stand and slip the panties down my legs, but I leave my bra on because it makes my boobs look good. Saint places his hands on the back of the sofa, and I climb on to straddle his thighs. It's early evening, but still light outside. I'm not a hundred percent certain that someone wouldn't be able to see us from the street if they tried hard enough. But I don't care about that.

I focus on the way I felt after I wrote my list. How I'm going to thrive. How I'm going to take this gift I've been given with Saint. I focus on the way his gaze makes me feel: Desired. Sexual.

He's so hard, it takes less than a second to position him at my entrance, and then I lower myself, enveloping him with my warmth. I toss my head back and sigh at how good it feels. Saint's hands grab my hips as he rocks me back and forth.

"Fuck, thought I could let you lead," he groans, lifting me and slamming me down hard.

He takes my hands and encourages me to kneel a little higher so he can fuck me. All the muscles in his abdomen tense as he thrusts up into me. I don't know if it's the places he's hitting or the intensity of his gaze and pace, but I feel myself riding the start of an orgasm in record time. "Don't stop," I gasp.

"Yeah? You like that?" he grunts. The frame of the sofa creaks. We might break it, but I don't have it in me to care when he feels so good.

"Saint," I say as everything in me begins to tighten. "I'm going to come."

"Do it," he instructs. "Come all over me. I want to feel you squeeze my cock."

And I do.

Stars form in my peripheral vision. I close my eyes and shatter. It feels good. Feels empowering. I really don't want it to stop.

As I slow down, he puts his thumb at the place where we're joined, gathers some of my cream, then licks it clean. His eyes narrow as he reaches for my neck and pulls my lips to his in a bruising kiss that makes me feel cherished and vital.

I taste myself when his tongue duals mine.

With little effort, Saint stands, walks us three feet to the wall, and slams my back against it. His body holds mine to it as he presses his hand to my throat, not hard enough that I choke, but enough pressure to feel it. "That day in your apartment, this is what I really wanted to do."

With no further warning, he withdraws and slams home hard. I feel my back inch up the wall. He does it again, with pace and precision. Each time he bottoms out hard, each time he goes a little faster. "Your cunt was made for me. Feels so fucking good."

His lips hit mine. It's messy. Sloppy. Too much movement. He bites down on my collarbone hard. I don't normally come twice, but I feel a second orgasm building.

I wrap my arms around him and hold tight.

"Ahh, fuck," he grunts at the side of my neck.

"Saint. Please. I need this."

I can't explain how it feels, as though the universe can be distilled to the one place his cock hits me inside.

"I've got you. Come for me, Briar. Soak me," he commands. And we come together. Me, with my mouth wide in a scream that has no sound. Him, repeatedly muttering *shit* over and over as he loses control of his thrusts and slams hard inside me.

I can feel him pulse.

I'm certain he can feel me do the same.

"Welcome home," I mutter as I slide my hands into his hair.

21

SAINT

"Yo, Saint, can we make a detour first?" Spark says two days later as we climb on our bikes.

He's been distant since he got back from his long ride. Which is weird, because today he actually looks happy. Not sure where the fuck his head is at. Was going to try and talk about it with him tonight over beers, before King asked if we'd do another cash run to Jasper Haven at the Port Authority.

"Sure thing. What are we doing?"

"Need you as a lookout while I have a conversation with someone. Have my back and shit."

"Whatever you need," I say as I start my bike. He starts his, and I follow him to an automotive repair shop, a small garage with grease up all the walls. A lanky guy in overalls is working on an old Buick, even though it's after ten in the evening. He has lights angled under the hood.

Spark looks around. There are neighboring buildings, but they are all closed for the night. "What are you thinking, Spark?" I ask.

He shakes his head and pulls on a single leather glove.

"Stay there and let me know if you see anyone."

I've never seen him dispense anything other than deserved justice, so I half watch the street and half watch Spark, who drags the lanky guy over the workbench.

"No. Don't. I'm sorry. I'm sorry," the guy yells as he fights to free his wrist from Spark's grip.

But Spark is unrelenting as he traps the man's fingers in a vise. The man's knees buckle, and he lurches awkwardly toward the floor.

I make a move to get off my bike. To intervene.

Spark says something too quietly for me to hear, then picks up a heavy industrial wrench in his gloved hand.

"I won't do it again," the man screams. "I'll do better." Tears and snot pour down his face.

Then Spark raises the wrench and slams it down on the man's secured knuckles.

"One," the man screams.

Jesus, Spark's making him count. And he repeats the action until the guy hoarsely says five.

Spark pats the top of the man's head, then walks back to me, tipping his head from left to right, then giving his shoulders a roll. There's a smile on his face. "Let's get out of here."

I want to ask questions, but he's right, we should go.

But once we're parked up in the lot we rescued Briar in, waiting for Haven to show his face, I ask, "You want to tell me why we just smacked that guy down on the way over here?"

Spark grins. "Nope. Other than his hand now matches his little kid's."

Jesus. I should have known he'd have good reason. For a moment I wonder what my life would have been like if someone had given my father a taste of his own medicine. My moral compass shifts again. I want the freedom to do that. I wish I was free of the shackles of the ATF and their rules. "Fair enough."

There's been limited traffic on the side road, so it's unusual to see two vehicles headed towards us. Even as I wonder if one is Jasper, they pass us and turn into a shipping container firm.

The first is a van.

"You see that?" Spark asks, and at the same time I realize the second vehicle is the black truck from Bethlehem with Nazi-loving stickers, the one Briar was in that night she found us.

"Saw it." I hand the envelope of cash to Spark. "Pay the man. I'm going looking."

"Bad strategy, Saint. We need to pay off this guy before tomorrow, but you going off alone is a recipe for a chest full of lead as you fall into the Hudson."

"It's a risk I gotta take," I say as I start to sprint. I need to know what those fuckers are doing. I bring to mind Briar's fears for her safety, the tears she cried, the dreams she's had. Rage consumes me. I'm judge, jury, and executioner. Stopping these men is the one thing I can give her.

Suddenly, a scream pierces the air, and I stop so I can listen.

Spark catches up to me. "Where'd that come from?" he whispers.

I shake my head. "Motherfuckers. I don't see shit."

We scramble between the fence and side of the building, avoiding years of built-up debris. As we hit the end of the wall and peer into the darkness around the corner, I see the truck.

My hand is on the hilt of my weapon, ready to draw, as I see five men climb out. They're armed to the teeth. So are the four men who walk out of a warehouse to meet them.

I pull my gun and step forward, ready to take out Joseph Hosea, when I am yanked back, my ass up against a wall before I have time to process Spark's fury.

"Where the fuck do you think you're going?" he whispers.

"They have women in that van." I think of them. Of women like Briar. We need to get to them. Get them out.

"Yeah, and they have bullets in those nine semiautomatics they're carrying. Lots of them. It's a suicide mission. Can't let you go in, brother."

He increases the pressure of his arm against my chest, and I suck in a breath, trying to reconcile the fact I know he's right to challenge the desperate need to take action.

"If we die today, it helps no one," he says.

I hate that he's right. It's a suicide mission. Nine heavily armed men against the two of us with limited ammo. I nod, but angrily shrug off Spark's hold. "Where's the van?"

Relying on the darkness of the shadows, we crane our necks and look around the building. Two of the men close the doors on a blue utilitarian shipping container, and I catch a partial number.

"I'm guessing in there," Spark says.

"Motherfuckers. What if there are women in there too?" I say. "We can't just let them be taken. We need to do something."

Unable to control my frustration, I let my voice grow louder, and two of them look in our direction.

"Move," Spark says, shoving me back down the side of the building.

I can't leave them, but Spark shoves me again. "Don't make me fucking carry you. Run."

So we do, before hopping on our motorbikes and evading the men on foot.

As we get back to Asbury Park, I pull off to my home. I know Spark is expecting me to follow him in to talk to King, but I can't let those women go unsupported. I dig my burner phone from its hiding spot and call Jensen.

"Jensen," he says roughly.

"It's Ryker. I need your help." I tell him every detail I can think of. There was a sticker with a partial number on the container. I tell him about the men. And then I tell him why I didn't feel like I could call Weicker, that he thinks this is a distraction.

"I'm on it. Go. Do what you have to do," Jensen says. "Keep safe."

I trust him to do the right thing. "Thanks."

The lot of the clubhouse empty when I finally park my bike next to Spark's and hurry inside. I can see him in King's office with Vex and Clutch. I stride to the office to join them, but Halo, the former Navy SEAL who is the club's road captain, puts his arm out to stop me. "No can do, preacher man. Private conversation."

"No. I was there with Spark; I know what's going on."

Halo shakes his head. "I can guarantee they ain't having the conversation you think they're having. King said admit no one. You know the rules. Go get a beer and chill the fuck out."

I see Spark jump to his feet and front to Clutch. They stare each other down until King says something that makes them both turn to face him.

King tips his chin, and Spark sits down.

"Halo. I need to go help Spark with whatever this is."

Halo shakes his head. "Trust me, you don't wanna get yourself mixed up in whatever this shit is until it's resolved."

I wish I could hear what was being said. It's obviously tense. And three of them against Spark.

They all look at Vex's laptop, and I see the color drain from Spark's features.

Vex says something apologetically as he runs his hand over his hair.

Jesus. This shouldn't all matter so much. I shouldn't care about any of them. But I do. I don't think King really wants Spark's blood on his hands. I don't think he'd cope with the guilt of it after killing Skylar. Clearly, whatever Spark was just told has shocked the shit out of him.

"Watch your hand, Saint. You don't want to do that," Halo says.

I look down and see my hand is on my weapon.

Shit.

I let go and raise my hands.

When I look back into the room, I see King is watching me. He raises an eyebrow, and I hope the look I pass him conveys what I want it to.

Spark slams an impassioned fist to his chest and grabs his cut, pulling the patch away from his chest and directing it at King. When he's done, he slumps back in the chair and rubs his face with his hands.

By now, I'm not the only one watching. Niro has stepped in beside me. I'm not sure whether it was at Halo's request or because he's concerned too.

"He's in shit, but King won't hurt him," Niro says. "He'll make him pay though. He's a vengeful fucker when he wants to be."

I take a deep breath. One day I'll be on the end of it.

Spark shakes his head and walks out of the office, headed to the bar. He looks ruined. I go to walk to him, but King stops me from following. "I know you're concerned, preacher. But give me and Clutch a minute first."

"He already carries too much," I say, knowing the burden of the unacknowledged PTSD he has.

King stares deep into my eyes. "He's not the only one, is he?" He doesn't wait for my answer before he heads to the bar.

Spark throws back a shot of tequila as Clutch places his hand on Spark's shoulder. He sits to Spark's left, King to his right.

It's only when I see the whisper of a smile on Spark's face that the tension across my chest loosens.

Finally, King stands and gets everyone's attention with a loud whistle. "Spark is claiming Iris. Little Irish just became one of our own. Because we aren't scared of the Irish mob. Because we're the motherfuckin' Iron Outlaws."

People cheer, shots are poured, and King grabs one and brings it to me. I take it, and King holds his glass to mine, one hand on my shoulder.

"Good news for your boy, yeah?" he says.

I glance over at Spark, who is smiling at something Clutch said. "You made the right call."

King studies me intently. "So did you. And if I ever see you go for your weapon again when I know it's going to be pointing at me . . . I'll gut you with a fishing knife before I fucking kill you without hesitation. Sláinte."

And with that, he knocks back his shot, then disappears with Halo.

I watch him go and blow out a breath. Fuck me. I'm getting sloppy. I'm gonna get myself killed.

"You good?" Spark asks as he comes to stand next to me.

"Yeah . . . yeah. Fine. What happened?"

Spark looks toward King's office. "The short version is Iris. The long version is I . . ." A smile crosses his face. It's fucking goofy.

"You love her."

"Yeah. But there's more to it. I'll fill you in over drinks. It's to do with who caused her accident. I got the plates and asked Vex about it. Anyway, Vex told King because it was proof I'm tied up with her. I don't know what it all means, but I'm sorry I've hidden shit from you. Was waiting to see if me and her was more than . . . well, you know. . . physical shit. Didn't want to bring problems to the club's door. Didn't want to go against my clubs' orders either. Didn't want to drag you into it. But she . . . she eases me, Saint."

He huffs and looks down at the ground, as if embarrassed by what he's shared.

Men. We're shit at admitting our feelings to one another.

"You deserve that, Spark. I'm glad King bent his rule." I also pray he'll bend the rules for me when the time comes.

"Can I ask you something?" he asks, looking up again.

"Sure."

"You know anyone who went through counselling with the VA?"

The truth is, I do. But I can't put Spark in touch with them because those people, if they speak to him, may give my cover away. "I guess I've known some guys who've gone through it, though not really anyone I'm close with. But if you're even thinking about it, my suggestion is to do it. Why now?"

"Because I had a moment yesterday when I wasn't this guy. A moment with Iris when I . . . fuck . . . when the world made sense again. When I didn't feel all this . . . weight, I guess."

I know how that feels. I wish I could tell him about Briar and have them both over for dinner. I wonder if Iris and Briar would like camping. I grip his shoulder. "Then I already love Iris for helping you feel that."

Two hours later, I can barely feel my lips. Spark is as drunk as I am. King sits next to me, as if our earlier conversation never happened. As we talk, I remember what happened in the garage before we hit the dock.

"You wanna tell me the full story of the guy and the Vise?" I ask. My words slur a little. I normally try to stay sober-ish, but I guess a member claiming an old lady is a big deal. Shots and beer have been flowing all night.

Spark places his glass on the table. "Iris teaches kindergarten, and one of her kids keeps getting beat on by his old man. It upsets her. Told me it looked as though the kid's fingers had been repeatedly slammed in a drawer. Fucker'll think twice before hitting his kid again."

"As the child of a Baptist preacher who routinely beat seven fucking bells out of his kids and occasionally whipped them for failing to remember Bible verses, I appreciate what you did."

King slaps my shoulder in a gesture. "No kid should go through that, man."

"You need me to go put *his* fingers in a Vise?" Spark asks. The last three words run together. "We could go slewing," he says, repeating the word I'd used earlier.

I'm about to respond when I realize what I've done. I planted seeds of the truth about who I am. The veins at the side of my head throb, even as I'm overwhelmed by these men who'd have my back.

And any kind of response gets stuck in my throat.

King mistakes my action for sorrow, and he grips me again, shaking me slightly. "Family always looks out for its own. You need to make that shit right, we'll all go with you."

And even as I sink as though my foot is tied to an anchor, my heart feels the tiniest flicker of warmth.

22

BRIAR

I t's early morning several days later, and I'm wide awake. Saint came home at some point after I'd gone to bed last night, and for the first time, I slept okay without him there to hold my hand. Now he's wrapped around my body, but I want to let him sleep. I have a meeting in the city later today, and he's agreed to drive me.

I know I should start to do things on my own. I could take the train. Heck, I could attempt to go back to my apartment. But today is not the day to do all those things, given my heart rate still spikes at the mere thought of it.

I ease his arm from over me, and he flops onto his back. His hair covers part of his face, but I resist the temptation to move it away before getting out of bed.

Once I've loaded the coffee grounds and pressed the button, the coffee maker splutters to life. Yesterday, I bought a much nicer blend, and I made the executive decision to toss the sludge he was drinking before. When it's done, I pour a cup, add some creamer, and go sit outside. A hoodie of Saint's sits over the back of the chair. It smells of him as I pull it on. The stones are chilled beneath my feet, but feeling the early morning sun on my face is worth the cool.

It's not the same doing this in the city. New York is noisy, no matter what time of day I sit outside on my tiny balcony. A car horn, a siren, voices of groups as they go out for dinner or return home from a nightclub. Here, it's peaceful.

I hear his footsteps before I feel him stand behind me. Saint slides a hand down the front of my hoodie—his hoodie—and beneath the tank I wore with my shorts. His fingers seek my breast, rubbing over my nipple as he wraps his other arm around me and nuzzles my neck. His erection pokes my back through jeans he's pulled on.

"Woke up and you weren't there. I didn't like it," he says. His breath is warm on my neck, and I tilt my head to allow him access.

"Didn't like it, or didn't know what to do with this?" I press back against his cock, feeling it twitch against me.

"Both. I mean. I could have jerked off and told you about it later but was wondering if that was my only option."

I thread my hands behind me to grab his hips. "Watching you do that would be hot."

"Watching you watch would be hot too. But I prefer audience participation."

His grumble makes me smile. "I'm nervous about the meeting this afternoon with the ad agency."

His lips make their way up the side of my neck to behind my ear; the action makes me shiver. "Well, I have the perfect plan to help you forget about it for at least ten minutes. And a morning quickie before breakfast is basically fasted cardio."

"In case you haven't noticed, I don't work out. The squishy bits of me don't appreciate fasted anything."

Saint laughs and takes my wrist, leading me to the

bedroom. "That's a good thing, because the hard bits of me really appreciate the squishy bits of you."

When we get to the bedroom, he tosses me onto the bed as though I weigh nothing. I've never been overly concerned about my body, but the fact I'm with a man who can toss me around feels extra special.

And Saint delivers.

Within minutes we're both naked; maybe four more minutes later, I come on his tongue. I love the way he throws his whole face into the endeavor. It makes me feel cherished and delicious.

The same way I felt when he encouraged me to ride his face. *You gonna hover there politely or are you going to fuck my face like you want it?*

"Saint," I gasp as he wipes his mouth along his forearm.

"Tastes so good," he says. "One day, we'll go somewhere hot where nobody knows us, and I'll tie you to the bed and do that over and over until you don't know which way is up."

I grin at the idea. "I like the sound of that."

"Good. But for now . . ." He reaches for my hips and flips me onto my stomach. I can't help but laugh as he puts on a condom. When he finally pulls me to my knees and enters me from behind, it's heaven.

He places his hand between my shoulder blades and pushes my forehead to the bed. "Fuck, you look good like this."

The bed creaks and the headboard hits the wall as he thrusts into me. I reach forward, pressing my hands against it to stop sliding forward. Saint kneads my ass, digging his fingers into my skin, holding me wide.

His thumb brushes over my other hole, making me tremble.

"Like that," I say. "Please . . ."

Using my own wetness as lube, he eases him thumb inside me a fraction and I feel so full.

In moments I come hard, reveling in the fact I orgasmed twice, even as stars dance in my peripheral vision. It's like my body is a cornfield in the middle of a drought and Saint is the rainstorm.

He grips the back of my neck and pushes me down on the bed again. "Wrists, now. Hands behind your back." His tone is raw with need.

I do as he says, and he grips them.

It takes him a moment to come, and I love the sharp shout of his release.

My body is sated, but my heart trips when he lies us back down and kisses my wrists, which still have the marks left by the cuffs and ropes.

"It's good, right?" he asks. "This. You and me."

I think about all the conversations I've had with my pop. I'm not sure how to trust what I'm feeling. It feels like the early days after a crisis are not the right time to fall in love. Heck, they aren't even the right time to cut your own bangs.

But he's right. I reach for this hand. "Yes, it does feel good."

We're yin and yang in so many different ways. Somehow, we're working.

I think about it as we drive into the city after lunch. "Do you love the energy of New York?"

Saint navigates the Manhattan streets to the address I gave him. The sidewalks are clogged, and the roads jammed. "Not feeling it right now, I gotta be honest."

I laugh. "I grew up in a Rust Belt city. Dad worked in the steel industry in Gary, Indiana. But the rise of foreign steel and automation meant less American steel, which meant fewer workers, which meant less businesses. He's always believed in honest pay for an honest day's work. Except the company he works for is always cost cutting. Dad just takes it; he's stopped being angry about soaring company profits and CEO salaries. He lives with the illusion of job security. As a result, there were times when it felt like I was living in a ghost town."

Saint takes my hand and squeezes it. "You wanted to get out of there?"

"I did. Don't think my parents will ever leave. Especially Dad. You know, he's never been on an airplane. He thought I was getting ideas above my station by going to college and that it was stupid to 'get a degree in drawing.' I mean, he was proud when I got a scholarship, but he still thinks people with degrees don't get the real world. And I understand his perspective, because the people shafting him left, right, and center are fancy consultants with fancier degrees. I wonder if his fears are because the world he's built for himself is all he knows, and there's safety in that."

"You see similar kinds of thinking regarding the army. Some of the kids who enlist are straight-up army brats. Grandfather was army, dad was army, and now they are third generation who want a piece of it. But others only enlist because they've been told since birth that this was their path out. And it works for some. It really does. Ask Spark and he'll tell you that he found a freedom in the discipline. I found freedom in the work. But it's never gonna work for everyone."

I look out of the window and see the deli, the laundromat, the bodega, the ballpark, all the yellow cabs, and the diversity of the people on the sidewalk. "At least they travelled with the army. Saw something of the world. Although there are better places to go than a war zone. If you're born in Indiana and encouraged to stay in Indiana, you never get the chance to broaden your worldview."

Saint bites down on his lip for a second. "I suppose it depends whether you are running from something or to something. Whether you are staying because you are scared or because you feel perfectly happy where you are. Like me, I was running from my homelife. The army was simply the vehicle. My dad believed spare the rod, spoil the child. He'd beat us with whatever was within arm's reach. A shoe, a whip, the Bible."

I turn to face him and place my arm on his bicep. "Ryker, that's horrific. I'm so sorry."

He glances at me. "*Saint.*"

"Shit. Sorry. But you can't tell me something so sad and not expect me to feel for you."

"And that's why we never use real names, so you don't feel compelled to. But there was a time or two when Dad would wave that Bible about and get folks at church to touch it for some reason, and I would bite back laughter, knowing the last surface the good book touched was my teen ass."

I laugh in spite of the story. "That's awful."

He shrugs. "So's beating your kids because they can't immediately bring 2 Chronicles 6:1 to mind."

I lean across the arm rest and kiss his bicep. "You had to remember all that?"

"Then said Solomon, the Lord hath said that he would dwell in the thick darkness."

"I'm so sorry you had to exist there," I say.

Saint chuckles. "No. That's 2 Chronicles 6:1. His approach may have been cruel, but it was effective. Twenty-five years later, and I still remember it."

A cab cuts us off, and Saint mutters a curse. "The traffic's a shit show."

"I wanted the chaos and the hustle and every TV show I'd ever seen about single women living here with all the shoes. Mainly the shoes. But it was a life so much bigger than mine. I knew at some point in my life, I was going to live here."

"And now?" Saint asks, turning onto the block the agency is on.

I look down at my bag with my laptop in it, the one filled with ideas I'm prepared to pitch. "This should feel like my best life. But somehow it doesn't."

Saint pulls up at the double yellow lines in front of the ad agency. A car honks, but he turns to face me. "Only you get to decide when you are done with this part of your dream. Don't let them take that from you."

I glance towards the building. There's a wide expanse of sidewalk between the truck and the entrance. It's maybe thirty feet. It feels like miles.

"Hey," Saint says. "Small steps. Literally and figuratively. Now go kick ass in your meeting, and I'll be right here."

"You shouldn't have to wait. You shouldn't have had to bring me. If I want to be here, I'm going to have to get comfortable with the train and the subway and the dark and—"

Saint presses his lips to mine. They're soft and comforting. "Steps, Rose."

The use of my real name shakes me out of the panic I was spiraling into. "Thank you."

"Anytime. Now go. I'll grab food for the trip home. Your work, it's good. Don't let them tell you otherwise."

And I remind myself of his words all the way to the agency's reception.

23

SAINT

Honestly, I hate New York.

As I lean against the truck, all I can hear are car horns and traffic and the rumble of the subway beneath my feet. There's a weird-ass yeasty smell coming from some nearby drains, and people are walking past a woman sitting amongst all her bags and belongings and her ratty sleeping bag as if she doesn't matter. As if she's inconsequential. I bought her a loaded bagel from the deli to eat, but she looks like she needs another fifty of them to fill out the gaunt hollow of her cheeks.

I can't decide what the fuck is wrong with this place.

The tall buildings with their flashy designs and glossy finish shout money.

The people sitting in their shadows are broke. Or broken.

Everyone's heads are down, focused on their phones. They have no clue of the world going on around them. I feel like sticking my foot out and tripping one of them to see what happens.

I look up at the building Briar went into. I know she's proud of her designs. I admire her ability to park everything else and focus on her work. On Tuesday, she was sitting on a stool at the kitchen island when I got home with a mild hangover. Her shirt was slipping off her shoulders, and I was feeling horny.

I stepped up behind her and slid my hand beneath her shirt as I kissed her neck. She tilted her head, gave me a little room to work, sighed, and then yanked her shirt back up her shoulder before asking me which shade of purple looked better. Not gonna lie, they both looked the exact same goddamn shade, but apparently that was the wrong answer. I got an eye roll and no sex.

I smile to myself, thinking about the way we came together later that morning.

"Preacher man." The Irish accent tells me exactly who is speaking to me. "What are you doing in my neck of the woods?"

I glance down at my watch before I turn to face Cillian Ó Ceallaigh. He's wearing a black suit, crisp white shirt, and shoes so polished you can see your reflection in them. Two men loom ominously behind me. The bulge beneath their jackets tells me they're carrying.

"An errand for a friend," I say. And, as if I'd planned it all along, I add, "There's a reason I'm not wearing my colors. Respect and all that."

Cillian studies me intently, then steps right up into my space. I'm taller than Cillian, but only by an inch or so. And I figure, given the cut of that suit, he's got a bare-knuckle fighter's build. "I find out King sent you down here to gather intel on us, I'm going to rip your balls off and shove them down your throat."

"Yeah. He sent a single man, without his cut, to stand on

a sidewalk in Manhattan on the off chance I see something. That really speaks to genius."

Cillian purses his lips. "You want to watch that mouth of yours, preacher man. Stick to Bible quotes. Leave my city to me."

"Thus I will punish the world for its evil and the wicked for their guilt. I will put an end to the pride of the arrogant, the insolence of tyrants I will humble."

There's silence for a moment. "I heard you were a Baptist, preacher man."

It's starting to bug me that he's using the name my club sometimes uses for me. "And?" I say.

"I've always thought Baptists favored the King James Bible. Shouldn't that quote be 'And I will punish the world for their evil, and the wicked for their iniquity; and I will cause the arrogancy of the proud to cease, and will lay low the haughtiness of the terrible.'"

My stomach flips, but I maintain the harsh grin. "Perhaps I thought it would resonate better with an Irishman if it came from a Bible he used at Mass on Sundays."

Maybe he suspects something, but the enemy of mine enemy is my friend. He hates the club. I'm meant to be on the other side of the club. It was one small slip. "Perhaps the words spoken should concern you more than the source."

I pull myself up to my full height and cross my arms in front of my chest. I want to retaliate so bad, I can taste it. But out of the corner of my eye, I see Briar jog down the steps of the building.

Fuck me.

She's wearing navy and orange. I think it's her favorite color combination. Her long blonde hair I love to fist swings in the watery sunlight.

"Hey," she says, when she reaches us. "I'm all done."

I see Cillian glance down her body, then back up. "And who are you, little one?"

There is uncertainty in her eyes as she looks between us.

"She's my neighbor's granddaughter who needed a ride for an important interview. And now we need to be going."

Cillian disregards me and takes Briar's hand. "*Conas atá tú? Cillian, is ainm dom.*"

"I'm good," she says without batting an eyelid. "Pleased to meet you, Cillian."

Cillian raises an eyebrow without letting go of her hand. I'm ready to rip his motherfucking hand off, but one of the things with bomb disposal, you learn that taking any unnecessary action can lead to detonation. Briar does not look distressed.

"You speak Gaelic?" he asks.

"*Nuair is gá in am riachtanais.*"

Cillian grins.

"We need to get going," I say.

"Not until I know why such a pretty young American speaks my language like she was born to it."

"Irish grandfather," Briar says. She looks up at me. "I told Pop I'd be back by one to help him get to the doctor's."

I make a show of looking at my watch. "Get in the truck."

She does as I ask, and I wait until I hear the door slam.

"What's her name?" Cillian asks.

"Like I'd tell you." Shit. Now it looks like she really does mean more to me than my neighbor's daughter.

"You Outlaws seem to be collecting Irish daughters and nieces and grandchildren."

I huff, as if indifferent. "She's not one of yours. She's not the daughter of anyone you know or care about."

"Maybe she is. Maybe she isn't. Maybe I'll find out

anyway. Rats are everywhere in every organization. You know this."

He means as an Iron Outlaw, because there is no way he's onto my cover. But my chest tightens at his comments anyway. "There is nothing to be read into me in the city with a woman who speaks Irish, you suspicious bastard."

"It's been . . . interesting," Cillian says. "Perhaps I should ask King to give me a courtesy call when you're coming over the border."

"Or perhaps you should chill the fuck out because we don't want New York."

Cillian straightens the cuff of his shirt. "But that's only because you're smart enough to know you won't win. Drive safe, preacher man."

"Asshole," I mutter as I get into the truck. Now what do I do? Call King and tell him I saw Cillian? He's going to ask why I was there. Or do I wait for Cillian to tell King, which I don't think is going to happen? "Fuck."

"Who was that man?" Briar asks.

I start the truck and glance at his back as he steps into a building behind us. "The head of an Irish crime family. The club has a very tentative peace with him."

"None of that felt peaceful," she mutters.

It wasn't.

We drive for the next hour in silence as I weave in and out of traffic I really don't want to be in. My frustration grows.

My head is reeling.

I can't put Briar unknowingly at risk. I need to tell her more.

The idea terrifies me. It's undercover 101 that you never tell a soul who you are. You don't reveal any details that might lead to your identification later.

More than that, it feels like telling her is the first step to an unravelling. She's the first thread, and if that comes unpicked, so does everything else. You see these movies about a sergeant assigned to a bomb squad and who is immediately hated for his maverick ways of dealing with his life and work. All of it is bullshit. Nearly every bomb disposal expert I know is measured. Sure, we ride the kind of high you get from extreme sports. The rush of exhilaration. The feel of doing something no one else wants to or can do. But the work? It's focused and calculated to the letter.

An extreme snowboarder doesn't want to die on the hill, we don't want to die in the field.

On my first two undercover assignments, I operated the exact same way.

But this one I'm fucking up left, right, and center.

By the time we pull into the driveway, I don't know what I want or need. I should go work out or go for a run, burn this off so I can think clearly.

I slam the door of the truck and jog up the driveway. Briar follows me and places her hand on my back. "Are you okay?"

Sliding the key in the lock, I realize I'm not. "No. I need to go out."

She follows me inside, and I hear her slam the lock closed. "You want me to make some lunch and we can talk about it instead?"

Shit. I got us bagels. They're sitting in the back of the truck.

I look at her eyes, trying to find some shred of sanity deep inside myself. "Thanks. But the mood I'm in, I'll say shit I don't mean."

"Did I do something wrong speaking to Cillian?"

The mention of his name tips me over the edge. "I don't want you talking to him ever again. I don't want to talk about him. I don't want any of this to spill over into our home."

She looks around, and I see what she sees. A shithole. A tiny house that I try to keep clean. She thinks I'm an Outlaw. It's all she knows. And yet she'd still rather be here with me anyway.

"Why the fuck are you even here, Briar? At some point, you're going to need to go home."

The words slip out without thought, even as I immediately want to retract them.

When I see her try to bite back her tears, I feel even more of a dick.

"Something obviously upset you during that meeting. But you can't talk to me like this."

I turn and look out the window before I lose my shit totally. "I am. Shit. Sorry. You need to give me some space, Briar. You aren't the only one trying to make sense of their fucking life."

"So talk to me then. Let me listen to you."

"I don't need to fucking talk. I need to do something. Fight. Run. Punch something. Clear my head so I can think first." I tug my hoodie over my head and stride into the bedroom. A run it will have to be. I'm too wound up to go use the equipment at the clubhouse. I yank my jeans down and rummage in the drawer for some shorts.

They're folded neatly because Briar did the laundry.

I shove my hand through the pile, and then sigh.

The door opens.

"Would fucking do it?" she asks. When she steps into the room, she's naked. Sunlight dances over her skin.

My cock needs only a second to agree, but I'm still

breathless with frustration she really doesn't need me taking out on her.

Yet I don't move.

She drops to her knees in front of me, and I didn't realize how badly I needed someone to look up to me and offer me something. Because everything I've done recently is for everyone else.

I've always carried the weight for others.

"Briar," I warn. "I can't be considerate in the mood I'm in."

She tugs my boxer briefs down my legs and exposes my cock, which bobs in front of her face. "I know. But let's try this first before you run out of here."

She doesn't waste any time. Understanding my mood, her usually tender touches are replaced with a rock-hard grip. When she spits on my dick, I almost come. Her playful licks of my cock are replaced with fat lips that engulf me, sucking me down to the back of her throat. She gags, saliva escaping down her chin. She uses a finger to catch it and stroke it over the head of my dick before repeating the action. This time she swallows me.

Deepthroat has never felt so good.

I place my hands on either side of her skull to hold her in place and begin to move.

"Pinch my leg if you need me to stop," I grunt.

I pray she doesn't.

My thumbs move to her neck, and I can feel the way she swallows around me. Her throat stretches to take me like an elastic band.

It's selfish, but I imagine she can't stop me. That she can't breathe. It's a fantasy, not something I'd ever really do, but fuck, it's such a turn-on. I can feel her throat cavity squeeze my head so tight, it makes my head spin.

Briar gasps, her eyes water.

"Pinch . . . me," I say as I pick up speed.

But she shakes her head.

I pull my dick from her throat to give her a moment. She splutters around it for a second, and then I'm back down her throat.

"Fuck, you feel so good, Briar."

She's worshipping me with her mouth.

Feelings of being a fuckup are replaced with a feeling of being cherished.

"You need to make me stop," I tell her, but she doesn't listen. "Or I'm going to come hard down your throat."

Her eyes flash to mine, daring me to.

And then I can't stop myself. I give into the sensations and take her hard, knotting her hair in my fist to hold her where I want her. I've given her outs. I trust her to use them. When she doesn't, I thrust harder, faster. I watch her eyes water even as they stay focused on mine.

The visual, the feeling, the fact it's Briar giving me this. Giving me something raw. Giving me what I need.

And I come. Waves so hard, my knees shake, and I have to reach back and hold on to the dresser as I thrust three more times.

I keep my eyes closed as she eases me down gently.

When I finally open them, she's kneeling in front of me. "Better?" she asks.

I am.

I tug my T-shirt over my head and clean up the mascara tracks and the wetness from around her mouth. "Now what can I do for you?"

Briar smiles softly. "You can tell me the truth."

24

BRIAR

I watch as Saint looks up to the ceiling and inhales so deep that his shoulders lift and his abs tighten. Then he blows it out in one long breath. The pause is *so* long, I wonder if he's going to do as I ask.

I'm turned on from what we just did, yet I feel a disconnect. "There's a distance between us. And while most guys can easily separate sex and emotions, I can't. I need truth and honesty more than I need orgasms."

"Fine. But let's get cleaned up and make coffee first."

I brush my teeth and wash my face while Saint cleans himself up and gets dressed. By the time I meet him in the kitchen, he's already made a pot of coffee with the nicer coffee beans I bought. If he's noticed the difference, he doesn't say anything.

He hands me a mug. "Let's go sit in the yard."

With his hand on my back, we step outside and sit on the makeshift bench. For a moment, Saint simply cups his mug and rests his elbows on his knees.

"My moral compass is shot, Bri. I've lost who I am."

Of all the places I was expecting him to start, that wasn't it. "Tell me."

Saint sits up, sips on his coffee. He doesn't say anything, but something tells me he's trying to figure out what to say.

And my earlier feelings of arousal from what took place in the bedroom are replaced by fear.

I wonder if he's going to tell me he's some kind of assassin.

"Please tell me you're a good person and not some mass murderer," I blurt.

Saint shakes his head. "I'm in this mess because I'm, more often than not, a good person. I work for the ATF—Bureau of Alcohol, Tobacco, Firearms and Explosives. I'm undercover with the Iron Outlaws."

I lean my head against his bicep, trying to figure out how I feel about that. "Okay. A noble starting point. I'm guessing much of this is lies." In the big scheme of things, whether what's between us is real or false shouldn't be the most important thing, but to me it is.

"Hey," Saint says. "Perhaps the only truth in all this is my feelings for you, Briar. Don't look at me like I'm someone else. Everything I've told you is true when it comes to you and me. My real name is Ryker Miller. My cover, Phillip York, was a real army chaplain who passed away after he left the service. I use his name with his father's permission because motorcycle clubs tend to check these things. That there really was a Phillip York enlisted and that he really was an army chaplain."

He shifts and tips my chin before placing his lips on mine. The kiss is soft and lasting. I sigh against his mouth. It calms the chaos racing through my mind.

"There are so many things I want to ask you," I say. "So many things I want to understand."

"Well, let me tell you what I think is safe to say, and then you can ask me if I don't cover something, yeah?"

I listen as he explains how he ended up joining the ATF after the army. He tells me about some of his other undercover work, especially the one about working with incels. It's horrific, and yet there are moments when he makes me smile. He's a natural storyteller. He tells me about his father, the malevolent preacher, and how he has nothing to do with his parents.

I say, "Your story makes me feel my parents aren't quite as bad as I imagined. Everything Dad said was from a place of fear. I feel like I should perhaps try to be a little more understanding of that."

Saint throws his arm over my shoulder. "You're taking this very well. I'm worried it's too well. And next time I go out, you're going to pack up all your shit and leave."

"I guess I had a feeling something was wrong. I don't know. A spidey sense. Hap picked up on it too and was worried about me."

"He's a smart guy. You wanna hear the rest of it?"

I nod.

"With the other undercover work I've done, the bad guys have been crystal clear. But with the Outlaws, it's been different. When I first signed up for this, I thought it was going to be easy. It's a lot harder to get into a motorcycle club than those other gangs. MCs are rigorous in their requirements and paranoid as fuck. You have to be recommended by someone. And then you move into being a hang-around. Then you become a prospect, which means you're basically a lackey to the club. You have to pretty much do whatever a patched-in member tells you. It's like frat boy hazing on a well-armed level. And if you pass all that, you become a fully patched-in member of the club. But someone has to nominate you."

"Who nominated you?" I ask.

"King. The president." Saint goes quiet again, and his shoulders sag. "I guess in a different life, I want to be a part of their organization for real. I believe in a lot of what they believe in. I'm fed up with living my life on everyone else's terms. Living by rules someone else decided and dictated. I love being on my bike. I love the camaraderie of the brotherhood. I love that there are consequences. What I came here to put a stop to, I feel like I've found a home in. I can't explain it any clearer than that."

"I'm guessing that's an impossibility given how you ended up there."

His fingers stroke up and down my arm. "I'm losing my edge on both fronts. I'm half out of the ATF, so I'm not bringing them what they need. And I'm half out of the Iron Outlaws because I could never be fully in. I've lost my place in the world, and it feels really fucking weird, Bri."

"I'm not surprised that this is the truth of who you are. There is such an element of trust about you."

He kisses the top of my head. "Because of all this, I really think the safest place for you might be back in Gary, Indiana, with your parents. Just while everything comes to a head. You don't want to be back in New York, and I'd hate for you to see Cillian again."

I laugh. "New York has like eight or nine million people living in it. The chances of me ever seeing Cillian again are slight. Plus, he probably won't even remember me."

Saint turns to face me and puts his hands on my biceps. "Cillian didn't become the head of an Irish crime family by forgetting about shit. He talked about rats in an organization. He's paranoid. He wants to know why you are mixed up with the club. He squirrels kernels of information away and stores them until they can do the harm. Plus, you and I both know you are never going back to your apartment, right?"

I do. "I emailed my landlord and asked if I could sublet it."

"And if he won't let you, I can pay it off for you. I have money of my own and access to cash through this."

I shake my head. "First, I can't allow you to use illegal money to cover my ass, and second, this is my problem, not yours. I'll fix it."

Saint looks at the yellow chrysanthemum for a moment. "Is there room for a we in there?"

"A what?"

"A *we*. You and me. I need to know if there's a we before I say anymore."

"I certainly hope so. But there won't be if you pack me off to Gary, Indiana, and face everything happening here alone."

"It's not safe here." There's a hint of annoyance in his tone.

I'm about to match it. "It's where *you* are. What are we going to do in the future? If you stay in the ATF and go undercover for years, am I to stay away then? Or let's say you manage to find a way to leave the ATF and have the Iron Outlaws accept you wholeheartedly. I'm guessing that wouldn't always be safe either, would it? And you forget, I've already survived worse than what has happened to you. I know what the worst case looks like, Ryker. And I want to face it with you!"

By the time I'm done, my voice is loud.

Saint looks over the fence in the direction of Hap before he places a finger over my lips. "We should stick to indoor voices," he says softly. But there's a look of admiration on his face that I haven't seen before.

He says, "When I've defused bombs or been undercover, I've always felt alone. Even though there was a bigger team backing me up. But you and me, it feels like a team."

"I'm sorry if I've seemed less than all in. I have a history of falling head over heels too quickly. I'm scared I'm doing the same here."

"Then let me fall first, Briar. I can catch you when it's your turn."

I smile and place my hand on his cheek. "I feel like we need a plan."

Saint takes our cups and puts them on the ground before he pulls me onto his lap. The bench wobbles, and we both grin. "I feel like I owe you an orgasm."

"Can we do both?"

He stands and takes me with him. "Definitely. But let's work on the orgasm first, because I've just about recovered from the way you sucked my cock down your throat."

I laugh and wrap my arms around him. "That's because your cock tastes so good."

He kicks the back door closed with his foot and carries me to the bedroom. But instead of throwing me down on the bed like I expected, he stands me on the end of it. His hands are gentle on my waist.

"You're sure about this?" he asks.

"About the orgasm or the fact your cock tastes good?"

Saint smiles, but it doesn't quite reach his eyes.

I run my fingers down his cheek.

"Neither. It's dangerous. More so now that you know. You weren't even mine, and it meant something when I found you in that parking lot. If I were to lose you again after everything you've come to mean to me, I don't know how I'd deal with it, Rose."

I love that he uses my real name.

Everything we are going through is becoming more real. Truer.

It's impossible for it not to.

"I'm putting extra pressure on you by staying, aren't I?"

Saint holds my gaze, but I know the answer is yes.

"By staying, I make it so you now have to worry about me as well as you. It'll split your attention, and that's deadly given what you do."

He cups my cheeks and kisses me like I'm already gone. "I want you with me, but you're going to have to agree to obey everything I tell you from here on out. If I tell you to run, you run. If I tell you to hide, you hide. And you're sure as fuck going to get comfortable holding a gun, because you need to be able to stand your ground."

I think about what he's saying. And he's right. "I'll do all that."

"And if I send a text, or call, or say in front of you the word *Judas*, you need to get the fuck out. I'll give you my real address in Maine. You just go."

"We can work out the details later. But I promise, Ryker. I'll do whatever you say."

And I mean every word.

Because if that's the only way the two of us get through this, I'd be stupid not to.

25

SAINT

"I found something based on the plates." Vex tips his head in the direction of the old pantry he operates out of. "Why's it so personal?"

"The woman Spark and I saved that night. She's on my mind. She told me the plan was for her to be delivered to some guy to be his wife. That's some fucked-up shit. If they're local, they could come for any of our girls: the girls who work at the strip club, the old ladies."

I think of Briar. She was worried about me heading out tonight. To help her relax, I left her in our hallway, with blush on her cheeks and bite marks on her shoulder after banging her up against the wall.

I didn't want to go. She didn't want me to leave.

And I feel it as much in my chest as I do in my cock.

We walk past Spark's room. He and Iris had a disagreement in the yard earlier that resulted in a furious Spark carrying her back into the clubhouse to sort things out. Given Spark's room is next-door, I stepped inside mine to make sure nothing got out of hand. As soon as I realized there was nothing going on beyond a whole lot of fucking, I got out of Dodge.

Vex flips on machines and the tech room lights up like the deck of the *Enterprise*. Perhaps I'm aging myself saying that. I wonder what Briar would make of it. She doesn't seem to care about the age gap. Neither do I.

"So what do you know?" I ask

Vex opens the files on his laptop. They're organized. Color coded. Detailed.

For a moment I'm entertained. "Strikes me that you have a million and one options with the skills you have. How did you end up full-time on the payroll of an MC?"

"Special invitation from Camelot, King's dad. I was messing around on the dark web. Hooked up with this group that would hack into places and hold them to ransom. Tried to pick organizations that weren't good social citizens. Corrupt politicians, that kind of shit. They were shit at paying me my share though. Then one day I get wind of them messing with the idea of hacking the Iron Outlaws. I figured the club would owe me big if I stopped it. So I showed up one Tuesday night and asked to see the man in charge."

I grin. "How old were you?"

"Seventeen. Spoke to Camelot. Told him what they were planning. He asked how much I would have made from the gig. I told him, and he said he'd pay me that if I could lock the club up tight. So I did. Cellphone encryption. Bank-level security of information. I wired up the clubhouse, their homes. Secured that shit right down. Was even able to show them the attempted data penetration the night they tried to hack. Good as his word, Camelot paid me out and asked if I wanted to join. Let's just say I had an easier path through prospecting than most, given they all knew I could undo what I'd done and steal their secrets."

I sit down in the chair opposite and ease back. "You never thought about doing something legit? With those skills you could make a fortune."

Vex laughs; his rich bass echoes around the room. "I'd get a suit instead of a cut, an office instead of a cupboard, and a nine-to-five instead of this. Never regretted the choice once."

"Fair. I get that feeling."

"You regret the army?" Vex asks.

Of course he thinks that's what I mean, when I'm talking about the ATF. "It was good for me. But I was drifting before I found this."

Vex nods. "I've managed to get a couple of pictures of who Joseph Hosea was with, the day King and Spark saw them at the diner bothering Iris."

"You did?"

His fingers fly over his keyboard. "Went and asked Bev, who runs the diner, if she had those Righteous Brother shit-heads on her security footage."

"You know Bev?"

"Wired her camera system. She kept getting broken in to. I've been trying to trace them by searching the web for their names."

I know a system that can deal with that. "Want to send them to me too? I'll see if I can help. I have a friend who's conversant with facial recognition." I can also show them to Briar. See if she recognizes either of them from the time when she was . . .

I find it hard to say words like *captive* and *abducted*, even if it's only to myself.

He clicks away, and my phone vibrates in my pocket.

"Done. Once we know who they are, we can hack bank information. How do these guys get paid? The club has a whole cottage industry to launder everything we have, but I wonder if these guys are quite as sophisticated. Could probably hack his cellphone if we wanted."

"For shits and giggles, let's say we do."

It would be illegal for a government office to hack a phone without clear cause. At least that's what they tell civilians while they do it all day and twice on Sundays for terrorist threats and subversive organizations like ours.

It would be hard for them to prove a cause right now.

But if Vex can do it and we can provide information to the FBI on their next intended victim, it could be huge.

"Okay." Vex squints at his screen. "The truck has travelled around Millhurst, Adelphia, and Howell. Wonder if he's looking for something."

"Property, maybe? If they are trying to get a property footing here, we need to know."

Vex nods. "I can check land and property listings. See what we get."

"Sounds good. I'll see what I can do with those images. Thanks, Vex."

"No worries. You okay, preacher man? You're looking tired."

There's concern in his voice. I hear it. I am tired. This whole fucking thing is starting to grind me down. The club is a marble bowl, and the ATF is a pestle. Davis didn't give a shit. Weicker is trying to keep the peace. But Vex actually cares.

"You know, I've got some shit going on," I answer honestly.

"Anything I can help with?"

I shake my head. If only he could. "Nah. But thanks for asking."

"Maybe you should go home. Get some rest."

I smile. "Yeah, maybe I'll do that."

I walk into the bar and look around the room. Halo is getting his dick sucked right there on the sofa by one of the girls who hang around the club. Bates is passed out, head down on a bar table.

King sits alone, so I hop up beside him. "Coffee," I say to the prospect behind the bar; he pours me a mug of steaming black tar. I take a sip. It's strong. I smile when I think about Briar on the first day she drank my coffee. And the sneaky woman thinks I haven't noticed how she got rid of my coffee and replaced it with her own.

King taps his cigarette in the ashtray. "You think I did the right thing?" he asks.

"Depends what thing you're talking about."

"Spark and Iris."

I rub my hand over my face as I consider his question. "Depends on how you look at it. If you start with the culture of the club and the happiness of those in it, then the answer is absolutely yes. The whole purpose of the club is to live outside the law and to live the lives you want, right? And if that's true, nothing should scare you as individuals or a club. But if you look at it from the perspective of your alliances and rivalries, who knows? I wasn't around the last time you and the Irish were actively on opposite sides. When your and Clutch's fathers wove a web that involved both the club and the Irish losing men over a weapons deal. But in balance, I guess what matters most is what do all these men and their happiness mean to you as their president?"

King takes a sip of the whiskey he's nursing. "That's a deep question," he says, shaking it off.

I shrug. "Not really. It should be easy enough to answer. Do you care more about the club or your men?"

"Can you answer that, preacher man? I mean, is it the army that matters or the men?"

It's a good question. "In truth, it's the USA or the men. For God and country. You have to believe in the bigger cause. But at a micro level, it's leave no man behind. It's the reason the Navy SEALs work. Take Halo. Bet he has stories where they had to do things that conflicted with his beliefs. Like following the bad guys and coming back for their own later."

King spins in his seat to face me. "You believe both can be important?"

"I have to. But I know for sure that the way you grow and develop loyalty in your men is by showing exactly what you'd do for them if they needed you. By not asking them to do anything you wouldn't do. What if you fell in love with someone you weren't supposed to? Imagine the wife of that Los Reyes gang member you killed walks in here and you guys have an immediate connection—what would you do?"

King huffs. "Fuck her sideways, then kill her and bury her next to her husband."

"You wouldn't do that." I'd like to believe he wouldn't, but I saw what happened to Skylar. His one-time girlfriend colluded with Clutch's father to kill King and his entire family. Then again, given he's done something like that, perhaps he's capable of so much worse now.

"You'd be surprised what I'd do, preacher man."

"You want to tell me you enjoyed putting a bullet in Skylar's head?"

"Not talking about her. But I'll say this. Skylar? Your hypothetical Los Reyes wife? They could be carrying my kid, but if they betrayed me, I'd kill them in a heartbeat. I'm over being betrayed. Dad let me down with his deal to save Cue Ball. Clutch let me down when he fucked my sister. Spark didn't listen to a firm order to stay away from Iris. And Skylar . . . well, you know what happened there. I feel like my control of the club is slipping away from me."

His words hit as hard as punches. I'm looking at a man who is at his limit of being betrayed. And here I am giving him advice. "You know. I hear all that. How you feel is how you feel. But there's room for compassion in all those stories. Your dad did a deal to respect the man who saved his life, to save him from death at the hand of the club by moving him somewhere out of reach. Clutch didn't mean to fall in love with Gwen. But as I understand it, it started before she ever left, in a sweet childhood crush, and has survived him walking in front of a hail of bullets to keep her safe. And Spark has been struggling with everything. You know this. Everyone says he's not been the same since he got back from Kabul. He's finally found someone who brought him joy. That shit's important, King."

"That shit is pussy."

I shake my head. Maybe a month ago, I might have had a different take on this conversation. But tonight, with the knowledge Briar is waiting for *me* at home, I want him to realize everything life can be. "Is it? Is your brotherhood *pussy*? 'Abhor what is evil; hold fast to what is good. Love one another with brotherly affection. Outdo one another in showing honor.' Romans 12:9-10. Doesn't that describe the club?"

"Doesn't the Bible also say thou shalt not kill?"

I nod. "It does. But it also says 'Greater love has no one than this, that someone lay down his life for his friends.' And you'd do that for one another in a heartbeat."

King tips back the shot placed at his elbow. "Bet you were fucking gold dust in the field, preacher man."

"I like to think I was." I was incredible at my job. Just not the one he's thinking about.

"You know, I never once doubted what brought you to our door. You're a rock-solid member of this club. Never once regretted the decision to nominate you. Go get some rest."

His words hit me harder than any punch could.

I want him to mean it.

I want this to be real.

My calm and leadership help him, help my friends, and help this club.

I feel sober enough to drive home, plus no one is on the road at this time in the morning. Once home, I send Vex's pictures of the guys to Jensen. Despite it being close to four in the morning, he responds.

Found the shipping container you asked me to go check out. Women released. Will track down the images for you.

There's a link to a press release in the media from one of the victims' families.

I send it to Spark and pretend like I found it while scrolling the news.

Tomorrow, I'll share it with Briar.

I used to think everything could be measured, calculated, and planned. The walk to a bomb site, the length of a detonating cord, the delay of a timing fuse.

But love can't be measured. It's as wild as fire and just as reckless.

I'm falling in love with her, and I know I shouldn't.

But I strip and climb into bed with her anyway.

26

SAINT

A week later, my breath comes thick and fast as Briar slides off me and falls to my side.

"Reverse cowgirl was never hotter." I grunt. "Could see your tits swing."

"Pervy old man," Briar says. And I laugh.

"Maybe, but this pervy old man made you come twice and watched your ass bounce while he was doing it."

"If that's what you do when I draw a sketch of you, imagine what you'll do to me if I draw a full-length portrait," Briar says as she snuggles beneath my arm and places her palm on my chest.

I chuckle and place my hand over hers. "It was an impressive sketch."

"You said your hair and beard are part of your cover. Do you have any pictures before you grew them out?"

"Not here. But when we go to Portland, I'll show you."

My phone rings, making Briar jump. I reach for it and see that it's Vex. "One second," I say to Briar, then put the phone to my ear. "Hey."

"I got a lead. I found a financial link to a warehouse. King's getting people together to check it out. Wanna ride?"

I look at Briar's pretty face, remembering the scratches down it when I first met her. "On my way."

I hang up and kiss Briar. It's deep and slow. Her tongue meets mine lazily. One day, none of this will feel quite so rushed. "They got a lead on a warehouse belonging to the organization that took you. I have to go."

She didn't recognize the other faces on the image I showed her, and it's been weighing on her. Her eyes follow me as I pull on my jeans and make sure I'm armed. "I'm proud of what you do," she says. "But, I'll admit, I'm scared for you. Infiltrating a trafficking ring alone would be frightening enough. But to do it with a group who would kill you if they knew who you really were . . ." She shivers dramatically. "Make sure you come back to me. Or at least call me and let me know you're okay if you don't come back tonight."

I sit down next to her and stroke her hair back from her face. "I'll do my very best."

"Good. Now go be my hero," she says with a smile that I'll take with me.

One kiss turns into two, then three. "Go," she whispers against my lips.

Fifteen minutes later, I pull into the parking lot and line my bike up in my spot. "What gives?" I ask King. "I thought you were of a mind that the women were the police's problem, not ours. And that at best, I could only lightly follow up with Vex. Now you're putting the full club against it?"

He tips his chin towards the corner of the clubhouse, where Gwen stands with Clutch. "Gwen caught wind of what was going on and said in no uncertain terms that Clutch and I better deal with it."

Feminine laughter has me looking in Gwen's direction. "I think you'll find what I said was 'you'd better pull your fingers out of your asses and do something about it before I castrate the pair of you with a dull butter knife blade.'"

Bates, our enforcer, laughs. "I can get you a better blade than that, sweet cheeks."

King slaps the back of his head. "Don't encourage her, you fucker."

"So now it's a club priority?" I ask.

"Only so far as them being here is affecting my city, and I want those fuckers gone."

I wish I could introduce him to Briar. Change his mind on the why of doing it.

Someone kicks the clubhouse door open, and we all turn to see Spark walk in, his face like thunder. He slams his keys down on the bar and scrapes a chair out from beneath a table before sitting down in a huff.

"What have they set up so far?" Niro asks, ignoring Spark's arrival.

Vex points to something on his laptop. "They bought this lot. Easy to secure and already fenced around the perimeter. Plenty of space to build if they want, but it has a large warehouse and an office building that's more of a cabin."

I tap the table. "How do we know for sure it's the Brotherhood's?"

Vex changes screen to a complex flow chart. "Shell companies. I've been trying to track as many of theirs as I can. Keeping an eye on real estate sales, anything with their name connected. This one's allegedly an auto supply importer. Anyone with half a brain would realize an importer of cars wouldn't set up a warehouse so far away from either import location, like ports or actual buyers of the products."

Switch looks to Spark. "What do you think?"

He's thoughtful for a moment, then sheds whatever was bothering him. "I think we give them notice that they won't get a minute's peace in our state. We go destroy the warehouse. Raze it to the ground. They got no other building, they can't move any of their shit here until they build a new one."

King nods. "Agreed. Can we make it look like an accident?"

"Fuck," Bates says with a grin. "Was looking forward to a face-to-face meet and greet."

Spark shakes his head. "Knives in case of emergencies only."

"Bastard," Bates mutters, and people chuckle.

"Think we'll see when we get there," Spark continues. "If we can save anyone, we will. Otherwise, if it's empty, maybe start a gas leak. Fuel explosion. Depends on what raw materials they've got in there."

"Let's do it," King says.

"Like taking candy from a baby," Bates says later as we park over the rise away from the warehouse a little after one in the morning. Switch pulls the van alongside. We brought it in case we find any of the women.

"Me, Niro, and Clutch are taking the rear," King says. "Saint, Vex, and Halo, you guys take the west side. Spark and Bates, you take the east. Switch, you stand guard out here. Meet the rest of you inside."

Spark uses night vision binoculars to take in the landscape. "Don't see cameras yet, but that doesn't mean they don't have them. Or proximity sensors. For all we know, an alert just went off in some command center. We need to move fast."

Vex hands earpieces to King, Spark, and me. Not sure why he picked me out of our trio. For all he knows, I'm an army chaplain, and there's a Navy SEAL standing right next to me. But I take it. It's trust in me, that I won't let my brothers down. I place it in my ear. "You hear me?" I ask, and King nods.

"Ready?" I ask Vex and Halo.

Both nod.

Halo leads us down behind the back of the building so we can approach from the east. We leave King, Niro, and Clutch at the rear and follow the wall. There's limited light, but a flicker of something close to the ground catches my eye. "Wait," I command.

Halo immediately understands the instruction. Vex takes another step before it computes. I pull my phone out of my pocket and turn on the flashlight, swinging it in the direction of what I saw. I crouch and throw the beam of light at eye level. "There," I whisper. "A wire, 'bout six inches off the ground. Trip wire maybe. Possibly a proximity sensor."

Halo crouches so he can see it too.

I switch to comms. "We found evidence of wires placed about six inches above ground."

"Got it," King says.

"Seems like there are four guys, two outside, two inside," Spark replies through our comms.

I look toward an outbuilding. There's a light on where there wasn't when we first arrived. "Got them," I say.

"Do you see anyone closer to the main building?" I ask.

There's static on the line that hurts my ear, and I wince.

"King?" I ask.

"Not me." His voice crackles. "Spark?"

I pull the earpiece from my ear, check the connection, then place it back in. "Spark, buddy. I know you're a focused motherfucker, but check in."

There's a hiss.

"I'll go check on him," King says.

"Help . . . fuck." The voice is Bates. It's quiet, raw.

"On our way," King shouts.

"Trouble," I say to my team. "Spark and Bates." And we take off at speed, retracing our steps to avoid any other trip wires. As we round the corner, three men are pounding on Spark. A sucker punch from one of them sends him to the floor.

Then boots to the face and gut follow as we run to help.

One of them notices us running in their direction. "Shit, there are more of them," he shouts and starts to run for the outbuilding.

Halo has his weapon drawn and drops the guy. With King and his team running from the rear, it's impossible to fire without risking a bullet going astray and hitting one of them. But our presence is enough to make the assailants flee.

Switch is on the floor checking Bates's vitals.

"Get Spark and his bike into the van," King instructs, and Halo and I help him stand. He's groaning, and blood is pouring down his face. We half drag, half carry him. He's a big guy, and we grunt under the effort.

"Said we . . . killed . . . his brother," Spark mumbles.

Once he's seated, I realize I would have killed a man for him. I had no thoughts about protocol or rules.

I need to resign my position with the ATF.

I need to get the fuck out.

Put some distance between me and the club for a little while maybe, then come back in a year or so.

When I can be who I truly am.

But as I get on my bike and follow the van back to the clubhouse, I realize that's stupid. Because to the MC, I'll always be Phillip "Saint" York. My road name is a lie. My name is a lie. My past is a lie.

When we get to the clubhouse, I help carry Spark to his room so Switch can do what he does best. He's busy getting stuff out of the medical kit. The first thing is a syringe. For painkillers? Antibiotics? Who the hell knows.

"Need any help?" I ask as I remove Spark's shirt.

"Just got to patch him up," Switch says. "I'm good."

The mood in the clubhouse is muted as I step into the bar area. Bates and Halo are mindlessly shooting pool. I see Gwen leaving the kitchen with a big-ass bag of ice. King is sitting at the bar with Niro, the two drinking whiskey in silence.

I grab my phone out of my pocket and step outside. It's foolish to use my main phone to call Briar, but I promised I'd let her know I was okay. Instead, I get her voicemail. It's a little before three a.m., she's probably fast asleep. "Fuck," I mutter.

"You good?"

Shit. I've definitely lost my edge if I didn't notice Vex sitting on the picnic table in the shadows.

"Yeah. That was something, huh?"

The red flare of the end of his cigarette cuts through the dark. "Yeah."

I step back inside and take up my position outside Spark's room, one foot on the wall.

"Where is he?" a voice yells in the bar. It has to be Iris. The slight Irish lilt, followed by the mass of brown hair tied up messily.

I stride over to her before anyone else can.

"Wait a second, Iris." I grab her arm gently as she heads to Spark's room, but she wiggles out of my grip.

"Is he in his room?" Her eyes flash wide. I can see the fear and sadness in them.

"He is. But he's a mess." I've always believed that being straightforward in difficult conversations is best. "You're going to have to rein yourself in for a second before you go charging in there. You go in all upset, he's going to feel worse."

"Fine." She stops for a second and breathes. Her shoulders drop, and she breathes again. There's an inner strength I can see as she composes herself. "Better?"

It's a move I've seen Briar make. "I see why he likes you. He's hurt but strong. He's gonna look a mess, tell him he doesn't. He's gonna push you away, love him harder, Iris. He's a good man. Let me know if you need anything."

And I stand outside, keeping guard, as Iris steps into Spark's room.

27

BRIAR

I wake with a start.

The pillow next to me has not been slept on.

I reach for my phone.

Five a.m.

And I breathe deep to bury the panic. There's a missed call on my phone but no voicemail. I don't ring it back. We never discussed what the protocol was for contacting Saint while he was working. And I don't want to do anything that might cause him problems.

Wide awake, I head for the kitchen and put on a pot of coffee. The sun hasn't risen yet, but the sky is that wonderful half-light before dawn. The only sound is the hiss and bubble of Saint's antiquated coffee maker. Maybe one day I'll get the chance to buy him a better one.

When the coffee is ready, I pour a cup and add a generous slug of half-and-half. I slide my hands around the mug and sip it slowly. It's too hot, and it burns my tongue, but I take another sip anyway.

I say a little prayer for Saint. I'm not overly religious, but I'm desperate. "Come home safe," I mutter.

I'm on my second mug when I hear keys in the front door. I reach for another mug and pour him some coffee. I know by now that he drinks it all day, regardless of the caffeine.

When he steps into the kitchen, he looks beat. There's blood on his shirt and anguish in his eyes. "I can't do this anymore, Bri." For some reason, I know he doesn't mean us.

I place our cups on the breakfast bar, then step over to him before sliding my arms around his waist to hug him tightly. "Are you hurt?"

I feel his head shake no.

"Come sit with me and tell me as much as you can." I take his hand and lead him to the stool. And he lets me.

I sit facing him; he faces the counter and holds his coffee. "You ever wish you'd lived an utterly different life?" he asks.

"The whole thing? No. Pieces of it? Yes. You?"

He places the mug down without taking a sip, then puts his head in his hands. "I wish I could go back to when I was leaving home and make different choices. I was so concerned with helping mom and Rae, my sister. Trying to get them out of Dad's house. My only thought was where could I make decent money. The military was it. But I never gave a thought to what I needed. There were other places I could find brotherhood, and money, and friendships. Where I could have defined my own life by my own rules."

I place my hand on his back and rub wide circles. "What you did for your family was good."

Saint shrugs. "Hardly. I was too far away to protect them every day. Mom didn't even leave."

"Yes. But that was her choice to make. You gave her the option, and she doubled down. But I hear you, Saint. That you want to live a different way. What made tonight the night you realized that?"

I listen as Saint tells me about what happened. About the raid. He keeps nothing from me. And I have a sense of pride in that. Our relationship is steeped in trust.

"I was about to kill those men. And it's not that I don't care. It's that I felt justified. If there were no rules of engagement, no societal rules and laws, I'd simply take out those fuckers. Save the police a job."

I reach for my coffee and take a sip. It's cooling down and no longer burns. "Morality is such a strange concept. No person's compass is the same as anyone else's. Same with justice. It's wild that a group of people, judges not even elected by the people, decide what is right and wrong. What constitutes a prison sentence or not. We all know those rules get applied differently based on factors like race, and people don't believe women when they are raped or assaulted. The whole system for justice is broken."

We sit quietly for a moment, sipping the coffee as the sky turns shades of deep purple and fiery orange.

"King offered to organize a ride out to take down my dad. Said if I needed help to make that shit right, the club would stand with me. It's going to crush him when he finds out I'm not who I say I am. It's going to crush me."

There are times when platitudes work. It would be so easy to say King will be fine once he knows the whole story. But we both know he won't. Instead, I place my hand on Saint's back, rubbing circles. Maybe comfort is not what he's looking for, but it's definitely what he needs. "So, what's your plan?" I ask.

"Plan?"

"Leaving the club is the bomb. You're on the edge of the perimeter. What's your plan?"

He looks at me for a moment as if he doesn't believe I'm real. I swear I see his love for me in his eyes as the corners of his mouth turn up in a soft smile. "One in a fucking million."

I wrinkle my brow in confusion. "What?"

He shakes his head, sniffs, and looks back out of the window. "You really want to hear my options?"

"Yes. You helped me with my stuff. Let me help you with yours, Saint. I know what you do is unsafe. I know what you want to do is probably illegal. I'm not stupid. But I'm here and in this with you."

Saint turns on the stool, and after a little maneuvering, we're facing each other, my knees inside his. The house is quiet as he cups my face and kisses me gently. It's tender. When he's done, his thumbs stroke my cheeks. "I'm used to doing everything alone, Bri. But you're like a lighthouse in this storm, and I'm really fucking grateful you're here."

A swallow the lump of emotion in my throat. "I'm glad I'm here with you too. So, your plan?"

"I could tell the ATF that I'm done, but they'd still expect me to testify and be a witness to everything I've already collected. I'm pretty sure they'd legally try to force me to. I'd have to find out what that constitutes. There're ways to hide who I am. You can don a disguise, use a pseudonym, testify in a closed courtroom or behind a screen. But at the end of the day, the club isn't stupid. It would take them all of five minutes to figure out who was present at all those events and realize I'm no longer there. Plus, I don't want to testify against the club at all."

"Okay, so that's option one with few pros and a lot of cons. Next idea?"

"I could tell the ATF that the club found me out and that I'm scared for my life and disappear. Again, I don't know how that works. If the ATF will try to track and find me. Or if they'll let me go. But then I'd never be able to come back to the club. Plus, I'd be looking over my shoulder for the rest of my life, which is not what I want."

"Won't that happen regardless of how things go? You're relying on finding an option where the club doesn't want to kill you. And I'm not sure that exists."

Saint sighs. "Exactly."

This conversation is going to need a lot of coffee. I head to the pot and top off my mug before doing the same for Saint. "So same as the first option. What about being a double agent or whatever?" I put the pot back and lean on the other side of the breakfast bar.

Saint shakes his head. "Nice thought, but if I tell the club I'm an ATF agent, I'm pretty sure I'm dead. The ATF won't let me remain with the club indefinitely. They're already getting impatient. I'll get pulled, and I won't have any future intel to share with them. But I did think I could clean up some of the evidence I've already submitted. Maybe the club knowing I did that will buy me some currency."

"Tampering with evidence is illegal though."

Saint looks up at me and raises an eyebrow. "Like all the rest of this is above the law?"

I can't help the chuckle that escapes. "Fair point."

"I'd have to check. Seem to recall tampering with evidence in Ohio was something like a third-degree felony with up to three years. I might be wrong. Would need to check what it is here."

"Can't imagine prison is a safe place for an ATF agent."

He shrugs. "Definitely not. But they often take that into account when choosing the prison. Likely wouldn't get sent to a USP, a high security federal prison. We're often kept segregated. Law enforcement can be sent out of state and sometimes given a fake name and backstory so only the warden knows who they really are."

"You know I'd come visit you."

"Prison isn't a place for you."

"It's not the place for you either. But this, you and me, Saint, it's bigger than temporary, bigger than prison, bigger than the troubles you're facing right now. I'm not making that up, am I?"

Saint reaches for my hands. "No, sweetheart. You're not making that up." There's a pause as he simply looks at me. "Plus, I'm a big guy. I'm not gonna get hurt. I'd like to think I could take care of myself."

"That doesn't make me feel better. I hate the idea you could get hurt."

He circles his thumbs over my knuckles. "I don't think any option is painless. Not even faking my own death and disappearing, which, believe me, I've considered. It's going to hurt, Briar."

"Then I'm going to be here to patch it all back up."

"You mean that."

"Yes. I mean that. Plus, we can role-play. If you get hurt, I'll be the hot young nurse. You can be the grumpy old man patient."

Saint grins at me. "Less of the old."

I laugh. "I'll even get one of those short, white nurse's uniforms."

"Stockings?"

"Sure."

"Fuck," Saint grunts. "Unless you plan to do something about this boner, you gotta stop talking."

Perhaps the kindest thing I can do right now is give him a safe place to land. Give him the warmth of my body, the security of the two of us intimately entwined in the safety of our bed.

I pull my tank over my head, smiling as his eyes go straight to my breasts. "Maybe I want to do something about that boner. We can come back to this conversation over breakfast." I turn, place my elbows on the counter, and lock my hands behind my head as my forehead touches the cool surface. My ass juts out.

The sound of his stool scraping along the floor tells me his answer.

When he drops to his knees behind me, biting my ass, I get my answer.

He needs to escape as much as I do.

And when he places his palm between my shoulders, stroking my skin as he eases his cock inside me, I wonder about the universe and everything that had to happen so I could be here for him like this.

So I could feel every inch of his length and the very depths of his heart.

No matter what plan we make, my life will never be the same again.

28

SAINT

Church. One hour.

The message on my club phone three days later is from Spark. I've never known anyone other than King to send a message calling for us all to get together. Over the past few days, I've seen Spark's strength come back. I've driven Iris to her school occasionally. With the splint on her arm from her accident and her car still in the shop, she's needed the ride and has been spending every night at the club.

Fierce woman.

Like Briar.

As I wonder why Spark wants us all there, I see the responses start to filter in.

Vex: *Will be there*

Thirty minutes away, I add.

Niro: *Is this legit, @king?*

King: *Is it @spark? Call me.*

Spark: *I've got good reason. Just trust me and show the fuck up.*

When I arrive, I see Spark and Iris, her arm still in the

splint from her injuries, waiting outside. They both look tense, but Spark is obviously trying to make Iris feel better.

I grab his shoulder. "'So do not fear, for I am with you; do not be dismayed for I am your God. I will strengthen you and help you; I will uphold you with my righteous hand.' And if for any reason Isaiah is wrong, and God won't . . . I will. Whatever this is, I've got your back, brother."

I feel like a fraud offering a Bible verse, but it's what he expects from me.

Everyone is already there. I sit next to Niro. "Fucking cockblockers," he mutters. "Literally just got naked."

Bates laughs. "Bet this is going to be more entertaining though."

"My aching dick doesn't agree," Niro complains.

King looks over at Iris and Spark when they enter.

"Irish," Halo says. "You causing trouble again?" He smiles as he speaks, and I appreciate his efforts to break the tension.

Iris sits in Spark's chair. He stands behind her. The Irish Mob and the MC. It's like some fucked-up power couple.

"She shouldn't be in here," Niro says.

Spark gives Niro side eye. "Well, she is."

"What's going on?" King places his elbows on the table.

Spark squeezes Iris's shoulder, encouraging her to speak. "Cillian thought what happened the night my dad died was an unplanned raid and pure bad luck. When he found out it wasn't, he wanted revenge."

Everyone begins to speak at once, offering their opinion. Bates is pissed. Niro and Rubble mutter something between them. What the pair needs now is time to explain.

"Why do you know this?" I ask.

"Because he threatened me." Iris raises the brace on her arm. "He caused the accident because he asked me to spy on you all for him, and I refused to help him. He also knew that if I were hurt, Spark would help, forcing us together."

Vex laughs. "Is that what we're calling stalking these days?"

Switch joins in the laughter. The speed at which these guys change mood is often entertaining.

"It was *protection*." Niro puts air quotes around the word.

"This isn't funny," Iris says.

Spark leans forward and whispers something into her ear that reassures her.

"What did he ask you to do?" King asks, and the club settles again.

Spark rubs the back of her neck, steadying her as she speaks. I'd do the same for Briar. Then he speaks. "He wanted some specific things. Wanted her to form a relationship with me so she could spy on me and the club. As sergeant at arms, I'd have the logistics to stuff, but everything is always secured."

Clutch's mood grows serious. "Did you compromise us?"

She shakes her head. "No."

"Because you couldn't find anything, or . . ." King lets the sentence hang and tips his chin at Spark.

"*Or*." Her answer is quiet as she looks up at Spark.

Niro, like the child he is, makes a vomiting sound.

"You two get any cuter, and you'll overtake Clutch and Gwen on the saccharine scale," Bates mutters. "And my teeth already fucking hurt watching the two of them."

I hear the slap as Clutch hits the back of Bates's head.

King nods. "I need you to wait outside, Iris."

Her eyes go wide. "No. I can tell you what he specifically asked. About routes and some other things. I can—"

"Out. Side," King repeats.

"I'll be right out, little chick," Spark says.

She whispers something to him I can't hear as he gently touches her chin with his knuckle.

"Safety is my specialty," Spark replies.

The door closes, but Spark remains standing. "I propose offering a payment to Cillian and Iris to close this matter."

"What the fuck?" Niro asks. "We don't owe them shit."

Spark looks to Clutch and King. "With respect, it's your dads who caused this. Cue Ball was stealing from the club. He should have gotten what's coming. But Camelot owed him a debt and arranged it so he'd go to prison, not die. When the Irish took part in the deal that night, they didn't know the club had deliberately put the delivery in jeopardy."

Clutch has the gray look he often gets when he thinks about his father's disloyalty to the club, and I feel for him. Because I'm the one currently being disloyal.

King puts his head in his hands. "Fuck me. The sins of our fathers."

I place my palm on the table and offer some verses. "'As for the father, because he practiced extortion, robbed his brother, and did what is not good among his people, he dies for his iniquity. Yet you say, "Why should not the son suffer for the iniquity of the father?" When the son has done what is lawful and right, and has been careful to observe all my statutes, he shall surely live. The person who sins shall die. A child shall not suffer for the iniquity of a parent, nor a parent suffer for the iniquity of a child; the righteousness of the righteous shall be his own, and the wickedness of the wicked shall be his own.' Ezekiel. 18."

Niro slaps my back. "Nice one, preacher."

I stand. It feels like a sermon. Like I can lead these men through darkness. "The rest of the 'sins of our father' Bible quote is about what it means for the children. It says the sons should not suffer. Neither should Iris. She's the daughter of the man who died. That includes you and Clutch. The club is wealthy enough to make this right. You should, so you can all move on with your lives."

"And if it's not enough, I'll pay." Spark walks over to me and hugs me before slapping my cheek lightly. He looks back at King but stays by my side. "She's worth more than that to me. I'll even hand in my patch if you need me to. Just help me make it right with Cillian, without years of violence, so he leaves us alone."

King sits back in the chair. "Five thousand a year for every year since her dad was killed to Iris. Sixty-five grand. Agreed?"

I watch as hands raise. Most without complaint. Niro and Rubble grumble but raise their hands.

King says. "Cillian, we round to one hundred."

"And I'll pay," Spark says. "Might need the club to bridge me. Reconfigure how much of a share I get. But let me make it right."

Halo groans. "Pray to God I never find pussy so good, I'm willing to toss a hundred grand for it."

I glance his way. "I've seen you toss more than that over the past year and a half at the strip club."

King laughs, and the mood is broken. "All in favor of the club bridging Spark while he pays off his old lady's uncle on behalf of the club?"

Everyone raises their hand, including me.

"Meeting adjourned," King says.

By the time I get out of the room, Spark is wrapped around Iris, and my heart fucking aches when I see the other brothers surround him.

I hear snatches of their conversation. "What did you do? . . . proposed we make it right with your uncle . . . club is going to pay . . . so fucking sorry for that . . . So, it's over?"

I feel the same way.

I need to come clean.

I can't face Spark right now, but I need to take stock of what's in my room here. Perhaps I should grab whatever I want to keep, just in case.

"Preacher man," King says, catching up with me. "What you said in there. Do you believe it?"

I place my hand on his shoulder, the man who had faith in me and thought I should be a member of this club. "Yeah, Uther. You have nothing to feel guilty for." I tap the patch on his vest. "You deserve this."

He surprises me by pulling me in for a hug. "Best nomination I ever made. Come get a drink."

"In a minute. Just got to take a leak." It's all I can manage.

Iris hurries toward me, and I grab her arm. "Iris. A word."

"Are you okay?"

I feel bereft. Adrift. "Spark. He's one of the good ones. And I just wanted to check, well, ensure that . . . fuck, do you feel as strongly for him as he does for you?"

She tilts her head, confused "I do. Every bit as much, if not more."

I let go of her arm and nod. "Good, then it makes what he's about to do mean something."

"What does that mean?"

"It might emasculate him if you knew, but you should. Can you keep a secret, Iris? No matter what the cost?"

Iris thinks for a moment. "That's the kind of thing you say to a child. They'll trust you blankly. But I don't know what you're about to say or what your motivation is for saying it. It's impossible for me to know if I'll keep that secret or not."

I smile. "I see why he likes you. The money for you is coming from the club. The money for your uncle? It's coming from Spark. He already lost three months of pay for disregarding an order so he could be with you. He's cashing in some of his investments to pay Cillian."

"He can't do that. It's not fair that he should—"

"You'll let him, Iris. And you won't ever tell him you know he did it. He's proud to take care of you any way he can. Let him have his pride. Don't beg him not to. Don't tell him he can't. Let him be who he is. A man who would do anything to protect any of us. I just . . . these are all good men. I only wish I were half the man Spark is. Some days, I feel like an imposter."

I look around the clubhouse and see my friends. Spark in discussion with Clutch and King. King grabbing Spark by the back of the neck and hugging him. King looks up and winks at Iris.

"Take care of Spark," I say and step into my room. I don't deserve to hang out with those guys.

I'm exhausted.

I lie down on my bed and put my arm over my eyes.

But I can't rest. I grab my second phone that I had hidden before the meeting.

"Rae-rae," I say when my sister answers.

"You good, Ike?"

"I'm . . . lost, Rae. Really fucking lost."

"Can you talk now?"

"Not really. Just wanted to hear your voice."

"Oh, Ike. Sleep. Eat. Shower. One step at a time. Mute your phone. I'll call back and leave some voicemails for you, yeah?"

She's done it before. Left me the very messages I need to hear. "Yeah."

"You safe?"

I glance to the door. "Enough."

"Okay. Promise me you'll sleep. You'll think more clearly if you aren't tired. I love you."

"Love you too, sis."

I hide the phone in the pocket I cut in the back corner of the mattress and try to do as she says.

It takes a while to fall asleep, but when I do, it's deep.

Chaotic hammering wakes me what feels like minutes later, but a glance at my watch says it's hours. "Iris has been taken," Halo yells as he busts open my door.

"What?" I ask, slamming upright, wiping sleep from my eyes. "How?"

"She'd gone home to pack. Was going to move in with Spark tonight. Big romantic gesture and all that shit. We were all going to go help her move once she was done. She's been taken from her house. Alarm went off. We're riding."

I grab my keys and phone and sprint outside. People are clambering onto their bikes and speeding after one another.

"What alarm went off?" I ask Niro before he peels away.

"Vex had given her a pocket alarm, she set it off. Spark checked the camera footage from her door and saw it. The Righteous Brotherhood have her."

My heart drops and I feel light-headed. I know what they did to Briar. What they probably intended to do to her, and I realize there isn't anything I won't do to make sure Iris comes home whole.

When we arrive at Iris's, I see two prospects being treated on the lawn.

I missed so much. I didn't even know why Iris was here and not at the clubhouse. "What gives?" I ask King.

"You gotta help me scrape him down off the ceiling. Anything happens to her, we might lose him for good."

King slaps my shoulder and steps up to the house.

I follow.

Spark's touching the shattered mirror with cracks and dents the size of Iris's head. The fuckers smashed her into it.

Briar had all those scratches down the side of her face. I know I'm conflating things. But I know how badly those men can hurt a woman.

"Where the fuck is she?" Spark groans, then closes his eyes and breathes deep.

I know the rhythmic box breathing we're all taught in the military. Four-second inhale. Hold for four. Four-second exhale. Hold for four. I do it with him.

Moral support.

Willing him to calm.

King looks around. "We should go back to the club."

Spark's eyes flash open. "I'm not going to the fucking club. I'm looking for Iris."

Clutch grips his shoulder, then tips his chin out toward us all standing in the front yard. Niro and Halo stand on either side of me, and there is the roar of more bikes coming down the street. "We're all with you. But we're better when we're organized."

"You holding up okay, brother?" King asks.

"Those fucking supremacist trafficker scumbags have her, so no."

King nods. "I get it. Felt the same when you told me Los Reyes had followed Clutch and Gwen last month."

Spark tugs on his hair. "They took her to get back at me for killing one of those guys. This is my fault. She doesn't even have a patch, not an official old lady yet."

King shakes his head. "We've still got both your backs."

"They're fucking cowards," I say, unable to keep it in. "Taking a woman." The bastards need to die.

Switch agrees. "Makes no sense they didn't come for us first."

Clutch pulls out his phone. "We should call in reinforcements. Want me to call the Allentown chapter, see how quickly they can hit the road?"

Spark looks utterly bereft. "Sure. But it's still too long."

"I'll start calling in nomads, see who's close by," King says, but Spark moves to take his phone.

"Cillian." It's all Spark says.

Shit. Cillian has men who are closer.

King and Clutch don't look convinced.

"I know. But if he cares about his niece at all, he'll help," Sparks says, echoing my thoughts. "Because I can't sit here and do nothing."

After finding the number, King dials, but Spark takes it from him.

"It's Spark. A trafficking group took Iris. We need manpower to find her. You're closest . . . Iris's house. But we're circling out now to find her. We'll text you . . ." Spark's face turns to fury. I step toward him, ready to intervene before he does more damage. "You motherfucker. You don't give a real shit about Iris, or you wouldn't have played her the way you have . . . I'll kill you first, you—"

"Stop," King shouts, grabbing the phone off him, saving me from doing it. "It's King. We've got a few start points. Come in wide when you cross into Jersey. I'll text you everything we have."

Halo joins us. "Got the plates from a neighbor. She also called the cops, so we need to get the fuck outta here."

I step towards Spark, King, and Clutch, but Halo stops me. "Let the club bosses deal."

When I see Spark's fist slam into the doorway three times, I feel the agony of it as surely as if he'd hit me.

Clutch hugs him, whispering words of comfort I can't hear.

"Cillian and his men are checking the highways headed northeast as they make their way here. ETA within the hour," King says.

"That fucker threatened to kill me," Spark replies. "He can choke on shit. It was a mistake to call him."

King grabs the back of Spark's neck. "The only important thing now is Iris. And the best way to find her, since neither of us has her, is to work together to get her back. Working. Together."

"Fuck. Fine. Let's go."

King approaches the top of Iris's steps. "This isn't a club vote. You don't have to come. But I'm going with Spark."

Clutch steps forward. "I'm riding with you."

"Little chick's one of us," Switch says. "I'm in."

I'm no longer an ATF agent. I'm no longer Ryker Miller. I'm Saint. Everything, for once, the club needs me to be. "'God himself will kill tens of thousands if it pleases him,' Samuel 6:19. I'm with you, brother. I'll help you kill 'em all."

One by one, everyone steps forward.

"Let's ride," King says.

And I'm ready.

Because vengeance is mine, sayeth the Lord.

29

SAINT

"Saint," Spark says as I collect what equipment I can to deal with trip wires and any other explosive devices we might find at the warehouse this time. It's the most likely option of where they have taken Iris.

"How are you holding up?" I ask, shoving wire cutters into the bag of supplies.

His face is stricken, pinched. "Sick to my stomach. I need . . ."

I place my arm on his bicep and squeeze. "Just say it."

"I need hope, preacher man. Because right now, I ain't got any."

I think back to my father's preaching, but it's the only verse I ever learned from Mom that comes to mind. She'd say it in those quiet hours when we ate pancakes and Dad slept off his anger. I paraphrase the quote. "But since we belong to this day, Spark, let's go get Iris, having put on the breastplate of faith and love and a helmet of hope and salvation. A version of 1 Thessalonians 5:8."

He swallows hard and lets his head drop.

I place my other hand on it, closing my eyes and praying that the confidence and hope I carry passes through to him.

"We'll get her back," I say.

Sparks breathes deeply, then lifts his head. "Thanks. Breastplate of faith and love. Helmet of hope. Got it."

He walks out of the armory, and King walks in. He starts grabbing ammunition, but he sees the things I have laid out on the table. "You wanna tell me how you know so much about explosives?" he asks in the dim light of the windowless room.

"Spent a lot of time assigned to bomb disposal." It's not a lie. I was. I keep it vague.

"Didn't think chaplains were allowed in the field."

"They're not." Again, it's the truth. But in between the two truths are so many lies of omission, and I struggle to hold my president's gaze.

King stares me down and takes another drag on his cigarette.

Cillian's voice carries through the bar to us. "That man is dead. A soldier who can't follow orders is a liability."

King runs his tongue over his teeth. "Those might be the only wise words from that Irish man."

And with that, he steps away.

King is suspicious.

Whatever happens next, this will be my last night with the Iron Outlaws.

It needs to count for something.

It takes an hour to get everything assembled. We park our bikes over the rise, so the engines don't give our arrival away. Slowly, we creep our way into the building. I deal with trip wires, and Vex takes out proximity sensors and cameras.

Bates deals with the two men at the small security building. A line of blood sprays along the window. Someone picks the lock, and we're slowly making our way through the rear corridor to the main warehouse space.

Screams ricochet throughout, then go silent. Spark starts toward a set of double doors, but Bates grabs him around the middle and holds him back.

"Think," Bates violently whispers.

Spark tries to peer through the gap in the door but obviously doesn't like what he sees. "We got to go in without intel," Spark says. "Just be ready."

Another scream is all it takes for Spark to go. Men flood into the warehouse, weapons drawn and firing. I take cover behind an old metal tool chest, and I gasp at the sight. A naked woman, who looks a lot like Iris from the back, is suspended, her hands tied, over a hook. She's no longer wearing her splint on her wrist. She must be in agony.

Joseph Hosea holds a gun to her head. "Stop," he yells.

"Iris." The agonized word slips from Spark's lips.

The man spins her, revealing the extent of her injuries. She's bruised. Bloodstained. Barely conscious.

It *is* Iris. But she makes me think of Briar.

The two meld in my mind.

We're here to save Iris and Briar and every other woman the Brotherhood has touched.

Confusion fills me. I've never been uncertain. Wires. Women. Weapons.

Suddenly, I want to kill every fucker in this room.

Guns are pointed everywhere.

"You're outnumbered," Spark says. I'm not sure how he's staying so calm when a world of rage is bubbling up inside me.

"I'm going to need you to leave," Hosea says. "You think your club is so powerful. Think you could kill some of our ranks and not receive any retribution?"

I get up from my place of cover and walk to stand alongside Spark, weapon raised. Clutch does the same. Some of us may die, but this fucker with three guns aimed at his head is going nowhere, no matter what he does next.

Iris stirs; through the haze, she sees Spark. Tears fill her eyes. I think of all the times Briar has cried for what she went through. I think of what Weicker says. It's not about what you know, but what you can prove. If all these men are dead and buried tonight, we can't prove shit.

The police need to see this and collect evidence. Iris needs to be able to speak and not be afraid.

I press my finger against the trigger, ready to take the shot, when a bullet sounds and Hosea hits the floor. I have a second to realize it came from Spark's weapon before all hell breaks loose.

I dive behind a pillar near Iris and provide cover, firing at those who would dare to shoot at Spark, who is trying to get Iris down from the hook. He's struggling, so I run to help lift her hands over the hook and gently lower them, so Spark can carry her to safety.

They hide in the corner of the room. I stand with my back to them, covering them.

It takes a minute for the club to kill anyone left.

In the smoke and silence, I hear Spark muttering softs words to Iris, dressing her in his T-shirt so she's no longer naked.

"I know it would be easier to be seen by Switch," Iris says, her words interrupted by sobs, "but I think I need an x-ray. I don't . . . I don't think I can pretend this didn't happen. I can't let Switch treat me and not report this to the police. There were four more women. They talked about selling perfect wives. Did you see them?"

Four more women. Four. Who are about to be sold to men like the one who wanted Briar.

I feel sick inside.

"I'm sorry," Spark says. "We didn't. And I understand. Give us a chance to figure out what we need to do to make that happen."

"I also . . . I don't think . . . shit."

Spark tugs her closer. "Whatever it is, tell me. We get through all this together."

"I was unconscious for chunks of time. I don't know if he raped me. He did other things . . . I . . . oh, God."

"Iris." Spark's voice is filled with anguish. "I'm so sorry. We'll get you to a hospital. Fuck everything else."

I know what I need to do. I'm out anyway. King suspects something now. I can't do this job anymore. And I can't worry about a gun shipment when there are groups of women being taken. I begin to concoct a plan. A way out.

My mind is rattling as Iris and Cillian reunite. As King, Spark, and Cillian discuss an opportunity for peace. I'm just an observer. On the outside looking in. I feel it as truly as if I'm looking at the scene through a window. The world does not change with or without my presence here.

I once got stuck in my car on the side of a highway during a snowstorm. It raged and was violent outside, but inside, all I could hear was a muffled silence. This feels the same.

I can't latch on to what they are saying.

I'm invisible.

I'm out.

I'm *out*.

But I *can* give Spark and Iris what they need to live their life as I leave.

"King and I made our peace," Cillian says. "It's settled."

As he speaks the words, Iris falls apart and collapses. Spark grabs her in his arms and hurries out to the van, which I'd driven at Switch's request.

I follow, leaving the others inside.

Her head is slumped on Spark's shoulder, and he holds her so gently, I could cry for the two of them. I know what it feels like to hold a woman you love while she falls apart because of this.

"Fuck, hold on, Iris," Spark mumbles.

"She's going to need to tell the truth of what happened here," I say.

"Can't think about that now. Open the door."

I do and help him get Iris comfortable. But when Spark tries to take the keys from me, I step out of reach. "I'm taking her."

"What the fuck, Saint? Give me the fucking keys."

"Do you trust me with your life?" I ask. I need to know. I need to be sure, before I throw all this away, that I have his trust. Because I'm going to need his help. Now, and in the future.

"Of course, but we're wasting time."

I grab his wrist. "Do you trust me with hers?"

"For fuck's sake. Don't make me hit you. Give me the goddamn keys." Spark tries to take the keys from my hand, but instead, I catch him off guard, pull him close, and hug him.

"I'm your only path out of this, Spark. The only path where Iris can be truthful, tell her story, have her day in court if the pursuit of this organization goes anywhere without incriminating you."

"What do you mean?"

I mark the sign of the cross over Iris, then close the door. "I'm not who you think I am. I'm an undercover ATF agent."

Spark goes for his gun but then pauses. It must be empty. "You traitorous bastard." He looks toward the warehouse, and I know what he's thinking. Draw attention. Bring help. But I put my hand on my gun in warning.

"Never fired a bullet tonight. Don't make me," I lie. He knows it's untrue, but he doesn't know how many rounds I did or didn't fire. "The woman we saved that very first night, the one who started all this. She gave me some intel. I passed it on to those who need to know. I can safely go on the record and put myself here, saying I followed a tip on the case of the other missing women. I can say I saw a shootout between two groups. Russians and Brotherhood. That I saw the woman, recognized her as Iris, and saved her. You can't do that without incriminating yourself."

Spark is looking at me like I'm a stranger. "You were my friend."

"Still am. Blowing up my undercover op and likely my career for this. Because you're a fucking good man, Spark."

The man looks so torn. "King will have you killed for this."

"Probably. But if you guys clean this up, Iris will be stuck, unable to talk about her memories of it." I think of Briar, terrified to tell the police, but desperate to prevent anyone else from experiencing what happened to her. "And if you guys clean this up, the lead on who is doing this goes cold. The first woman we saved—she's my fucking Iris, Spark." The confession lifts the weight on my chest. "So much has happened, but I know what you're going through right now. I know what these bastards do. I know what it feels like to . . . to love someone who has been through what Iris has. I can't let this fucking lead go cold while you try to hide the fact you were ever here."

Spark is silent for a moment. "I don't even know you."

"Still the same guy. But I gotta go. Jump on your bike, but then go hang out at a bar near the hospital and wait until I call. Give yourself an alibi."

His eyes take on a sheen of hurt. "I can't watch you drive off with her. She's my fucking world."

"It's half an hour now, or a lifetime if you end up incriminating yourself and going to prison. Text King in five minutes that you see police cars headed his way. Get the club out of there. The Iron Outlaws aren't the bad guys. I'll call King myself once I'm clear of the hospital."

"I still don't understand why."

I huff. "What would you give to find all the men who hurt Iris?"

He jams his hands into his pockets. "Everything. I'd kill those fuckers in a heartbeat."

I grip his biceps firmly. "Then let me go do what I do. Let me do this. I'll even feed you what I know. If you get to them before me, you tell me. I want a piece of them as much as you do."

"You're an ATF agent. You can't just kill 'em."

"Was. I *was* an ATF agent. After tonight, who the fuck knows what I'll be. Trust me, Spark. I gotta go. And while you may not feel the same way about me after tonight, the past two years have been the best of my fucking life. Redefined who I am as a man. I'm better for your friendship, man. I'll drop Iris off at the hospital and report to my handler that I'm out," I continue. "Trust me, it's the only way Iris and Br—well, it's the only way they get justice. And I'd rather get the real scum. The traffickers who prey on women."

Spark looks at me, then the van. I can feel his indecision, but then he relents. "Take care of her."

"With my life."

"Don't make me kill you."

"That will be your choice. But I won't give you reason beyond those I already stated. This gets you all out of there. Besides, 'love each other as I have loved you. Greater love has no one than this; to lay down one's life for one's friends.' John 15:12-13. It was good knowing you, Spark."

I climb into the driver's seat, my gun still steady. And Spark lets me go. In my rearview mirror, I see him peel out of the lot, following the van. About seven minutes from the ER, he peels away.

My faith in myself grows at his trust in me. Even though we are on different sides of the game, he knows I'll take care of Iris.

And in doing so, I'll find justice for Briar.

I dial Weicker. Screw not using your phone while driving. I've broken bigger rules and laws tonight. "Weicker. I'm out. I've been made."

"What the fuck, Ryker. You good, you safe? What happened?"

"Can't speak now, but I'm about to drop Iris O'Connor off at the hospital and give them your number."

"Is it recoverable?"

"You were right. After rescuing that woman, I became preoccupied. That preoccupation blew my cover. I'd been investigating with the help of the club. Found a building connected to the group. Iris was taken, so I went there and found the Righteous Brotherhood in a legal wrangle with some unidentified Eastern Europeans. While they fought, I saved Iris."

"You need to come in. To debrief."

"No. For now, I need to get safe." I blow past a light as it turns red. Time is all I've got right now. "Gotta drive now, but I'll be in touch."

Dropping Iris off is stressful. I need to leave her with no papers, no insurance details, no nothing. Once she's on a stretcher, I give them Weicker's number then run. In the van, I text Briar the word I hoped I'd never have to.

Judas. Home in 20. Pack what you can.

As I drive, I call Spark.

"Saint," he says.

"Pretend you're getting the call that Iris is hurt," I instruct.

"What the hell happened to her?" he asks.

"I've been undercover all this time to stop the shipments of weapons and explosives. Now say something else about Iris loudly."

"Where have you taken her? Which ER?"

"But I couldn't do it. What I found with you guys was the kind of shit I found in the army and lost when I left it. The brotherhood that just doesn't exist anywhere else. And my focus changed. The woman we found changed my life, just like Iris changed yours."

"I'm on my way," Spark says, and I hear the scrape of a stool or chair.

"I'm out, Spark. Take care of yourself and Iris. Be happy, yeah? Let her heal you."

There's a pause. My emergency vehicle, the one I've had hidden all this time, is in sight. I'm about to give all this up.

"I want to kill you," Spark says as the noise from the bar disappears. I'm guessing he's outside.

"I'm sure the others will too." I kill the engine and step out into the cool evening air. Stars shine optimistically in the inky black.

"But I also owe you, preacher man. I'll do what I can to ensure the punishment is lenient and swift."

"Thank you." I fumble beneath the non-descript truck's wheel arch for the small lock box with the key.

"One thing. Your girl. Is she okay? You know, after . . ."

I know what he means. "We're working on it. It's not easy. It's part of why I want these guys, Spark."

"On that we agree." I hear the roar of his bike come to life, and he kills the call.

And now, I'm officially out on my own.

30

BRIAR

*J*udas. *Home in 20. Pack what you can.*

"Breathe, Briar," I say as I run to the bedroom, grab my suitcase, and throw it on the bed. I toss everything in, cramming dirty and clean clothes together. It doesn't take long. It's not like I live here. I pack up all my work stuff and cables, tucking everything away.

Then I start on Saint's things.

I find a case under the bed and throw a mix of his clothes in there. If he doesn't have time to pack everything, this might be enough. I drag both our cases to the front door. Then I begin to pull food together. Snacks. Water. Things that are easy to eat on the way.

Every time panic rises, I bite it back down. It's a constant battle against the metallic taste of fear in my mouth and knowing Saint trusted me to pull this all together before he got home.

I feel like I have purpose in this.

I'm nearly done when Saint runs into the house.

He hugs me tightly and kisses the top of my head. "I'm

going to get Hap to drive you somewhere. You need to be away from me for a little while."

"What? No. Where you go, I go."

Saint shakes his head. "Not right now. I'm at risk. You being with me puts you at risk too. I can't have that."

I pull out of his grasp. "You don't get to dictate that. I feel safer with you rather than away from you." He reaches for me, and I bat his arms away. "This wasn't part of our deal."

"Yeah, well, blowing up everything tonight wasn't either. If they come for me, I don't want you caught in the cross fire."

"You're scaring me, Saint."

This time I let him pull me close. I wrap my arms around him and take comfort from the feel of him against me, the smell of fresh air, and the scent of him…leather, cigarette smoke, musk. "You should be scared. They know. I told Spark. The men who kidnapped you took Iris. We got her back. Did what needed to be done. But I didn't want Iris to be stuck like you were. Unable to tell anybody, because the club wouldn't want anyone to know they were even there."

I cling to him harder. "We go together. I trust you, Saint. I know you'll keep us safe. You have a plan, right?"

"It's better if you don't know it. Safer. In case . . ."

I look into his eyes. "In case what? In case the Iron Outlaws find me? I'm coming with you. You can spend five minutes arguing, but it'll take us longer to get on the road."

"Don't. You promised. You said you'd obey me."

"You said *Judas*. I'm running. Stop arguing with me. I'm terrified, and you're making it worse."

"Fine." Saint grips my face and kisses me hard. "There's a truck out front. Start putting stuff in there when you're done packing up here."

He grabs a sleeping bag, a tent, and a fishing rod from the hall closet and takes them outside. I follow him out to the truck with the first of the cases. He takes it from me and tosses it with ease into the back.

"Fuck. Fuck. Fuck," I hear him mutter as I follow him back inside, and he begins to hurry around the apartment.

He has a backpack in his hand, and he's grabbing things, collecting weapons and cash from hiding places. He adds electronics and wallets and cables, plus a flashlight and a fishing knife.

I have time to grab more of his clothes, and he hands me a big sports bag. I throw a few towels in the bottom first, then pile more clothes in. He disappears into the bathroom, and after a bunch of banging around, I hear the hum of a beard trimmer.

It takes five minutes, but by the time he comes out, his beard is gone, trimmed close to his face, and inches have been cut off his hair. He tosses a bag containing all the medical supplies from beneath the sink into the sport's bag.

"Think," he mutters. He stuffs his fleece, waterproof clothes, and hiking boots into the second suitcase he pulls from the hall closet.

His phone rings, and he looks down at it.

I want to ask who it is. I want answers. But now is not the time. Not when we are obviously running for our lives.

Instead of answering *that* call, he makes a call of his own. His eyes are on me as he speaks.

"Listen to me and listen good, King. You've got about an hour. I know you are at the hospital for Spark and Iris, but you need to get the weapons out of the warehouse. You've all got to clean down your homes and vehicles. Cash. Weapons. Fake IDs. All of it. You need to get Track out of town. Send him and Tessa to Philly, just for now. He was the only one dumb enough to talk on tape."

"On tape. What the fuck, Saint? What did you do?" King's yelling, and I can hear every word.

"I did what I had to for the women. For Iris. For Br—"

He nearly says my name but catches himself. He reaches for my hand, and I take his. We're in this together. He didn't abandon me that night in the parking lot. Or the next day. Or the next day after that.

He's walked every step of this with me.

Now I get the chance to repay him.

I'm going to stay with him so he knows he isn't alone.

"You're undercover?" King snarls, and Saint takes off his cut. My heart hurts as he lays it down with such reverence.

There's anguish in the corners of his eyes as he gently runs his fingers over his patch.

Saint.

"Doesn't matter who I am. Just promise me. They'll come for the club. I blew everything up today so you guys don't go down for what happened in the warehouse when we rescued Iris. So they'll try to close in on what they've got."

"And what have they got?" King asks hoarsely.

"Everything, King. They've got everything."

Saint hangs up. "Guess I'm Ryker and you're Rose."

I muster the courage to make peace with where we're at. "Meh. You'll always be Saint to me, and I kinda prefer Briar over Rose. Rose always had her petals crushed too easily. Briar has more thorns."

"We need to go."

"Are we likely to camp?"

He shrugs. "I packed for all eventualities." He moves his

bags off the bed, and I grab the two pillows and the quilt. We start to drag things out to the truck.

"If we're camping, we'll need more than one sleeping bag."

Saint huffs a laugh, despite our situation. "I don't know, could be fun."

"I've seen your hips move. You need room."

"You young 'uns headed on a trip?" I jump at the sound of Hap's voice.

I look up to Saint, uncertain how to answer. Thinking we'll lie. Instead, he shakes Hap's hand. "Some shit went sideways."

Hap places his hand on top of Saint's. "I'll keep an eye on your place."

Saint nods and I wave. "Thanks, Hap," I say.

We load the rest of our things into the truck, and Saint pulls a beanie over his hair. I climb into the truck, and he hands me the quilt and a pillow. "At least one of us should be comfortable."

Once we're underway, I turn to face him. "What happened, Saint? The details."

I tell Briar everything. Every detail Spark. Iris. Their relationship. Cillian. Joseph Hosea and the Righteous Brotherhood. "Everything was supposed to be solved, until it wasn't. Iris went home to pack to move in with Spark. And those fuckers who took you took her."

I sigh and glance out of the window. I remember those moments after I was taken. "Would it help if I talked to her?"

Saint reaches for my hand and pulls it to his lips, kissing my knuckles. "I love you," he says.

It catches me off guard. His actions have shown me. But to hear the words . . . "You do?"

He smiles softly. "Yeah. Despite the shit show we're in, you're insistent on sticking with me. You care about Iris enough to offer to speak with her. You're smart and clever and resilient. What's not to love, Briar?"

I grin. "I love you too, for the record."

He glances at me before returning his gaze to the road. "Given we're on a six-hour drive to evade people who want to kill me, that's perhaps the best news I've had all day. Why do you love me?"

"Because you're loyal. And selfless. You didn't need to save me that day, even though you were shot at. You've served in the army. The ATF. You have courage and depth. You make me feel safe, cherished, and extremely hot at times."

Saint chuckles. "You *are* hot."

"Maybe *horny* is a better word."

"*Horny* is a terrible word when we've got a long drive ahead of us. Adrenaline has my cock retracted up into itself right now. Let's leave him there."

I can't help but laugh at the turn of the conversation. "Only you could make me laugh on a night like tonight."

He squeezes my hand. "We'll get through this, Briar. Because we don't have any other options. I promise you that at the end of this, it'll be the two of us. No matter what gets thrown at us, we're in it together."

I settle down and curl up beneath the blanket I grabbed. "What's the immediate plan?"

"Drive to my home in Portland, Maine. Swap out the truck. Get some sleep. Pack up properly. Fuel up, then leave for Michigan. My sister, Rae, lives in Ann Arbor. We'll sit tight there for a little while."

My eyes start to feel heavy. "If you need me to drive at some point, wake me up and I'll take over."

"Get some rest," he says. "You're going to need it the next few days."

And in spite of the chaos, I do as he says.

31

SAINT

I take a last look around my home, and I swallow deeply at the idea I may never come back. I take in the ledge over the fireplace that I stripped and sanded, and the rug Rae had delivered when she was horrified to learn I didn't have one. It's still a pain in the ass to vacuum though. Who knows if the spot in the corner will ever hold a Christmas tree again.

I hope it does.

I dial the one person who can fix it. "Rae-Rae. I need your help. Can I come stay?"

"Of course. When are you getting here?"

"I'm in Portland. It's like a thirteen-hour drive. Probably fifteen with a couple of stops." I look at my watch. We arrived in Maine a little after four in the morning and fell into bed. It's now ten. The sun is shining through the window in the breakfast nook I built myself. "It'll be late when we arrive. Early hours of the morning."

"That's a lot to process. You're in trouble? And *we*?"

"We are. And her name is Briar. Well, Rose, but her nickname is Briar."

"You don't even need to ask. Bring her. I'll leave a key taped to the roof of the mailbox."

My gut flips at what I'm going to say next. "My will is up to date and—"

"I can't have this conversation with you, Ike." Emotion clogs her throat. It clogs mine too.

"My will is up to date and has everything left to you. All the savings, pensions, and things. But do me a favor. If it comes to it and Briar is still alive, split it with her."

There's a pause, the sound of a gentle cough. Then another. "I'll do what you ask. I better see you for breakfast. Is there someone I should call if you don't show up by a certain time?"

"I'll message you a name and number. And some details of the trip. Routes we are taking. We'll be safe. I promise."

"Okay. Send me a picture of Briar, just in case."

"I will. See you tonight. I love you, Rae-bear."

"I love you too, Ike."

Briar steps into the room and wraps her hands around my waist from behind me. I feel her forehead press against my back. "I'm sorry you have to leave like this."

I place my hands on top of hers. "Shit was going to tip one way or another soon. I'd gone too deep. At least, that's what the ATF will think. That I got into my role too much."

She steps in front of me. "And is that the truth of it?"

I shake my head. "No. I found something with Spark and King. Found something in myself. I thought I was meant for a life of service. Went into the army to escape home." I cup her cheeks. "I hate to say it, but I feel more alive now than I ever have. I'm following no one's rules but my own, and it's liberating."

"If I said I get it, and that I understand, does that make us Bonnie and Clyde?"

I laugh at the analogy. "Unlikely, sweetheart. Unless you plan on robbing banks and shit on the way to Michigan."

"What about Thelma and Louise?"

"Again, unlikely. Not sure how many cliffs there are to drive off between here and Michigan."

She raises an eyebrow at me. "Niagara Falls."

"Still no. Let's go. It's a solid thirteen hours, even in good traffic."

"That's such a dad thing to say. Next, you'll be asking if I went pee because you don't want to stop."

"Briar," I warn.

She winks at me and walks in the direction of the front door. And yeah, I track her ass as she flounces away.

"What the hell kind of shit is this?" I ask ten minutes later, as Briar leans back in her seat after connecting her phone to my truck's sound system.

"It's called pop music, old man. Let me guess, you want easy rock. A bit of Elton John? No, Chicago." She starts singing one of their popular hits.

"I don't know what bothers me most. The fact you keep calling me an old man, or the fact you know the lyrics to 'You're the Inspiration.'"

She smiles and makes no effort to change the music that will probably make my ears bleed in an hour. With her elbow resting on the door, she runs her fingertips over her lips. Lips that I love. When they're speaking, when they're laughing, when they're wrapped around my cock. I shift in my seat and try to focus on the highway ahead of us. A boner would not be helpful right now.

I'm surprised it's even stirring, because I fucked Briar on the stairs up to my bedroom last night. Couldn't wait once we got home. Call it an adrenaline high or something. Made love to her this morning and kissed the bruises the wooden stairs had caused.

"I'm scared," Briar admits. "Aren't you?"

I reach for her hand, glancing over at her briefly. She's curled up on the passenger seat in one of my hoodies she found in the house and claimed.

"Fear exists in each and every one of us," I say, even as I acknowledge the sparks of fear in my stomach, waiting to detonate. "But it's how we deal with it that defines whether we act scared or not. Whether we let that fear erode our ability to make good choices."

"What do you mean?"

I pull out and blast by a white sedan that can't decide which lane it belongs in. "They say there are three key steps to staying calm during explosive ordnance disposal."

Briar squeezes my hand. "Jesus, I almost forgot you did that for a living. I'm lucky you're even here."

I smile. "The first step is to avoid the panic hole. Kill the what-ifs. Instead, you need to ask what kind of problem you're facing. It requires objectivity. You need to think through the catalog of times you've faced something similar for insight. The second step is to simply look on the bright side. You're still alive. It's just a bomb. You're trained for this. It's optimism, but it fires something in your brain that makes you believe it's possible. And the final one is to get comfortable with not knowing how it all ends, but how to get through the next step. So, what are your what-ifs?"

"I've got a lot of them. It'll take forever."

I point out the windshield to the long road ahead of us. "Babe, we've got thirteen more hours in this car. What else are we gonna do? Play I Spy?"

Briar smiles. "That would be funny, given spying is basically what got you into this mess. Okay, here I go. What if the people who took me come for me again and you never find me? What if King kills you for what you did? What if the ATF arrests you or sends you to prison? What if we—"

"Briar, take a breath between sentences."

She stops and does as I say. "You get the idea."

I nod. I do. "Okay. So instead of all the what-ifs, let's reframe them, see what we're facing. What did you say first?"

"What if the people who took me find me again and you never find me?"

"Right. Good to know you realize I would come for you. But there is no one left to take you. We left all those dead bodies in the warehouse. I know Spark. He won't let what was done to Iris rest. With Vex's help, they'll shut down the rest of them. But even if they didn't, your experience tells you that you can escape. Your experience tells you someone will help. The second key step is optimism. You're safe right now. You are more informed than you were before. We believe the Iron Outlaws will take out the rest of this ugly chain. And the third step is realizing we can't control whether everyone is caught right now, but we know all the right immediate actions have happened. We're hiding you, and the club is on it. So the first what-if isn't a fear we need to give in to right now."

"That makes logical sense. But the man, the one I was supposed to go to—he still exists." The scratch of fear in her voice reaches the tight bands of my heart.

"Maybe. But he has no team left to get you. These kinds of rings aren't easily replaced. He can't call up another trafficking ring and get them to grab you again. So, let's tackle the next thing on your list. What was it?"

"What if King kills you for what you did?"

I pause and think about it for a moment, and I realize

that never getting to be an Iron Outlaw again would suck more than dying. "Okay, what was the first step?"

Briar bites down on her lip. "Avoiding the panic hole. Asking what problems you're facing. Reframing."

"Right. I'm facing an appropriate response to my actions from King. A man who is so angry, he wants to kill me. I've been there before. Every time I walked out to diffuse a bomb, there was a real risk that insurgents or locals would go to the nearest tower with a rifle and take me out. I have skills to help me avoid that. Right now, the ATF has my back. That might change, but right now, they are still with me. I think I have Spark as an ally. What was the second step?"

"Optimism," she says, but she rolls her eyes.

"Why the eye roll?"

"I don't know, it seems hokey."

I shrug. "Yeah, but most of us don't understand that our thoughts don't control us, we can control them by observing and reframing. Like, nervousness and excitement feel very similar in the way they are experienced in the body. Did you know you can talk yourself into believing your nerves are actually excitement?"

"Mind over matter shit. Got it."

Now I roll *my* eyes. "My optimism is I'm alive. I have a plan. You are safe. We're away from trouble. Tonight, we'll get to my sister's. And it will all be good because it's us."

She moves closer to me and loops her hand around my bicep. "You're such a sweet talker. Carry on."

"What was the third thing?"

I feel the warmth of her breath on my arm as she laughs. "What is this? Kindergarten repeat-after-me?"

"Spaced repetition learning is a well-respected technique. Just tell me the third step before I get the urge to spank your naked ass."

"What kind of messed-up kindergarten did you go to where your naked ass got spanked?"

I can feel the mood in the truck lighten with every mile. Even if she thinks it's childish, she's shaking the fear. "What was the third thing, Briar?"

"Fine. It was comfort in not knowing the ending, just knowing the next steps—which, I know." She adopts a tone I assume is meant to mimic me. "I'm on my way to my sister's, we know what we are doing and where we are staying for the next two days. Those are the steps, blah, blah, blah."

"That's it," I say with a grin. "Definitely getting a naked spanked ass for that horrible impression of me."

She looks up at me and smiles. "Can't wait for it, Mr. Miller. Although, I'm so not having sex with you the first night in your sister's house."

This makes me laugh. I think about that. Sex in other places. I want it. I haven't really taken her anywhere because I was following her lead on when she wanted to leave the house. "When this is all settled, I'm going to take you to the kind of place where you have to get dressed up to go."

"A date. Sounds lovely. Still not having sex with you in Rae's home."

I slide my hand along her thigh, higher and higher until my pinkie finger rubs along her seam. She grabs my wrist firmly. "Saint," she warns.

I chuckle and remove my hand. "I've got plenty of time to persuade you."

Time passes. We chat. We laugh. She sings. I try. Briar grabs us subs while I fill up with gas. I take a bite once we're back on the road. "By the time we get there, I'll be so tired, I don't think an armed raid will be able to wake me once I climb into that bed."

"Too tired for sex?" Briar asks playfully.

"Fuck. That's it," I say, sitting up in my seat. "A raid."

Briar's eyes are filled with confusion. "What? What raid?"

"The enemy of mine enemy is my friend. Shit. I should have thought of this sooner."

"Ryker, I have no idea what you're talking about."

"I need to call Cillian when we're at Rae's."

"Iris's uncle?"

I take another bite of food. "Yes. Because he's the head of an Irish crime family. A friend in the FBI was looking into Cillian. We shared some mutually beneficial intel. But if I could find out what he's planning to do next, I can call Cillian with it. Offer him the information in exchange for him backing me up with King."

Briar places her hand on my shoulder as I pull out to pass a truck. "Aren't we in enough of a mess, without adding another party to it all?"

My mind is racing with possibilities. "There is a fragile alliance between Cillian and King. They've been enemies, co-conspirators, and friends. He was there the night we saved Iris. It might work. Cillian is never going to escape the mob life. If the FBI don't get him this time, they'll pick him up in the future. It will blow their current case but won't stop the FBI from trying again. But if the information is useful to Cillian, he'll owe me. He'll owe us. And he can mediate when the time comes."

And perhaps Spark will help too.

It's the flicker of a plan, not even well constructed.

But it's all I've got.

32

BRIAR

"**O**h my God, please tell me this isn't a mirage," I say as we pull up onto the gravel drive of Rae's home.

It's dark, and I can't make out the details, but it's a pretty enough single-story home surrounded by trees. There is a porch light giving off a warm orange glow that reveals a cute seating area with thick cushions.

Saint yawns. "Not a mirage. We're finally here."

Once the engine is off, he tries to stretch his arms above his head in the cramped quarters of his truck. It's nearly two in the morning. I feel like I've been awake for days, even though I managed to snatch the occasional nap in the truck.

"We'll take what we need for tonight and leave the rest in the truck, yeah?" He puts his arm over my shoulder and kisses the top of my head.

"Sounds good."

We do as he says, and he grabs the spare key from the mailbox. When we let ourselves in, there a sweet smell of cinnamon, and Saint smiles. "Had a feeling she wouldn't rest until we got here. Come on."

With our bags lined up in the hall, he takes my hand and leads me through the house to the kitchen. "Hey Rare-bear."

A woman lifts a tray of cookies out of the oven and places it next to a second tray on racks on the counter. "Hey, Ike," she says turning around before stepping into his arms. "God, I'm glad to see you."

He kisses the top of her head. "Those oatmeal raisin?"

She looks up at him. "Of course they are. They're your favorite. Figured you wouldn't want a meal this late, but that you might be grateful for a glass of milk and a homemade cookie."

"Sounds perfect. Rae, this is my girlfriend, Briar."

He's never used the word *girlfriend* for me before. I like it. I like the way it sounds when he says it.

"Briar, this is my sister, Rae."

The first thing I notice is how similar the siblings are. They have the same wide blue eyes, the same dark hair, but while Saint's was a wild mess when it was longer, Rae's is blown out into a sleek long bob.

"It's lovely to meet you, Rae," I say, offering my hand.

Rae ignores it and hugs me. "It's *so* good to meet you too." She turns to Saint. "Girlfriend? I like it. We can talk in the morning. I left a container for any cookies you don't eat. And I put you in your usual room. Made up the other bedroom in case it wasn't a girlfriend you were bringing me. You're adults. Sleep wherever the hell you like. I'm going to bed."

I can't help but grin. "I like your sister."

Saint pulls me in and gives me a soft kiss that turns heated. "Want to role-play? You go sleep in the other room, and I'll pretend to be a guest who can't find their way to their own room. Maybe feel you up a little." His hands slip beneath my T-shirt, his thumbs brushing my nipples.

I glance in the direction Rae went and raise an eyebrow. "How about you get some milk and eat a cookie like a good boy?"

"How about you let me take you to bed and fuck you like a good girl?" I'm about to respond when he looks over at the baking trays. "After we've had some milk and cookies."

I can't help but laugh. Maybe it's a sense of relief we're safe for now. Maybe it's the fact we just got out of the truck. Maybe it's because we can both be ourselves. But I'm buoyed by his mood. It's playful. He dunks his cookies; I don't. They're still warm and taste delicious.

When we're done, I rinse the dishes, and Saint moves our bags to our room.

He comes back for me and switches off all the lights before we head to a bedroom that is thankfully down the hall on the opposite side of the corridor from Rae. Saint closes the door and leans back against it.

"Take your clothes off for me, sweetheart."

I tried to convince myself while we ate that I would refuse. That I'd feel uncomfortable having sex with him with his sister so close down the hall. But now, with our troubles momentarily halted, I want to slip into this moment with him.

He folds his arms across his chest. His biceps stretch the sleeves of his T-shirt. I like the scruff more than the beard; it suits him better. You can see the strong line of his jaw.

I pull my shirt over my head, revealing a simple nude bra. But the look in his eyes heats quickly as he watches, and I find myself becoming aroused. I kick off my sneakers, then slip my black sweatpants down my legs. My socks come off with them.

When I'm standing in my underwear, he drags his gaze down my body and back up again. "You know, I spent a fair chunk of the drive trying not to think about how I was going to fuck you when we got here."

"And what conclusion did you come up with?" I unfasten my bra, guide the straps down my arms, and let it fall to the floor.

His eyes track me as I remove my underwear. As I step out of them, I widen my stance a little and let my fingers skate between my legs. It feels good. Soothing. Gently arousing.

"Fuck, Bri. Slide two fingers inside for me." His voice is rough.

"If you tell me how you're going to take me."

"Somewhere by Hershey, I figured I was going to fuck you standing up against the door." His voice is low as he unzips his jeans and pushes them down his hips a few inches. "Somewhere outside of Pittsburgh, while you slept, I decided I was going to make love to you, slow and deep. Missionary, with your legs up around my back." He dips his hands into his boxer briefs and palms himself. He sucks in a breath. "Cleveland, I was so tired, thought you'd have to do all the work and ride me. Then, in Toledo, I remembered how you sucked me down the back of your throat. Now, slide those two fingers into your pussy, pull them out, and suck on them."

It's dirty, the way he's talking to me. And I love it. I do as he asks, focusing on my own pleasure as I dip two fingers into my warmth. I slide them back and forth three times before I pull them out and hold eye contact with him as I dip them into my mouth.

Saint goes slack-jawed as he watches me through hooded eyes. "Now what?"

"Do it again, but this time put them in my mouth."

I do as he says, my body coming alive at my touch. When

I remove my fingers, I take them to him, and place them to his lips. With his other hand, he grips my wrist and feeds them into his mouth. Heat pulses through me in waves. The look in his eyes is hungry. Feral.

He licks between them before he releases them with a pop. "You taste so fucking good."

In one swift move, he grabs my hips, lifts me, then sets me down on the edge of the bed. Saint drops to his knees between my legs and pushes me back so he can get to my pussy. "Oh, God, Saint," I groan and grip his hair.

"Inside voice," he grunts. "And ride my fucking face."

I don't need telling twice. The feel of his rough palms against my thighs is such a turn-on. As is the magic he's currently working with his tongue against my clit.

It feels raw and intense.

I want it to last, yet I want to come.

He adds a finger, then another. His tongue licks and sucks my clit. It's noisy and messy. I want all of it.

My legs begin to shake as I detonate for him, my hips lifting, then he holds me down on the bed.

"Knees," Saint says. As I climb onto all fours, he tugs me right back to the edge of the bed, where he stands behind me. Within seconds, he's sheathed and thrusting deep inside me.

I hear the hiss of his breath as he does so.

He pauses, seated deep. Almost too deep. I can feel him throb inside me. It's too good. "Jesus, Rose. You feel so fucking tight like this."

I place my forehead down on the bed, but as I move to stretch my arms past my head, Saint grabs them and holds them in one fist behind my back. I'm completely at his mercy, unable to properly support myself.

"You don't like this, call me Ryker. Otherwise, don't make a sound." Saint grunts. And without warning, he slaps my ass, hard. The sting burning as I clench around his cock. "That's for breaking your promise to do as I say and to leave without me."

I try to raise my head to say something, but he slaps me again. "And that's for calling me an old man."

He isn't moving his cock. It's deep inside me, stretching me wide. The feelings are confusing. The pain and the heat. It's like ice and fire.

"Please, Saint," I beg.

He slaps me again. "That's for speaking when I said not to."

I can feel a second orgasm building. I'd forgotten how much I enjoy this. How much I needed it.

"Fuck, I can feel how much you want this," Saint says. "You need some more."

I nod. Following his instructions. He slaps me again, then runs his palm over my ass, making it burn more. "Feel good, Rose?" he asks.

I turn my head so I can see him out of the corner of my eyes. He looks consumed. By me. It's the headiest of feelings. To know you can do that to another human being. With our gaze connected, he slaps me again, and this time I come hard.

And as I do, Saint begins to move, thrusting hard. Holding me in place. My cheek scratches back and forth along the bedding.

"Fuck, Briar. Yeah. Make me come. Can I feel you squeezing me."

And with that, he comes deep inside me. He lets go of my hands to grab my stinging butt, the sensation bringing a third, milder orgasm. Or aftershock. I'm not sure which.

Either way, when he flops down on top of me with a grunt, I can't help but grin.

"What happened to inside voice?" I say.

I feel Saint's rumble of laughter. "Fuck it," he says. "Don't care who heard that."

A few minutes later, when he's disposed of the condom and I've found something to sleep in from our hastily packed bags, we curl up in Rae's guest bed, I realize I don't care either.

Because fear has a weird way of making you appreciate all the things that are life affirming. And this, with his arms around me and his lips on my neck, kissing me good night, is as life affirming as it gets.

33

SAINT

I'm praying that the code of silence surrounding undercover operations still stands, and that Jensen has no idea that I've blown my cover.

There is a message on my phone from Weicker telling me to call in or get my ass back to the office. I text a response saying I'm safe and I'm taking a couple of days. It's all the time I need to plot my future and do one last thing that might save my life.

I step out into Rae's garden. November is just around the corner, and there's a cold bite to the air despite the muted early morning sun. I miss my cut. The leather was worn and kept me warm.

The borders of the yard are well tended and makes me wonder what Rae would think of the garden Briar and I started to build.

Dialing Jensen's number, I wish I'd brought a cigarette outside with me. But I've decided to quit.

Again.

But I'm rethinking the timing.

Maybe I should quit when I know everything is settled.

"Jensen."

"Hey, it's Ryker."

"Ryker. I was going to call you today."

"Yeah. What gives?"

"One of those photos you sent me. He's a cop."

My mouth goes dry. "Yeah. Where from?"

"Crime Suppression Central Unit. A detective. Michael Callahan."

"Has he got any form?"

"No. The opposite. He's been Trooper of the Year. Honor above all honors and stuff. He's squeaky clean. Is he your suspect for one of the two cops involved with this ring?"

"I guess so. Sit tight. Let me check in with Weicker."

"Okay. I'm gonna check he's not involved in the trafficking or any other ongoing investigation. Last thing we need is the guy who's involved out there with warrants for search. Fuck knows what will go missing."

"Good idea. Speaking of warrants for search, I wanted to talk to you about Cillian Ó Ceallaigh. He's getting closer with the club. They did a deal to broker peace between them. Want to know if I should stand clear of the fallout if you guys are thinking about picking him up."

I know I'm fishing. Jensen probably does too. There's a pause and the sound of a door closing. "No pickup any time soon. We have an informant. A senior leader. It's a dirty deal. Inform versus a heavy sentence. It's gonna be a long process to take it down. But this is the first time we've got a guy in the organization willing to flip."

"What did the guy do?" It matters to me. Because what I intend to do will surely end the guy's life.

"Beat the shit out of a homeless guy. Died in the hospital two weeks later. No ID. No next of kin. No missing persons."

I reconcile my thoughts. Fucker has it coming. It amazes me how quickly I'm able to pass judgment.

"I'll send you what I can. Try to get more details about the pact between the two clubs, yeah?" I say.

"That would be helpful."

We say our goodbyes, and I end the call.

The next call is harder.

"Spark," I say when I hear my friend's voice. It's gruff with lack of sleep.

"Saint." That's it. No warm greeting or stupid pun about it being too early to be calling. "You could get me killed, calling me on a phone you know Vex could trace in a heartbeat."

"I need Cillian's number."

There's a sigh. "Haven't you done enough damage to the club?"

"One day I hope you'll sit down for a beer with me and listen to my reasons. They're as complicated as your own. Please give me Cillian's number. It could be the only thing that keeps me alive." Even though it's true, it's wrong of me to say that. Spark's need to protect those he cares about is unlimited. But I know this is the one thing that will cut through all the bullshit and get him to pay attention.

"Motherfucker," Spark mutters, then does as I ask, and I enter it to my contacts.

"How's Iris?"

"A mess, but alive. We've got you to thank. I'll do what I can to help you, preacher man."

And with that, he hangs up the phone.

I take in a deep breath of air and look over to the open window where the curtains are still drawn. Briar's asleep still. It's been less than a month since I found her in that parking lot, and yet so much of my life has changed.

I dial the number Spark gave me.

"Who the fuck are you, and how did you get this number?" The Irish lilt and fury make me smile in spite of the chaos.

"It's Saint."

"Preacher man. You've got balls calling me."

I shrug, even though he can't see me. "Way I see it, I saved your niece."

"Way I see it, we were all there."

"You insult me. I'm in this mess so Iris could get her peace. So she could talk to the police, and they could follow the leads of the organization."

"You sound like you have a vested interest. The girl? She wasn't your neighbor's granddaughter, was she?"

I glance back to the window where Briar sleeps. "Who she was is none of your business. But as a man, an uncle, and a godfather, I'm surprised you aren't a little more thankful for how I helped Iris."

There's a pause. A silence. I don't fill it.

"Aye. You're probably right. How grateful are you expecting me to be?"

"I need you to broker peace for me with the club."

Cillian laughs. "I'm grateful, but not a miracle worker. King is ready to hang, draw, and quarter you."

"Would you be more grateful if I told you there was an informant in your organization?"

There's another pause, and I swear if I didn't know better, frigid air blew straight out of the phone into my ear. "What?" Cillian manages, his tone strangled.

"You heard."

"Who is it?"

"As I see it, I have two choices. I need to either disappear to where the club will never find me. Or I make it so the club won't kill me, and I get a pathway back in. If it's the former, I don't give a flying fuck what happens to your organization or you. If it's the latter, as a member of the club and your friend, well, then I have skin in the game."

"You bastard."

"Given my father, I wish I were."

"What do you want me to do?"

I smile. "Broker peace. Figure out a path, and I'll tell you what I know. Tell you how to identify the person. I'll call you back in a couple of days."

I hang up the phone.

"Want some more coffee?" Rae asks, stepping out into the yard with my coffee cup in her hand.

"Thanks." I take it from her. Caffeine isn't quite nicotine, but I take a sip.

"On a scale of one to ten, how bad is it?" she asks.

I look down at the mug. "The first cup was better, but this is a solid seven."

Rae punches my arm. "That's not what I mean, and you know it."

"I know." I sip some more coffee, enjoying the sound of the birds. I didn't realize how much I missed the peace and quiet until this moment. With a sigh, I put my arm over her shoulders. This whole time, it's always been me and her against the world. "Let's go inside, and I'll tell you about it."

As we step inside, Briar enters the cozy kitchen. She's wearing my hoodie over the sleep shorts and tank she insisted on pulling on. I like sleeping next to her naked body, but after we fucked, she wasn't having any part of that in my sister's house.

I'm half tempted to move us to a hotel.

Except I don't want to use a credit card to check in, and the nice hotels don't take cash.

"Morning, sweetheart," I say, letting go of my sister for a moment to kiss Briar gently. Her lips are always so plump in the morning, still soft with sleep.

She sighs against my mouth.

It would be so easy to slide my palms around her and cup her ass, pick her up, and walk her back to the bedroom. But despite the desire to ease into a lazy morning of making love to this beautiful woman, I pull myself back. "Coffee?" I ask. "It's better than mine."

Briar grins. "That's not hard. Yours tastes like sludge."

I fix her a cup the way she likes it. "I was about to tell Rae what's going on. You okay if I tell her the full story?"

"Of course. She's your sister and deserves to know why we're here."

I run a finger down Briar's cheek, about to kiss her again, when my sister makes a gagging sound. "Never thought I'd see the day Ike Miller had a thing for a woman." Then she chuckles.

"Yeah, well," I say, not taking my eyes of Briar. "Sometimes the right woman has the power to both knock you on your ass and knock some sense into your head."

"Feel like I've been trying to tell you that for years," Rae mutters.

We sit down at the table, and between Briar and I, we tell Rae everything. Rae reaches for Briar's hand as we tell her about how we met, and what happened before Briar escaped.

As a trained psychologist who now works as a counselor and therapist, Rae knows all the right things to say that I fumbled my way through when Briar and I met.

She reaches for Briar's hand and holds it while offering both soothing and pragmatic advice.

It takes Rae a moment to compose her thoughts when

we're done. "I think the two of you should tell all this to Weicker."

I look at Briar, knowing how she doesn't want to involve the police. "Briar's story is hers to tell. And she's worried about the police connection." I place my hand on her knee and squeeze it.

Rae nods. "I hear you. I'm not suggesting for a second Briar go to the police. But if Weicker understood why ruining the case for this was so important to you, you might get a much fairer hearing. Otherwise, it looks like you went rogue for no apparent reason. Even if he was the only one who knew, he might be able to provide air cover for you both."

There is no way in hell I'm dragging Briar to the office to lay bare to a stranger what was done to her. "I'll tell them Spark and Iris became my friends. And how the woman I met in the lot that night stayed on my mind. It'll be okay." I'm not sure I truly believe those words, but I don't want to put any of this on Briar's shoulders.

"She's right." Briar takes my hand. I see the shift in her eyes. A quiet confidence. "I appreciate you trying to protect me, but Rae is right."

"We'll get through this, Briar. It'll be fine. It—"

"Can I make a police report here in Michigan for a crime that happened in New York?" Briar's words cut me off at the knees as Rae quietly leaves the kitchen to give us space.

"Briar, babe, we don't need to do this. It will be enough to—"

She cups my cheeks. "It's been a month. I packed the dress. It's in my case. Whatever happens next, we're protected. Either the police believe us and protect us, and you find a way back to the club because Cillian owes you. Or we move here, buy the lot down the road, change our names. I don't know. But if this helps you get out of trouble and me being a witness helps women like Iris . . . then it's worth it. Don't you think?"

Her last words are uttered so softly and sincerely that my heart melts all over again for this special woman. "Have I told you today that I love you?" I ask.

Briar shakes her head. "You didn't, but your actions just now did. Let me do this for us, Ryker, because there's nothing I wouldn't do to keep you safe and whole. To help secure a future for us."

"You're willing to do that?"

She strokes my cheek, and I lean into the feeling. I've not allowed myself any real peace in the last two days. "You'll be with me while I give my statement, right?"

I nod. "Of course I will. But I meant all the rest of it. You and me. In this for good, not just for now."

Briar has the audacity to laugh.

"What?" I ask.

But she can't stop. And her laughter makes me laugh too, even though I don't know what the fuck is funny. When she pulls herself together and wipes the tear that's escaped her long lashes, she takes a deep breath. "How can you sound unsure? We've shown how good we can be under pressure. You think a nice home in a quiet spot with jobs we like and kids who keep our lives interesting is going to be harder than this? We have a foundation most people aren't capable of building, Ryker. It would be utterly foolish to walk away from that."

I sweep her out of the chair and pick her up, my palms holding her ass. "The universe certainly has an ironic sense of timing."

"Yeah?" she says, tipping her head to one side so I can kiss the soft skin of her neck. "Why's that?"

"Because a month ago, I would have thought losing my job, my cover, and my club was the worst thing that could have happened to me."

"And it isn't?" she asks as I guide us back into the bedroom and kick the door shut with the heel of my boot.

I throw her down on the bed and tug my T-shirt over my head. "No. Because it led me to you." She wiggles her hips as I tug her shorts down her legs. "Plus, I'm going to be unemployed shortly and will need you to support me."

Briar snorts. "You can pay me back in orgasms."

"I feel like I still benefit from that." I unzip my jeans and slide them down my legs. I'm naked beneath, and Briar's eyes go hungrily to my cock.

"That's it then," she says. "You can't ever go back to work."

34

BRIAR

The following morning, after an exhausting afternoon giving statements and speaking to detectives, I convince Saint that he should absolutely take Rae grocery shopping. I'm fine here.

In fact, I feel liberated by sharing what happened.

I didn't think I'd feel that way.

But now I have a plan of my own.

I checked Saint's phone while he was in the shower and grabbed Iris's number.

They left half an hour ago, and I'm stalling. I take a deep breath and video dial.

A man with long wild hair answers, shirt off. He looks at me like he can't place me, but I remember him. He's the man who saved my life. "Fuck me," he says.

"Hey, Spark." Unexpected emotion catches in my throat. I don't know why. I was feeling invincible only moments ago. "Thank you. For saving my life."

There's a long pause. So long, I wonder if it's deliberate, to get me to hang up. "If I'd known where it would lead, I might have thought twice."

Relief floods me when he speaks. "From what Saint has told me about you, I doubt that's true."

He raises an eyebrow. "He shouldn't still be using that name."

Like a rock in the river, Spark is solid. Steadfast. But I hope one day I can wear him down enough to accept my thanks. "And you don't need to know his real one. I need to talk to Iris."

"You two need to stop calling me."

I shrug. "Technically, I called Iris. Is she there? I thought I could . . . help."

Spark tugs his hand through his hair, pulling hard. "One second. But make her cry, and I'll hang up on you."

"What I want to talk to her about are things I couldn't speak to Saint about for weeks. Let me help her. If I can."

The frown on his face turns to sadness. And I swear to God that if I didn't know better, I'd say the threat of tears hangs in his eyes. "Feisty little chicks," he mutters. "Be the goddamn death of me. Give me a minute."

The camera points up at the ceiling as he walks to another part of the house he's in. Upstairs. I hear soft words of comfort, asking if she needs more pillows, asking if she's in pain, asking a million questions before he asks if she wants to speak to me.

She must have agreed, because I see her face appear on screen. I bite down the gasp. Her face is a mess of scratches and bruises.

I put my hand to my own cheek. "It took a couple of weeks for mine to get back to normal," I say before I even introduce myself.

Her eyes fill with tears, but she puts her hand out to someone off screen. I assume it's Spark. "I'm okay." Her

voice is hoarse and raspy. Mine was too after all the screaming. "I need some privacy."

He obviously tries to refuse.

"I know. I love you too. But, please . . ."

Her eyes track him off screen, and I hear a door close.

"Hey," she says. "I'm Iris."

"I just realized. We're both flowers. I'm Rose. How are
you feeling?" Saint would probably be mad I trusted her
with the truth of my name. But the woman has dealt with
enough without deceit from me.

Iris shifts herself up in the bed. "Numb."

Cold creeps down my spine. "I remember that feeling.
Then it would try to process in my dreams. One night, I was
having a nightmare, and I screamed so bad, Saint had to
come and wake me. I scared him as much as I scared
myself."

"I keep seeing his face in the moment before he slapped
me."

"The one with the slicked-back hair? Joseph Hosea?"

Iris nods. "He's dead. They all are. At least, everyone
who was there in that warehouse."

Saint told me they were, and I honestly thought I'd
believed him, but it all hits in a different register when Iris
confirms it. "I was taken before you were. And I can't help
thinking if I'd reported it, it would never have happened to
you. I'm sorry, Iris."

"Why didn't you?"

I wipe away a tear. "Because I heard them talk about
how they had police officers on their payroll, and I was
scared. They had my purse, my keys, my wallet. Everything.
They knew where I lived. If I got free, they would know
where to pick me up all over again. I even met the man I was

supposed to be given to. Sold to." Tears spill over my lashes, and I dash them away. I didn't come here to unload on Iris.

Iris sighs and leans back on her pillow. "You did what you had to do. I understand why you feel like you couldn't process it. I can't. People from the club want to come see how I am, and I miss my kids, but I can't face any of them. Not while I look like this. Not when they are going to look at me with pity." Saint had told me about Iris being a teacher of young children. I can imagine her struggle.

I think about the early days with Saint and my experience yesterday of sharing what had happened to me with the police. "It's hard. But it improves. Every day. I promise you, Iris."

She glances over to the door, as if she's checking something. "I'm not even sure I can handle Spark looking at me the way he does. Like I'm about to break. Even though I feel like I am. It's messed up."

"From what Saint told me, Spark won't waver. Not once. He's all in with you, Iris. And I know it's hard. But learn from my mistake. Share how confusing it all is with him. He'll want to know."

Iris sighs. "I'm fed up with crying."

I remember that feeling too. "Then don't. Decide right now you are going to stop. And if you start again anyway, be kind to yourself. It's so early after what happened. And you're still healing."

Iris touches her bruised eye gently. "I don't know what I'd do without him, without Spark."

"In the middle of the night, when you're fast asleep, I bet he feels the same way about you. Saint shared some of what Spark has gone through and how you changed him for the better. It's why Saint made the choices he did, even though he's probably going to pay for them." The hitch catches in my voice.

"It's not fair. You've already paid enough of a price. It's always the women who get hurt."

I nod and try to compose myself. "We're okay. We're trying to come up with a plan. What he did for the two of you that night was the right thing. He thinks the world of Spark and King. It cuts him up inside that he's lost their friendship. But the fact he's a good man is the reason I love him. Your happily ever after carries a heavy price for him."

"And for you."

"I didn't call you to make you feel bad or to get pity. We're getting off track. I wanted you to know I'm here for you if you need me."

Iris shakes her head. She perks up a little. Less sad. More . . . what was the word Spark used? Feisty. Yeah, that.

"No. We stay on that track. You shouldn't be in hiding."

I huff. "I'd rather hide for the rest of my life with him than find out what it's like to live without him."

"Saint helped save my life. The club might have forgotten, but I haven't. King is furious. Demanding loyalty from members. Spark is torn. The club is his life. I got sixty-five thousand dollars from the club for the death of my dad. It's Saint's if he needs it to pay back the club."

"Holy shit, Iris. For real?"

She nods.

"I think Spark'd be glad to see it save his friend."

"That's so generous and kind and unexpected. Is money all it will take? Because I have some, not much. I have about five thousand in savings. I wanted to get a place of my own. It's barely anything."

The bed sinks next to me. I was so engrossed in the conversation, I hadn't heard Rae come in. She looks straight at me. "My brother's bringing in the groceries. But if you need money, quietly, I can re-mortgage the house. I bet I could get about fifty or sixty thousand out of it."

My eyes sting, and I grip Rae's hand.

"I'm going to call my uncle Cillian," Iris says. "I don't know if Saint told you about him."

"Some." I don't tell her what I heard through the open bedroom window this morning.

Iris nods. "He should pay too. I'll ask him for fifty."

"That would take us to one hundred and seventy. Is it enough?"

I see a small wince of pain as she shrugs. "Who the hell knows. They're men and they're stupid."

Rae grins next to me. "Never a truer word spoken. There's a reason I'm still single. Let me go help Ike so he doesn't get suspicious. I'm assuming you're going to tell him about this."

"Eventually." It's the best I can offer.

Iris waits a moment. "Saint's real name is Ike? I thought it was Phillip. Oh, shit. The undercover thing."

"It's not Ike, but it's probably wise I don't say what it is."

When she smiles, it changes the shape of her bruised face. "I hope we get to meet in person, Rose. I hope we get to be friends."

For a moment, I allow myself to daydream. "I'm gonna hold on to that. It's going to get rough again before then. But I promise, I will hold on to it."

Iris makes a move to get out of bed. "Shit, that hurts," she groans.

"Stop. Where are you going? Don't hurt yourself."

"You sound like Spark," she says with grim humor.

"Spark." She tries to shout his name into the hallway.

I wince as she does. "You should get back in bed," I encourage.

"Fuck me, little chick." I hear the boots and the voice before I see him. "You need me to tie you to that bed?"

"Not while I'm still on the phone with Rose."

I bite down on my lip at the comment and can't hear the words Spark murmurs as he tugs Iris into a hug, which I hope for her sake is gentle. The world goes into a blur as the phone gets squashed between them.

"We're going to save Saint," she says. "And you're going to help."

35

SAINT

I straighten my shoulders and crick my neck from left to right, kind of like a boxer when he steps into the ring. But as I catch sight of my reflection, I see the clothes are utterly different. I'm in a gray suit and a white shirt.

Briar smiled when she saw me. Said something about billionaire role-play when I get back home. Or secretary and boss. But she also said she preferred me in jeans.

And I agree.

Because this feels like a costume. I run my finger beneath the collar of the shirt to create a little more room to breathe.

We drove back to Briar's apartment from Rae's yesterday. It was hard to say goodbye to her. But I promised her when this is all wrapped up, and after Briar and I have taken a long and well-deserved vacation, we'll go see her again.

I pull out my phone and text Briar.

You doing okay?

It's the first time we've been back to her apartment.

When we got there last night, she felt uneasy, but a couple of glasses of wine helped her relax.

Plus, she's armed. Took her to a gun range while in Detroit to get her comfortable with the gun I left her with. She's not a crack shot by any means. But she knows to point it at someone's body rather than try to aim for their legs to slow them down. That shit never works. The body is a bigger mass. Easier to hit the target.

I'm doing fine. You worry about you. Good luck today. There's a four-leaf clover emoji. Then a second line of text. *Wait. Should the clover be code for the Irishman who shall not be named.*

I'm sure Cillian wouldn't appreciate it.

After today's meeting with my bosses to explain my actions, I'm going to call Cillian and see what plan he's come up with to help save my ass.

Now I just have to keep all the stories in my head straight while I face the ATF.

Funny. He'd hate that. I really love you, B.

Good. Because I'd hate to feel like this about someone who didn't feel the same. Hurry up and come home.

With a deep breath, I step inside the building to chaos.

People are hurrying around. There's shouting and frantic movement of individuals.

I head to where I'm meant to meet Weicker, Davis, and other members of the team. "What gives?" I ask as Weicker glances up at me.

"A hit piece on the ATF in a national newspaper. Accusations and shit about this office. Everyone's on high alert, trying to figure out where the leaks are, how much is true. It's a shit show. Bit like our op."

I pull out a chair, put my bag with my laptop in it next to me. "Can I talk to you first? In confidence. Without everyone in here. There's something that needs to be known, but not by everybody. Not yet at least."

Weicker looks around the room and nods. I take a deep breath while the room clears. When it's empty, I take another one. I'm banking on Weicker putting himself in my shoes.

"Rose Whittaker was the girl I rescued that night at the docks. When she ran to me, she was barefoot, wearing a slip of a dress, and was a beaten mess. Her wrists were torn to shreds from being bound. We got her free from the men who held her, and I offered to take her anywhere, the ER, the cops, home. A friend's place. She said she needed a safe place to stay for a night. And asked if I could help her find clothes and money. That she'd pay me back. And in that moment, she reminded me of my mom and my sister, who would routinely suffer beatings like I did at the hands of my Bible-thumping father. Back then, I just wanted to get them out of there; and when I met Rose I felt the same."

Weicker places his fingers and thumbs on his temple. "Jesus, Ryker. You're meant to remain objective."

Thinking of that night gets my heart racing all over again. What if I hadn't been there? Would they have killed her? What if someone else had found her and then abused her all over again? I catch the doom spiral and endeavor to stop it.

"I know. But you need to hear this for the next part to make sense. I took her home, patched her up, preserved the slip she was wearing. She wouldn't go to the police because, like I told you before, she heard the men who took her saying there were police on payroll. Speak to Jensen. We got an identification on one of them. He was with the perpetrators at a local diner one day. Camera footage places them chatting at the same table. Anyway, I advised Rose that she was washing evidence down the drain when she tried to scald her assailant's touch from her body."

Weicker curses.

Desperate to do something other than stare at him, I stand and go to the window. The glass is cool to the touch, the world carrying on outside like normal. "She never left. At first it was a function of her not feeling safe enough. And when we eventually returned to her apartment, there were signs someone had been there looking for her. And that was the first day I kissed her."

I rest against the window ledge as Weicker closes his eyes and tips his head back. "You blew all this for a woman?"

I itch the side of my scruff. It's soft because I haven't clipped it in five days, and it grows fast. "Not just one woman. Let me finish before you pass judgment."

"Fine, continue." There's exasperation in his tone.

"I started to investigate. The club placed trackers on Joseph Hosea's truck. We were able to narrow down homes and locations. Where he was spending his time, that kind of thing." Up until now, it's all been the truth. I want to keep the lie down to as few sentences as possible. I struggle to frame them in my head. "When Iris O'Connor went missing, I was already checking out the address of one of the warehouses. I was unaccompanied and on my own time. When I saw Iris, I knew she was in grave danger and didn't have time to call for help. Her hands were tied and were looped over a hook that hung from the ceiling. She was naked and unconscious."

"Fuck me," Weicker says, with disgust at what he's just heard.

"There were men associated with the Righteous Brotherhood there, but also Russian accents. Faces I didn't know and haven't had time to worry about. Guns were drawn. In the confusion, I knew I had one chance to save Iris. Was it reckless? Yes. Did I put my life on the line? Yes. But in a heartbeat, Iris O'Connor became my sister, Rae, and she became Rose. Both women I love. And I simply needed to save her. After that, I got her out of there and called you. I had to reveal myself, and Iris heard me. She told Spark and now I'm made."

"That's the report you want to put in?"

I huff a laugh. "No. The one I really want to put in asks questions. Your wife, Weicker? How far would you go to keep her safe? Would you trust the cops? Hell, look outside that door. Would you trust us? We take the moral high ground, let the badge speak for us, but do we really act that way? We do deals with bad guys to get to more bad guys. I love Rose. Gonna fucking marry her at some point. If there is ever a question between the right thing for the op, and the right thing for a woman in distress, whether it be Rose, my sister, Rae, Iris, or any other woman, I'm gonna make the same call over and over. Which is why I'm also resigning as of today."

Weicker looks up at that. "Sit the fuck down. I'm not accepting your resignation."

I do as he asks and pull out a chair. Now that I've said it, I can't take it back. I've put it out into the universe, and it feels right. "I'm afraid you don't have a choice. I won't do this anymore. Not when I'm told to compromise my values. To stay focused on a weapons investigation when I see women in danger. And I realized, as I saw myself in this suit on the way into the building, a desk job isn't for me either."

I stop there. For now.

I hear Weicker's pen hit the table in a steady drumbeat. "You're one of the best I have."

"Had. And unfortunately, on this op, the organization never treated me like that. Especially Davis."

"You could move."

"I'm going to. But it won't be within the ATF. I can't do that to Rose. Let me tell you the pieces I'm not going to tell everyone else who walks in here. She was abducted on her way to her apartment by a man she'd met on a dating app a week earlier. She was held in a concrete room, forced to strip in front of strangers and put on lingerie. She was told she was going to become some cunt's wife. A *perfect* wife. When that man arrived and she tried to protect herself, he beat her so hard that she could barely remain conscious. I've seen her claw her way back from a huddled mess on the floor of my shower into a woman willing to go to the police she dreads to make this easier for me, so I could tell you. She also reported it in another state so it couldn't get covered up. She's a warrior. A survivor. And I won't put her through anything like that again. I can't be disappearing into undercover ops."

Weicker leans back in his chair. "You're giving up an exceptional career, Ryker."

I smile. "Let me ask you that question again. If this were your wife, how far would you go to keep her safe?"

Davis blusters into the room. "What the fuck were you thinking?" he shouts.

I don't answer. I simply look to Weicker, to see if my friend will come through for me, or whether he will protect himself.

"Well?" Davis says, walking closer. "We're having to clean up this mess, talking to prosecutors to see what we have that is worth charging because you recklessly blew your cover."

I still don't say anything.

Weicker draws in a breath and looks at me with a stare that conveys that while he obviously thinks I'm an asshole, he's here for me. "Sit down, Davis. There's shit you don't know."

"There better fucking had be." He grunts as he sits.

And from there out, I let Weicker lead.

Four brutal hours later, it's settled. Before my resignation is official, I'm going to update all my reports, which I plan to amend to minimize all intelligence. I roll back what I know, anything I can feasibly get my hands on. I know the rules of evidence tampering, but I also know how to do it so subtly that it will go unnoticed for years, which is how long it will take to arrest, charge, and then await trial. By then I'll be long forgotten and out of the system.

When I get back to her apartment, Briar is sitting at the small round table by the window, her tablet in front of her. She's sketching some scene for what looks like a book cover.

"*One Day Like This*?" I ask, peering over her shoulder before kissing her neck.

"Hmm" she says, tilting to the left so I can get the spot behind her ear that always makes her shiver. "It's a rock star romance. Best friend's little sister."

"Is that what it sounds like?" I slide my arms around her.

"If you think it means the rock star hero fucks his best friend's little sister, then yes."

I laugh. "I don't want to think of anyone fucking my little sister."

"Which is why the trope works." She places her pencil, a stylus that she gushed about having pixel-perfect precision, down on the table.

When she smiles at me and touches my cheek, my heart trips like it always does around her. "How did it go?"

"We have a plan. And I'm out at the end of the week."

I feel the air leave her lungs. "Good."

"Why don't you go put on something nice? I'll even trim this," I say, smoothing my hand over my beard. "Then let me take you out for dinner."

Briar glances out the window, a frown on her face. "Is it safe to do that?"

I shrug. "The Outlaws don't hang here. Cillian lives over in Brooklyn. It's a coincidence he saw us that day. I want a date with you. A normal one. We don't need to go far or fancy." I take her hands. "Just come make a memory with me, Bri. One that doesn't involve anything other than the two of us."

She softens at my words, then looks down at the leggings and the hoodie of mine she's wearing. "I should shower and change."

I tug the hoodie over her head. She's naked beneath. Not even a bra. Does it make my cock hard to think of her nipples brushing up against my hoodie all day? You bet your fucking ass it does.

"I'll do you a deal. You clean me and I'll clean you. Then I'll take you out to dinner."

Briar smiles as her tension eases. "Okay. Deal. As long as that's a euphemism for shower sex."

I take her wrist and lead her to the small bathroom. "It can be a euphemism for whatever you want it to be."

36

BRIAR

Four days later, I erase the lines I've drawn. They aren't quite right. Didn't flow. Didn't give the piece movement.

There's a bang out in the hallway, and I jump. We've been back in my apartment for five days, and I still can't get used to it.

On Monday, we went out for phở. On Tuesday, we grabbed subs and ate them on my tiny balcony. And last night, the two of us curled up on the sofa and watched a rom-com that made Saint groan at the cheesiness of it. We bought pre-prepared food and nibbled on cheese and crackers.

He's gone to the ATF offices every day. I went with him yesterday, and we talked to Weicker. He was sympathetic. It felt sincere. Today is Saint's last day.

Then we're going to Mexico for four weeks. I can work anywhere, and well, Ryker needs a bit of time. He tries to be strong, but I can tell it's all wearing him down. We need some rest, in a safe place. Our world is up in the air, but as

long as I can fall asleep in the same bed with him at night,
I'm okay.

I try to keep busy, packing up the rest of my stuff. I'm
subletting my apartment to one of the women who works at
the ad firm. She recently split from her husband and is
looking for a place to lie low for a while. I've told her I can
be flexible. I'm leaving some of my furniture, so it's one less
thing for her to worry about.

Packing should have made me happy, but every clang of
the ducts or slam of a door has my nerves on edge.

I thought work might help, so I started a new project. A
second book cover for a romance author who wants a
graphic design for a Christmas novella. But I can't even get
the simplest idea for Christmas baking to take shape.

I hate this place.

My phone rings, and I slam my palm to my chest.

I don't recognize the number. Usually, I ignore it. But
Ryker told me his cell phone doesn't work when he's in the
basement of the building, and that he might call from a
work phone. "Hello."

"Rose?" I feel like I know the voice, but I'm not sure.

"Who is this?"

"It's Spark. I need to get a hold of Saint. Is he there?"

I look at the clock on my laptop. "No. I guess he'll be
home in another hour or so."

There's a pause. "Tell him to call me when he gets back.
And . . . tell him no matter what, no matter how it might
seem, I've got his back."

"Should I be worried, Spark?" My stomach flips, and my
breath becomes shallow.

"Trust me," Spark says. And with that, he hangs up.

Trust me. Not the most reassuring.

I turn off all my equipment and move to the sofa. There's no way I'm getting any more work done today.

Clouds scud by outside my window. The first moment I stepped into this apartment, I had a great feeling about this place. It was a new beginning. An exciting life. In some ways that is true—I never would've met Ryker if I hadn't moved here—but I'm not ready for the old "every cloud has a silver lining" chestnut yet.

I think about Iris and what she said. It's always the women who get hurt in the cross fire. I wonder how many more of us there are. I close my eyes and try to nap.

I jump when there's a knock and Saint walks through the door. "Hey, sweetheart," he says, dropping his bag and climbing on top of me. His legs hang off the edge of the sofa, but he slides his hands beneath me. His lips brush mine.

"All done?" I ask.

"All done."

He's filed his final reports, made some updates to previous ones. While he can't delete evidence and reports that have already been filed, he can edit them. He told me he planned to drop weapon classes, numbers. With a half-decent lawyer, none of the club would face anything serious. And there is a history of so many of these cases falling apart at the eleventh hour because of everything from entrapment claims to flaky evidence trails.

"Good." I kiss him back, letting my hands slide over his strong shoulders, down his back. "You have a phone call to make. You need to call Spark."

Saint jumps up. "What? How? Spark called you?"

I nod. "He did."

Concern wrinkles his brow. "How did he get your number?"

"I called Iris."

Saint jumps to his feet. "Jesus, sweetheart. Didn't I make it clear enough? Vex can track anything. Maybe King is having Spark's phone traced in case I call him."

I sit up and cross my legs beneath me. "Is King really that paranoid? Would people agree to being tracked to find you?"

Saint tugs a hand through his hair. He went to a barber yesterday to sort out the botched job he did of it the day we fled. He wants to grow it long again. "I'm a federal agent. Of course King is that paranoid. And who says he'll tell Spark he's doing it. I saw King lock Spark in an office with Halo guarding the door because he thought he was fucking Iris. And when I tried to step in, to save him, King said to me, 'I ever see you go for your weapon again when I know it's going to be pointing at me . . . I'll gut you with a fishing knife before I fucking kill you without hesitation.' Then he had the audacity to clink his glass to mine and say cheers."

"Why do you admire him so much?"

"It's complicated, okay? I think he's a good man, a thoughtful one, beneath the façade. I don't want him to lose his humanity. I'm fed up with rules I need to follow. The army. The ATF. I want to be free of all that bullshit. I like the edge of it, Briar. I want to fucking thrive. I'm chasing that feeling of being completely at home in my own skin. Why did you call Iris?"

"Because I wanted her to know it would get better. What she's going through right now. And you thought it was sweet I cared about Iris enough to offer to speak with her."

"Didn't mean you should do it right now, sweetheart." Saint tips his head back and sighs before rubbing his hand over his face. "Your kind heart is going to get us into trouble."

I stand and take both his hands in mine. "Don't you see

that it didn't? Spark and Iris want to help. And that's what he said on the call. For you to call him and know that no matter what, he's on your side. We've got some money. It's in my account. Iris has given us the money from her father's death. She says she's going to ask Cillian for more. Rae has given us fifty thousand. We're at a hundred and twenty thousand. We have something to offer to help you get out of this."

His hands go straight back into his hair. "No, Briar, this is my problem to solve. I can't take all that money off you. And where did Rae get that money?"

"She remortgaged the house, but—"

"Fuck," he mutters. Then he repeats it, more quietly this time as he tugs me into his arms and kisses the top of my head. "I appreciate what you are trying to do, sweetheart. But let me navigate this, yeah? Only because you don't know all the players."

"Fine. But you should call your sister and thank her."

Saint grips me and tugs me close. "Is that before or after I spank your ass for conspiring with her?"

It makes me grin. "Definitely before."

He pulls out his phone and video calls her. "What have you been up to?" he asks when her face appears on screen.

She looks a little stricken, so I step in. "I told him about the money."

"Oh. Right." Rae grins at someone off-screen. She's not in her home. "I'm with company. We should talk about this later."

"Oh," Saint says. "*Oh*, right. Got it. Well, you didn't need to do it, but I love you for it."

"You'd be surprised what I'd do for you, Ryker. I'm so damned lucky I got you for a brother. Love you too."

The screen goes dark.

"Was the subtext there that she's with a guy?" Saint asks.

"Umm. I think so. I mean, there's a small possibility she was thinking about who might overhear what you were about to say. But it's probably a guy."

"Urgh," he says, shivering dramatically. "That grosses me out."

I go to the drawer I keep the takeout menus in. "She's a grown woman who didn't get any while we were staying over. Why shouldn't she be out with a guy?'

"'Cause she's my fucking sister," he answers playfully.

The exasperation in his tone makes me laugh. "Who is in her mid-thirties. Calm down, big brother. She can have sex whenever she likes."

He puts his thumb on my lips, pulling down slightly before kissing me. "You wanna put that smart mouth of yours around my cock instead of giving me sass?"

"We can add it to the list, somewhere between spanking my ass and making me orgasm at least twice."

Saint laughs and kisses me once more before letting me go.

We order Chinese food and plan to eat in front of the television again under the promise that it won't be another rom-com. I get the plates while Saint pops two bottles of beer from the fridge.

The intercom buzzes, and I answer it. "Hello."

"Got your Chinese delivery."

"Apartment forty-eight, fourth floor." I buzz him up while Saint gets utensils.

When there's a knock at the door, I open it and am met with the barrel of a gun.

I can't think or breathe beyond it. I force myself to look up. Spark, four other men in leather, and Cillian stare back at me. A man with a scar down his face is holding the gun, and he has a finger over his lips.

My whole body begins to shake. "Don't do this," I say softly, my eyes on Spark.

I back up into the room and see Saint ready to move for his weapon. It's suicide.

"Touch it and I'll drop her," the man with the gun says.

"Niro. Don't hurt her and I'll come with you," Saint says. He raises his hands.

"Y'all have got no fucking class." The soft Irish lilt seems at odds with Cillian's suit, but after what Saint told me, I remain on guard. "You're scaring the girl." He comes over to me and ducks slightly to look in my eyes. "*Beidh sé go breá, beagaidín. Coinneoimid slán é.*"

It's going to be alright, little one. We'll keep him safe.

"I don't believe you," I say, my throat raw and dry. I glance at Saint, whose eyes are fixed on Niro. I love him, and I'm not certain if I've told him enough so that he knows it to his very bones.

Cillian touches my cheek, and I shirk away. "I know."

"Clutch. I'll make this right," Saint says, looking at a tall man whose patch reads *vice president*. "Don't bring Briar into this. What happened to Gwen is nothing compared to what Briar has gone through."

"Let's take Saint and go," Spark says. "Niro, lower the gun."

Niro shakes his head. "King said the girl comes with us."

I see the look that passes between Spark and Cillian. "He wants Saint." A man I don't know says this. His patch says *Bates*.

"He also wants insurance, and he knew none of you would have the balls to take her," Niro says. "Bates, take the girl."

The man named Bates has the audacity to place the Chinese food on the counter before gripping my arm.

Spark walks to Saint and puts his hands on his biceps. "Jeremiah 29:11."

"What the fuck is that?" Niro asks. "The man isn't even a preacher."

But when I look to Saint, his shoulders have relaxed, and he nods.

The only sign that tells me I should go with these men.

37

SAINT

Niro grips my arm as I climb into the van. "Don't give me a reason to kill you or your girl, preacher man. I don't want your death on my conscience. We're armed; you're not. There are five of us and only two of you. Now, do I need to tie you up for you to behave?"

"No. We're good."

I help Briar inside, then climb in after, pulling her close to me as we sit. She's shaking uncontrollably, and I need to remain strong enough for both of us.

Spark climbs into the driver's seat but winks in the rearview mirror as he adjusts it. Clutch joins him in the front. Niro sits behind us. The others climb on their bikes. I don't know where Cillian went. I don't know what he said to Briar. As people get settled, I kiss the top of Briar's head. "There's hope," I whisper.

At least, that's how I interpret what Spark told me.

Because Jeremiah 29:11 is about that. Hope. *For surely I know the plans I have for you, says the Lord, plans for your welfare and not for harm, to give you a future with hope.*

And it makes me do something I haven't done in a long

time. I pray. I'm not entirely sure who I'm praying to. Maybe they are pleas to the universe, because this is not how my life was meant to end. I'm meant to be in the sun with Briar, her in a turquoise bikini that matches the color of the water. She's sun-kissed and so fucking happy, it hurts my heart to witness it.

I thought my life flashing before my eyes would be all the things I've done, not all the things I would never get to do. There are kids. Three of them. Two boys and a girl, in that order. And a dog. No, make that two. One is a great guard dog, the other is a dumbass who finds sticks three times the size he is. I ride my bike; I'm part of this club. And at the end of every ride and every day, there's Briar.

"Remember the camera feed to your apartment," I whisper. "Use it."

Briar's hand grips mine. "Don't make me have to. Please."

I see the ink on Spark's hand as he steers the van. An iris in deep purple, and the letters of her name across his knuckles. I want to carry the mark of Briar with me every day too.

I'll get it done by someone other than Niro.

Maybe I'm going to face my death, but I'm so fucking calm. Like the days when I walked the last two hundred meters to a bomb.

When the van finally pulls up outside the clubhouse, I take a moment to look at Briar one last time.

"I love you. So much," she says.

"Don't ever doubt how much I love you too," I say.

"I'm scared," she replies.

"I know. But trust Spark. If anything goes to shit, trust him."

Tears sting her eyes. "We were so close to figuring it all out."

"There's still time. Remember. Step one. Avoid the panic hole. Step two. Be optimistic. Step three. Control the steps, not the outcome."

Niro chuckles in the background, and I turn to face him. "How you got that scar on your face will be nothing compared to what I'll do to you if you harm her."

He shrugs. "Can't wait, preacher man. That was a great motivational pep talk by the way."

I let the anger fill me. But like the first step in any bomb disposal, containment is key. I save my fuel wisely. There will be a time when I need it. Some bombs can't be disposed of. They're too cleverly and tightly wired and planned.

Sometimes, all you can do is let them detonate.

The lot is filled with bikes. Every member is here to witness this, and I breathe in slowly. Keeping my heart rate down is going to be crucial. Stress won't help me make clear decisions. Stress won't make what's about to happen hurt any less.

When they lead us around the back of the club, my heart sinks. We're going to the shed.

"You okay, sweetheart?" I ask, squeezing her hand.

She shakes her head without saying a word.

Spark falls into step alongside me. "We've got her," he whispers. "Cillian's men are going to take her from the two prospects guarding her while you're inside. She'll be at my house. He has his men there to protect her."

"Good. Tell Cillian I'll tell him what I know if I make it through tonight. What is this?"

"The best I could do. It's gonna hurt, but you'll live."

Briar slams to a halt. "Whatever this shit show is," she

says, "you look at me. Not them. They don't exist. Just you and me. Right?"

I cup her cheek and move to kiss her before Niro shoves me away from her. "I'm done with the lovefest. Just get inside."

And then we're separated. I see Cillian has Briar by the shoulders while Niro and Bates drag me into the shed.

I hear her scream my name, the fear of it jacking the heart rate I tried so hard to control.

The concrete sound-proofed chamber is clad in old wood to make it look like a derelict building. The floor is ever so gently sloped into a drain in the middle of the floor. Above it is a giant hook. From it dangle two long, heavy-duty wire cables.

King stands in the middle of the room. Thinking about the way they picked us up, I realize it's the first time I haven't seen him lead from the front. Usually, Saint has to remind him about how at risk he is. I'm surprised he didn't come get me himself. The other patched-in members stand around the walls of the room.

I shake free of Niro and walk under my own steam to face King. He stares at me until I'm literally two feet in front of him.

"Thought you could hide?" King says.

"Aren't we all hiding who we really are in some way?"

He takes a minute to light a cigarette. "Answer the question."

"No. I needed to give you time to cool down before I could speak with you rationally. And I needed to make right what I'd done."

He huffs and blows out a ring of smoke. "Make right? How do you make right that you lied to us, Judas?"

Two things hit me. He has seen my messages to Briar, to

know the word we used was *Judas*. I glance at Vex, who is looking at the ground. And I think about my dad.

Dad would ramble about Judas's betrayal of Jesus ad nauseam, but one thing always stuck, and I voice it out loud to King. "Judas was not forgiven because he never repented. When I joined the Outlaws, I was lost. I'd spent years literally wandering the desert with the army. The ATF capitalized on that. But it was only here that I found my fucking family. I stopped reporting in. Stopped giving them information. Never shared the weapons drops. But then Briar came into my life, and all I cared about was finding the people who took her. And I knew they'd never see real justice in the current legal system. Abduction charges, sexual assault charges. Shit that goes away with a good lawyer and a clean record. I could only deliver that justice here. So I fixed my reports and evidence the best I could. I've quit the ATF."

"But the ATF have information on us they didn't have before you joined us, right?" King asks.

I nod. "They do."

There are mumbles of complaint.

King steps away from me. "You must have something pretty big on Cillian for him to come out in your defense."

I don't acknowledge what he says.

"Iron Outlaws, we have a choice. Kill Saint now. Or do the one thing Jesus couldn't apparently do and forgive our Judas."

There are a few chuckles at this. Niro is loudest.

I hate that fucker.

"So, now you have to make your choice." King steps back up to me, but he's talking to them. "Put twenty grand at his feet. After all, Judas betrayed Jesus for thirty pieces of silver. The money will go to the club for future legal bills as a result of his actions. Or exact a punishment on Saint. Show him what his betrayal means to you."

Hands begin to slap against the concrete wall.

"At the end, we'll count. More punishments means he dies. More cash means he can live, and, if he matches the amount of cash himself, at some point in the future, he can re-join the club." He grips my chin. "Fight back, and the vote counts double." He turns to the others. "Iron Outlaws. Today be ours."

There's cheering like a gladiator fight.

Spark takes my shirt. "Just fucking breathe."

I can see the pain in his eyes. The man wants to protect everyone. It's in his nature. "None of this is your fault," I say.

Niro runs a tattoo parlor, but he's also a piercing expert. When he steps up with two huge hooks in sterile packs, I feel sick to my stomach.

Spark turns me so my back is to Niro. I draw in a deep breath.

It feels like it takes forever for Niro to decide where the hooks should go.

When the first hook pierces my skin, I drop my head forward. The second is no less painful. I breathe until I start to feel lightheaded. But all worries about my knees collapsing pass into insignificance as Niro connects the cables to the hooks and winds a winch, which slowly lifts me, by the skin, until my toes scrape the floor.

"Judas," Niro says, and walks away.

Bates comes next; he's got a knife. He walks behind me and drags the blade down my back, the agonizing burn of metal through skin makes stars swim in my eyes. The iron-rich scent of blood fills the air.

I swallow deeply. I can't feel faint this early in the process. There is too much to come.

"Judas," Bates says.

Clutch is next. He steps up in front of me. "You helped save Gwen. Now we're straight." He drops a brown envelope at my feet.

Switch follows. "I'm a fan of redemption arcs." He tosses an envelope down.

Track is wearing a knuckle duster. I told King to send him away because he's the only one on audio talking about being at a weapons delivery. He draws his hand back and slams it into my ribs. One cracks, I'm sure. The skin on my back feels as though it's ripping. Then he draws his hand back and does it again.

"You said one punishment," Spark says to King, stepping forward between me and Track.

"That one was for breaking Tessa's heart if they come for me," Track says.

"It's fair," I manage to say.

Spark turns and faces me. So, this is how we meet again after everything went down at the warehouse. I want to talk to my friend. Reassure him.

He reaches for an envelope in his cut. He taps it against his palm as he struggles with what to say. "Iris . . ." he says, finally.

"I know," I tell him.

He nods and drops the envelope in front of me.

And so it goes.

More envelopes in between beatings. I watch the blood trickle down the drain.

I lose count. The envelopes begin to blur. Pain consumes my every breath.

Finally, King steps forward brandishing a knife. "This is going to hurt," he says.

"Not worse than anything my dad inflicted," I manage to grunt.

He carves something into my stomach. Letters.

An I and an O. Iron Outlaws. As if pain of the blade slicing through my skin isn't enough, he empties a container of salt over the wound.

"Judas," he states as I pass out from blood loss and pain.

38

BRIAR

The sound of a key in the lock makes both Iris and I jump.

It's a little over a week since Iris was taken from her home, and I can tell she's uncomfortable in Spark's house, despite the metal security gate and camera he installed for her. Her bruises have turned yellow, finally fading from the first time we spoke. But I know the mental scars take a lot longer to heal.

I've spent the past hour looking at a surgical-type bed that the club's medic, called Switch, had apparently set up hours before this shit show began.

Cillian has tried to reassure me that this is the best way to resolve things. The fact there is a giant tarp to protect Iris's wooden floor and rug is not reassuring. Saint's going to be a mess when he's returned to me, which I've been assured he will be. And I'll be here to care for him like he cared for me.

Because he won't be reporting these people to the police either.

I run to the door and hold it open as Spark and Clutch carry Saint into the living room.

Bizarrely, from the neck up, he looks totally fine, but from the shoulders down, he's a mess. I reach for his hand and pull it to my heart, where I clasp it tightly. "Oh, God. What did you do to him?"

Others follow. I read the names on their leather cuts. Switch comes in first, and I'm glad to see him move into action. The trays of medical supplies are slid into place by a tall, jacked man with the patch *Halo*.

"How . . . many?" Saint's voice is ragged. His breathing in between each word is harsh.

"Ten envelopes, nine beatings," Clutch says.

Saint smiles softly, then looks up at me. "It's going to . . . be . . . okay."

I feel a little faint at the sight of all the blood. "How could you do this to him?" I ask Spark.

"No one in this room did this," Spark replies. "But it's an old-school MC punishment. A club vote that extracts vengeance and dishes forgiveness. Now it's done. Over. The club won't pursue any further repercussions."

Now my head really does feel woozy. Saint took this so we can get on with the rest of our lives. It's too big a sacrifice to comprehend, but he did that for us.

"What can I do to help?" I ask.

Spark squeezes my hand. "Just be here for him."

Switch inserts an IV into Ryker's arm. "It's pain relief," he says, as if sensing my concern. "And a heavy-duty sedative. The less of what happens next he feels, the better it will be for all of us."

"I love you, Rose," he says as he floats under.

"I love you too," I whisper at his temple before kissing his forehead gently.

I don't let go of his hand. Not when Clutch and Spark move him so Switch can clean up his back and stitch him up. Not when they clean out and sew up the initials carved onto his stomach. Not when they are finally done, and Saint is still sleeping.

Cillian brings me a cup of milky tea. "Here, this will help. I put sugar in it."

I'm really not in the mood for sweetened hot tea, but I don't have the energy or will to fight the Irishman. It goes down surprisingly easily. "Thank you."

Iris steps forward and places her hand on Saint's forehead. "I owe him my life. I know the others were there that night. But the rest of it—I needed to be able to tell the police. He gave me the ability to do that without incriminating anyone else in this room. He deserved better than this."

Spark steps next to her. "I did the best I could, little chick. It was this or . . ."

He doesn't say the rest of it. He doesn't need to.

She looks up at him. "I don't doubt it."

Halo has his back to the wall, one foot resting against it. "Good to see you on your feet, Irish," he says.

Iris smiles. "Good to be on them. Thanks to all of you. Sorry I haven't been up to company."

"*Conas atá tú?*" Cillian asks me.

"*Táim ag fanacht le haghaidh an saol daor,*" I reply. It's true. I really am holding on for dear life. I have anger and nowhere to place it. I feel sick from what was done. I don't know what to make of all the people in this room.

"Holy shit," Clutch says. "Don't tell me we have *another* Irish?"

I shake my head. "My grandfather, my pop, was Irish. He wanted me to speak the language."

"I feel like we should invoke a no-Irish clause," Halo says with a grin. "Feels like you're scheming."

I smile. I can't help it. "Yes. What I actually said was 'You shoot the big one, and I'll take the medic.'"

Cillian chuckles. "More of the Irish in her than not, I say."

And I remain by Saint's side as people come and go. As Saint moves upstairs to Spark's spare room. As he gets better day by day.

I leave the room at one point so he can tell Cillian who the rat is in his organization, a decision I've already made my peace with. With the clues he's able to provide, Cillian has a very strong clue who it is.

One night, Ryker and Spark stayed up talking around the fire pit in the yard while Iris and I sat inside together. I adore her. And from the way Saint and Spark hugged each other before they went to bed, I think their friendship, while currently fragile, will survive too.

We collect the matching payment. A mix of the money we'd been given and cash Saint had hidden in the lining of one of his bags. Money the club paid him that was supposed to serve as ATF evidence. Only he and I knew that was where the money came from.

And in the times in between, I focused on my work. I become a pro at doing work in snatches so I didn't lose any clients.

Seven days later, I'm busy packing. Saint had his stitches removed. The bruising has faded. He finished the course of antibiotics Switch gave him. And we both want some sunshine before winter hits. Mexico is calling. We have flights in the morning.

"Babe," Saint says as he checks out my pile of shoes. "I thought we were travelling light."

"This is light. I narrowed it down from seven pairs to four. Plus my sneakers. And my flip-flops."

He laughs as he playfully knocks me down on the bed and then sits next to me. His ribs still hurt. Switch says it will take three to six weeks for them to fully heal. Saint is pretending he's fine, but he forgets I can see him wince. I wiggle up close to him, keeping my head on his bicep rather than his chest. We've not had sex yet because of it. The blow job I'd tried two nights ago at his request was great until he came, tensing his abs as he cried out in a mix of ecstasy and agony as it pulled against his ribs.

"I can reduce the shoes," I admit.

He kisses the top of my head. "Meh. You're good. I was teasing. Plus, your legs look good in those heels. I'm gonna fuck you in them somewhere we shouldn't on vacation."

I can't help but chuckle. "Is that before or after your ribs heal and you can perform in a way you don't throw your back out, old man?"

Saint laughs but then stifles it and grabs his ribs. "Shit. Don't make me laugh."

"You sure you're up for travelling? We could wait another week."

"Heal here, heal there. Whatever. I feel like some sun and a sun lounger are the best choice. Although, you might have to haul that case full of shoes off the baggage carousel yourself."

"Good practice for a few more years when I need to push you around with your walker."

"Fuck, Bri," he mutters as he shudders with muted laughter.

The distant rumble of bikes turns into a roar until they all seem to stop outside the house. I jump up and check the window. "It's Spark, Clutch, Niro, Halo, Switch, Vex, Bates, and some guy with black hair."

Saint sits up slowly. "That'll be King."

I met all the others over the last week, except King. Some have been nice. Clutch came with Gwen, and we hung out together. I learned I'm now an old lady. I said I should be considered a young lady given my age relative to Saint's.

Gwen laughed. So did Halo and Spark. Saint spanked my ass later when we were alone, and I loved it. It was all the more exciting when he told me I couldn't move because it would hurt his rib. Hence the almost aborted blow job.

"You wanna wait up here?" Saint asks as he joins me by the window.

I shake my head. "I've got my head around the idea that if they were going to kill either one of us, they would have done it by now."

"Always the optimist, eh?"

I lean my head against Saint's shoulder. "Isn't that step one? No, two? Stop the doom spiral. Be an optimist. Control next steps, not the outcome?"

Saint grins. "See? Getting you to repeat it in the truck that day helped you remember it."

I roll my eyes. "Whatever."

He takes my wrists and kisses me with more heat than the situation asks for.

Saint bites my lower lip. "Let's go see why King's here."

I know King's reaction has cut him deeper than the blade he carved into his stomach. Personally, I want to stab King in the eye with a rusty needle. Maybe one day I'll feel more forgiving than I am now.

"Fine, I'll come with you."

By the time we get downstairs, most of the men are in the large kitchen.

"Preacher man," King says. "Although, guess I can't call you that anymore. You must be Rose."

As King's cut opens, I see his gun. It dawns on me that Saint is not armed. I glance over the knife block.

"You won't be needing those, Rose." King holds my eye contact for a moment.

There's something unnerving in the way he looks at us. Like he won. And I don't know why.

He turns to Saint. "Some of my men voted for you. Some of them didn't. But you paid your dues. Earned respect." He tosses Saint's cut onto the kitchen counter. "You come back, but you start at the bottom. Not as a prospect. But you don't get a vote. You don't come to church. You don't get any information before anything happens. You will not be told where anything is stored. You won't have access to any supplies. You can keep the strip club. Makes more money under you anyway. The only money you get from the club for the first twelve months is your management salary from the strip club. You don't get a cut of anything else we do. Your share goes to our legal fund, just in case. Keep your nose clean for those twelve months, and we'll review. Is that understood?"

Saint reaches for the leather. I see the way his fingers dance over his patch the way they touch me when we make love. With reverence.

He slides it over his shoulders.

Spark catches my eye and winks. With a smile.

Relief slips through me.

The sight of the cut back on his body means the worst really has passed. He's got what he wants. And I'm happy for him.

"Go on your trip. Come to the clubhouse when you get back, and we'll talk," King says. "There will be checks and balances to make sure you don't fuck up again."

Bates looks at Niro, and when their eyes meet, Niro grins but looks down at his shoes as if to hide it.

King runs his tongue over his lip. "One last question, Saint. What would you give to be a full member of this brotherhood again?"

Saint shrugs. "There isn't much I wouldn't give."

King nods as if considering something. "There may come a point in the future where you'll need to remember that answer." Then he shocks me by tugging Saint to him and hugging him. "Welcome back, preacher man."

King hugs me too before I can stop him. "Welcome to the club, Rose. I'm sorry for what you had to go through."

"Thank you." It's all I can come up with. King is mercurial. All the impending doom energy lifts almost immediately.

"It's over, isn't it?" I say to Saint as conversation erupts around us.

"Yeah, sweetheart. It's over. God, it feels good to have this back."

"If we're staying, could we buy our old place next to Hap?"

Saint grins. "You want to live in that old dump?"

I shake my head. "No, I want to build a home in it with you. I want to rip out the kitchen, and finish the yard, and buy a new coffee maker when we can afford it. Maybe grab a rug and a new bed."

Saint kisses me. "I'll talk to the realtor, see if the owner will sell it. Although, fuck, we'll have to see if the bank will approve a mortgage based on a job managing a strip club."

I can't help but laugh. "Then I'll apply for the loan. I run my own business, pay my own salary."

He taps the end of my nose. "Over my dead body are you paying for the house."

I look around at all the leather cuts and weaponry in sight. "I mean. The dead body part might still happen."

"Nah, this means they have my back. Even if they don't want to right now." Saint pats his cut. "Have I told you today that I love you?"

I shake my head. "You told me I was packing too many shoes, which sounds a lot like you don't."

"Take 'em all. We'll pay for extra luggage. Because I love you, Rose Whittaker. Today is the first day of building our new life."

Sincerity radiates from his eyes, so blue and pure that I can't help but melt into a puddle. "I love you too, Saint. Thank you for saving me that day."

Now it's Saint's turn to look around at the brothers milling around. "It's my pleasure. Because I think you saved me right back."

EPILOGUE: SAINT

I wake up and realize this morning is the first morning I've woken up without any pain.

Nothing aches.

Nothing hurts.

It's only taken three and a half weeks, and I literally have four days left before we fly home.

Sunlight is diffused by the mosquito net hanging around the four-poster bed. The heat of the sun and time spent on a sun lounger has helped me physically and mentally heal. But it's time to get back to reality. My money won't last forever, and while Briar might think she's going to support us financially, she's wrong.

She's worked while we've been down here. Getting up early in the morning for a few hours. Then, during afternoon siestas, when we've dodged the hottest part of the day, she's done some more.

Plus, she's begun to rebuild her relationship with her parents. It started with a message, then a teary video call where she explained what happened. We're going to see them when we go visit Rae. It's only a few extra hours' drive.

The realtor was able to negotiate a way for us to buy the house next to Hap. Plans for the strip club are coming along nicely with events I can run and people I need to hire. The first is Rose. She's going to take over all the social media graphics and rebranding of the club.

And I'm going to try and rebuild the MC relationships I ruined, because I want to give Rose something stable. I want her to feel the sense of brotherhood and support from before I broke everything. It's taken a lot of conversations for her to understand that I was the one out of line. That I caused the problems.

I think we're both looking forward to going back now. And I'm glad. Because after all this, if she told me she couldn't see herself as an old lady, I would have handed in my cut. Because to be honest, there isn't much I wouldn't do for her.

Which makes me think of King in the kitchen. That there isn't much I wouldn't do to join the club. No matter what he makes me do, it won't be as bad as getting stuck as a prospect.

Rose's asleep in my arms and feels so good there. Her ass is tight up against my dick; my hand cups her breast. Gently, I rub my thumb over the nipple. It's a lazy start to lovemaking. Easing out of sleep, stirring into arousal, and knowing you can take all morning with it.

We've had a lot of sex since we got here. Sex that protected my ribs the first week. Sex that blew my mind. Sex that soothed my heart. Sex in those goddamn heels. One day, she'd told me that *odaxelagnia* is the term for getting aroused by biting. It's a mild form of sadomasochism apparently.

Live and fucking learn.

She also did the math on our age gap and decided it

rounded up to a decade and a half, which makes me sound like the dirty old man she teases I am. I spanked her ass fifteen times in celebration, and she came three times that night.

We also got a noise complaint from the bungalow next door.

I slide my palm over the softness of her stomach, and she stirs.

"Morning," she mumbles.

Now that the nightmares have passed, I've realized Briar is like me. A night owl rather than an early bird. A loner who needed to find their person. She turns in my arms and, without opening her eyes, purses her lips for me to find them, which I do. I slip my hand between her thighs.

She's already wet.

"I was dreaming about you," she says as her eyes flicker open.

I slide a finger inside her, then a second as she raises her knee over my thigh. "What was dream me doing to get you this wet?"

She grins. "We were renovating the kitchen, taking out the kitchen counter, and you bent me over and took me from behind one last time before we ripped it out."

My lips curve against hers. "Glad that dream me can deliver."

"It was watching you wield a sledgehammer. Something about your arms at work I think."

Watching her smile does something to my heart. She single-handedly brought it back to life.

Her robe sits across the bottom of the bed, and I reach for it to pull the belt out of its loops. "Remember how I once told you we'll go somewhere hot where nobody knows us, and I'll tie you to the bed? Hands over your head."

I love the way her tits rise when she does that, but I park the urge to bite them while I tie her up. Her hips roll as I do.

She's a greedy girl that way, and I love it.

I run my lips down her neck and over her chest to her nipple. I lick it twice before sucking it into my mouth.

Rose bucks beneath me, her clit seeking the pressure she needs to get off.

I start with a wide, gentle bite then start to narrow it until it's just her nipple between my teeth. I know how much pressure to apply for it to work for her. Not so hard it hurts, but not so gentle it's only playful. She loves it as much as I do.

"Ryker," she gasps as I blow cool air over the red peak.

I repeat the action on her other breast, and this time she groans. "Please."

I move my fingers to her pussy.

"Fuck, I love how much you love this." I dip two fingers into her and then rub some of that wetness on my cock. We got tested before we left, and both of us were clear. Plus, Rose has a contraceptive implant. When I ease into her, I thank the universe. Because skin on skin with this woman is everything.

"Fuck, Rose." I stop, seated deep inside her.

"Mmm," she says, sighing.

Sex can be a lot of things. It can *mean* a lot of things. But as I cup her cheek with one hand, as I begin to move, I think this is my favorite. Unrushed. Deep. Intense. When I'm staring deep into her eyes, watching every feeling flicker through them, I feel connected to her on a level I've never felt with any other human being.

"Have I told you today that I love you?" I ask.

When she smiles, it's the kind that shatters my heart while fixing it. "Not yet today, you haven't."

I kiss her lips, soft with sleep, and encourage her to open so I can taste her.

Our hips start to move; our breath comes a little faster.

But my eyes stay on hers.

And hers stay on mine.

Even as her cheeks grow pink, even as I feel her come around my cock.

Even as I come deep inside and bite down on the idea that I can't wait for her to carry our kids. That I want to feel her stomach swell with a child of our own.

Perhaps the best bit of not using condoms is the ability to stay in the moment with her. To not have to move and clean up, but to simply come down from the high together.

"Morning," I say, and kiss her again.

"That will never get old," she says. "Unlike you."

I can't help but laugh, and the action causes me to slip from inside her. "Careful. You want another fifteen spanks?"

"Not right now. But ask me later." I untie her wrists and place a kiss to the underside of both of them.

"Want some juice?" I ask.

"Please," she says.

I push the mosquito net to one side, place my feet on the cool white tiles, and pad to the kitchen. The sun is hitting the lush garden outside, and it makes me think of Rae. I haven't checked in properly in a few days. And when I have caught her, she hasn't been able to stay on long for one reason or another. When I asked her about it, she told me to stop being so nosy about her private life. There must be a guy on the scene.

I dial her number, and when she answers, she's sitting in a place I don't know. Wood panels line the walls. It's a cabin or something.

"Hey, Raester," I say, and step out into the garden. She looks tired. And then I think of the way I woke Rose up.

"Morning, Ike."

"Where are you at?"

She glances up at someone off-screen, but her eyes assess whoever it is coolly. "I'm staying at a friend's place."

"A guy friend?"

Her smile is enigmatic. Like the Mona Lisa where you're never quite sure. "A none-of-your-business friend. Anyway, how's the trip? Ready to come home?"

My sister wouldn't stick around wherever she is if she wasn't happy. It was one of her guiding principles after getting away from Dad. She was never going to stay anywhere or with anyone that caused her pain or brought her anything other than joy.

I turn the camera to face the garden and the sun. "Going to be hard to leave this, but I'm ready."

There's silence for a moment. "Gardens really are the most amazing thing. You can take the most barren piece of land, something that looks so sad and unhappy, and with a little tender loving care, turn it into something so beautiful."

There's so much truth to her words. "Just wanted to share it with you. Are you good?"

"Yeah. I'm good."

But there's something about the way she says *good* that makes me wonder.

"You wanna talk?" I ask.

"And make you miss one of your last moments in paradise? No. I'm fine. And remember, I know you're going to face some difficulties when you get back, fitting back in with the club. But know you have my blessing, for what it's worth."

Her words catch me off guard. "Yeah?"

"I know how much it means to you. And there isn't much I wouldn't do for you to be happy."

"Thanks, Raester. I love you. You need me, call, yeah?"

"I love you too." And with that, she ends the call, and I go get Rose her juice.

Because Rae is wrong. Paradise isn't a place.

I grab the juice and walk back into the room. Briar is sitting up with her back to the headboard, her tablet and pencil in hand.

Paradise is anywhere she is.

EPILOGUE TWO

"Thanks, Raester, I love you. You need me, call, yeah?"

Saint's voice grates on my last nerve, but Rae convinces him she's fine, and they hang up.

She looks up at me with a face so filled with grace, I want to choke her. How dare she look at me with guileless blue eyes like I matter to her.

Eyes so like her brother's, I want to carve them out.

She sure as fuck doesn't matter to me.

She's a tool for control. I no longer need to point a gun at her head. There is no misunderstanding between us. If Saint realizes I have her before he walks back into my clubhouse, he dies.

So does she.

"Good girl," I say without thinking. And I see the light flicker on in her eyes.

A week I've had her.

A week since I made the trip to Michigan with Niro and a van.

A week since I decided Rae Miller was going to be the insurance that her brother didn't fuck up.

And in that week, I've realized she has a praise kink a mile wide.

But that isn't going to save Saint.

I'm going to extract my pound of flesh.

I'm going to make him pay for every betrayal I've suffered.

And I'm going to do it through her.

"What was all that garden bullshit?" I ask.

Rae sits calmly. Of course, she's some kind of psychologist. Or therapist. Or some kind of mind-fuck do-gooder. "Did I say anything untrue?"

I hate when she answers a question with a question. I tug my hand through my hair. "Don't try and mess with my head. I'm the one who controls what's happening here."

"I understand. Why is that so important to you?"

"Why did you talk about fucking gardens?"

Rae looks towards the garden outside the cabin wistfully. The sun catches her face, making her brown hair glint red. "Because I miss mine. Because that one out there is crying out for some preparation before the worst of winter hits. Because soil on your hands and the feeling of a good day's work mean something to me. Why does it bother you so much that I like them?"

Damn, if I don't hear the sadness in her voice. Not that I fucking care. "I don't give a shit one way or another. Stop the mind games. Go get back on that bed and show me how grateful you are I didn't kill him. And make it good, so I don't change my mind."

As easily as if I'd asked her to go run me a bath or cook dinner, she rises from her seat and walks past me.

As if she's better than me.

And I follow with the sole intent of making her realize she's not.

I KNOW, I KNOW ...
IT'S KING!!!

I'm so grateful to you all for taking the time to read Saint and Briar's story and would love you forever if you would take a minute to rate or review or share it if you loved it.

And, yes, book four is THE BONDS WE BREAK. King and Rae's story. Oh my gosh, it's a good one. King kidnaps Rae as insurance against Saint's actions. But he's never met a woman so much smarter than him, and a psychologist as well. It's not long before she manages to undermine his upper hand, as he fights falling hard. Read on for an excerpt.

And please, please sign up for my newsletter here. Don't forget to double opt in.

THE BONDS WE BREAK EXCERPT

KING

Twenty-five days.

That's how many have passed since my club let me down.

Not all of them, but as I sit in my office, the room we use for church, the gap between them and me couldn't be any wider.

I reach for the bottle of Jack on my desk and take another chug. The alcohol no longer burns. It no longer numbs, either. Because since the vote went in favour of Saint, I'm wondering if I actually know the men on the other side of the glass.

Clutch, my VP, the man who loves my twin sister, Gwen, knocks on the door, even when I had told him not to.

I gesture for him to come in,

"You coming out to join us?" he asks.

I reach for the packet of cigarettes only to find it empty. A full packet, still wrapped in film, lands by my hand.

"I got you covered," he says.

I glance up, nod, and then remove the packaging.

"Okay, I'm done with this shit," he says, tugging out his

seat next to the big table that seats us all. "You're the president of this goddamn club. It's time you started acting like it."

If my best friend realised how close I was to blowing up the whole world, he'd watch how he spoke to me. As it is, I let the rage swirl internally. Externally, I light my cigarette and lean back in my chair. "Why don't you say what's on your mind?"

"You ready to listen?" he asks.

"If it's going to be some misplaced pep talk where you get all life-moves-on with me, then you can shove it up your ass."

"The men can feel you pulling away. It's causing a split in the club. You've got Niro and Bates walking around like they have a direct line to you. Like they are the only ones you trust. Then you got the others who felt Saint did enough for us as a club that he deserves a chance at redemption. You offered him that. You told the club members to vote with their conscience. If you didn't mean that, if you wanted the fucker dead, you should have said so. But pouting away in here is not going to build a better club. And I know you're a better president than that."

I feel the tide.

The one that pushes me to be club president then drags me under, feeling like I'm worthless.

It eddies. Tugging me back and forth.

But like a riptide, no one sees how dangerous I am on the surface. "Noted," I say.

Clutch leans forward. "Noted? That's all you've got?"

I shrug. "What do you want me to say? We allowed a fucking ATF agent to become a member of our club. We look like clowns."

The slap of Clutch's palm hitting the table top echoes

through the room. "Snap out of it, brother. The men out there need you to lead. You won't step up, I will."

That makes me stare at the man I've been friends with my entire life. "You took my sister. Now you want my fucking club too?"

"I love you like a brother, but you're behaving like a cunt. I don't know what to do to reach you."

"Should have thought about that before you dropped twenty grand at the feet of a traitor."

Clutch stands and pulls up the waistband of his jeans. "I'm giving you two weeks, then I will ask the club to vote on whether you are doing your job or not. If not, I'll stand. I'll even hold the position until you feel ready to step back into it. But this..." He gestures around the office with the stack of empty bottles and the scent of stale cigarette smoke. "You gotta get your head on straight."

He leaves the office and slams the door so hard the partition wall shakes. I see some of the men crowd him when he steps outside. Halo grips his shoulder and shakes hard. Spark sits next to him at the bar and shoulder-checks him in support.

I want that.

I want the camaraderie of my club.

I want my brothers back.

But then I remember I didn't flake out on them. They let *me* down.

Vex taps on the glass, and I wave him in. "For the record, I think this is a really bad fucking idea," he says, tossing the manilla envelope onto the desk.

I open it up, and there it is.

Or, there *she* is.

I place the tip of my finger against her cheek. Rae Miller is one attractive woman.

Without a doubt, this is Saint's sister. They have the same blue eyes, but while Saint's hair is wild, Rae's is smooth and long.

My dick stirs in my jeans, and I'm pissed at myself for appreciating the shape of her tits, even as I wonder what they'll feel like wrapped around my dick.

Because Rae Miller is about to become my personal insurance policy. She's about to become my payment for every betrayal I've faced. I'm going to claim my pound of flesh from her body.

And she's going to let me if she expects me to keep her brother alive.

And I'll watch as it drives Saint insane that I've taken the only thing he valued outside of Briar.

I'll watch him crack as he sees her turn into a shell of her former self.

"Don't do this," Vex says, his eyes on me.

I gave him no choice. I told him I'd take his patch if he didn't find her for me.

"Send Bates and Niro to me, " I say, gesturing to the door. "And breathe a word about this and you'll be kicked out of this club faster than you can blink."

I see doubt cloud the dark eyes of one of the smartest guys I know. It unnerves me, seeing it there, but it won't change the course of action I'm about to take.

Vex leaves the office and within minutes, Niro, my treasurer, and Bates, my enforcer, arrive together. They are as different as chalk and cheese. Niro with his dark hair, broad frame, and scarred face. And Bates, with his short hair, pretty face, and deceptive street fighter's build.

"What do you need, Prez?" Niro asks, taking Clutch's seat next to me.

I look out to the bar and catch sight of Clutch looking in

through the glass. It doesn't bother me that I see concern etch his features.

"I don't like the way the vote went over Saint," I say.

Bates nods. "Fucking wild that so many felt he deserved a second chance."

"So, what do you want to do?" Niro asks, placing his palms on the table.

"I need some insurance for when Saint gets back to keep him in line."

"Have you asked Vex to dig up dirt on him?" Bates asks.

I shake my head. "I asked him to find me Saint's sister."

Niro howls like a fucking wolf. "I love it."

I think back to something Dad once said in jest. He told me if I was ever in agreement with anything Niro said, I was probably standing on the wrong side of the argument. That logic flickers through me for a second, but I can't bring myself to not do this.

"He has a sister?" Bates asks.

"Just one, younger than him. Her name's Rae. She lives in Ann Arbour, Michigan. I want to go get her, then keep her...show Saint when it's time that I have her."

Bates leans back in his chair. "That's a lot of logistics to worry about. How many brothers need to know? Who keeps guard when you aren't there?"

I shrug. "I think it's pretty simple. I get Vex to wire Dad's old cottage up while I'm gone with cameras from every angle on the exterior property. The only risk we have until I actually tell Saint is making sure Rae knows I'm a heartbeat away from pulling the trigger on Saint. I'll need to tell her and have her believe that she's the only thing keeping Saint alive."

"In my experience, bitches are not the most rational human beings," Niro says.

Bates chuckles. "Maybe if you weren't such an asshole to them..."

Niro flips the bird across the table.

"She'll believe it. I have something that'll help convince her."

Niro raises an eyebrow. "How dark are you going with this, boss?"

"As dark as it needs to get her compliance and Saint's obedience."

Bates nods in approval. "So, what's the plan?"

"Go home. Sober up. Get some sleep. Tomorrow, early, we take the van. Pack for a few days, just in case she isn't immediately home. We'll plan the rest on the way. Soon as we have her, we bring her back. Pick me up from Dad's cottage. I'll ride up there and leave my bike so I have it when we get back."

"On it, Prez," Bates says, standing. "I'll take the van home tonight. Swing by and pick you up around five in the morning. It's a ten-hour drive, maybe eleven with breaks and traffic. Let you work your magic. Then drive back. Faster drive home. Less traffic and fewer cops. We can rotate."

"Good enough. See you in the morning."

I watch their backs as they leave. I notice Clutch does too.

I stub out my cigarette and pull on my heavy leather jacket with my patches on the back. Hard to believe it's nearly December. So much has happened this year that I can't wait to see the end of it.

As I head to the door to leave, Clutch stops me. "You got something going on you need help with?" he asks, as if he wasn't just in my office, threatening my presidency of this club.

"Nothing you need to be worrying about."

When I step outside, there's bite in the air. The kind that gets under your skin and into your bones.

I like the sting of it on my face.

As I climb on my bike, I think about Saint, in Mexico, all fucking loved up with Briar because he thinks he's got what he wants. The girl. The club. His life.

I grin. Because within twenty-four hours, I'm going to destroy everything he holds dear.

ACKNOWLEDGEMENTS

I'm so grateful to all of you for taking the time to read Saint and Briar's story and would love you forever if you would take a minute to rate or review or share it if you loved it.

Thanks to my amazingly talented team. Manu, Isabel, and Michele for making the story shine. Letitia, Wander, and Alex for the incredible cover. And Dani for her marketing wiz.

Thanks to Rachel Hamilton for reading a super early draft for assuring me that the shed scene wasn't too much!

Thanks to the wonderful Michelle Rattigan for her Irish language help.

And thank you to T, F, & L ... I love you all.

ABOUT THE AUTHOR

Scarlett Cole is a contemporary romance author that calls both Toronto, Canada and Manchester, England home. A born city dweller, she periodically quashes the urge to live in the country by hiking up a mountain to remind herself that living away from people would terrify the pants off her.

She believes everybody deserves their love story to be told and loves her heroes on the rough and rugged side...and usually tall (because she married one of those 6ft 6" men you read about in romance!). She's an A-type personality and Scorpio star sign, so good luck getting her to do anything she doesn't want to.

When she isn't writing, she's happy to talk about hot men and expensive shoes while drinking a cold gin and tonic. Don't bring up olives. As far as Scarlett is concerned, they are the devil's food. As long as you don't bring up olives, she's happy to hear from you any time.

ALSO BY SCARLETT COLE

Excess All Areas / Sad Fridays Series

One Day Like This

Next Time I Fall

How Good It Was

Love You Like That

Let Me Love You

Love Distilled Series

Love In Numbers

Love In Moments

Love In Secrets

Preload Series

Jordan Reclaimed

Elliott Redeemed

Nikan Rebuilt

Lennon Reborn

Second Circle Tattoos Series

The Strongest Steel

The Fractured Heart

The Purest Hook

The Darkest Link

The Greatest Risk (Novella)

Love Over Duty Series

Under Fire

Final Siege

Deep Cover

Made in the USA
Columbia, SC
17 July 2024

38778072R00185